CRAFTY CAT

A CRAZY CAT LADY MYSTERY

BY MOLLIE HUNT

Crafty Cat, the 11th Crazy Cat Lady mystery
by Mollie Hunt

All rights reserved. This book or any portion thereof may not be reproduced or used in any manner whatsoever without the express written consent of the author except for the use of brief quotations in a book review.

ISBN: 9798340449023
Independently published

Copyright 2024 © Mollie Hunt

Editing and Design by Rosalyn Newhouse

Published in the United States of America

No generative AI has been used in the conceptualization, development, or drafting of this work.

This book is a work of fiction. Names, characters, places, and incidents either are products of the author's imagination or are used fictitiously. Any resemblance to actual events or locales or persons, living or dead, is purely coincidental.

Cover Art: "Greetings!"
© by Leslie Cobb, Cat Artist
www.lesliecobb.com

Other Books by Mollie Hunt

Crazy Cat Lady Mysteries
Cats' Eyes
Copy Cats
Cat's Paw
Cat Call
Cat Café
Cat Noel
Cosmic Cat
Cat Conundrum
Adventure Cat
Cat's Play
Cat House

The Tenth Life Cozy Mysteries
Ghost Cat of Ocean Cove
Ghost Cat on the Midway
Ghost Cat at the Mystery Hotel

Other Mysteries
Placid River Runs Deep

Cat Seasons Sci-Fantasy Tetralogy
Cat Summer
Cat Winter
Cat Autumn

Memoir
There's a Cat Hair in My Mask: How Cats Helped Me through Unprecedented Times

Dedication

This book is dedicated to all the creative people who quilt, sew, draw, paint, take photographs, write, sculpt, color, or stare out the window watching the birds. We all have a capacity for creativity within our hearts, and whether we produce to sell, to donate, or merely to satisfy our soul, our imagination is a positive influence on our world and our universe. Keep it up!

Chapter 1

There are reasons we can't go back to the past, and we shouldn't want to. People get hurt. People get killed. Time flows one way on purpose. Trying to relive some golden moment will only get you in trouble.

My name is Lynley Cannon, and as the years pile on since my big six-oh, those facts become clearer to me every day. Not the part about people getting killed... That revelation came only after a series of unexpected events about which I will tell in due time. For now, I'll just repeat the old adage: *You can never go home again.*

It started innocently enough when my best friend Frannie Desoto invited me along to her quilting club, a group of cat lovers who get together to sew cat-themed quilts for animal shelter auctions. The idea sounded fun, and being a long-time shelter volunteer myself, the cause suited me. I knew nothing about quilting, but Frannie assured me that Pauleen and Paulette Hart, seasoned quilters themselves, would have no trouble taking me through the basics. The mother-daughter duo had tutored many a would-be seamstress while running their business, House of Quilts.

To look at it from the outside, House of Quilts was just what its name implied, an old residential house off Hawthorne Boulevard in Portland, Oregon. The only thing to distinguish it from the homes to either side was the colorful signage depicting a log cabin patchwork quilt that hung above the front porch. With the building nearly obscured by a lush vine maple tree, I would have passed right by it if Frannie hadn't yelled for me to pull over.

I swooped my little Toyota into an open parking spot on the street and turned off the engine. Peering out at our destination, I shook my head.

"I don't know about this, Frannie. I haven't picked up a needle and thread for eons, let alone sat down at my sewing machine." I pictured the vintage model given me by my mum some decades back which now sat latched in its case on a table heaped with flotsam.

"It'll be fine. You don't have to sew if you don't want to—you can just watch. But I bet you'll get inspired once you see what the gals are doing."

Gals, I thought to myself. An outmoded term, but so Frannie Desoto. Though her outfits, always impeccable and expensive, were of a current fashion, there was something about Frannie that harked back to a gentler era.

Frannie and I had met years ago through our volunteer work at Friends of Felines cat shelter. Being more mature than many of the twenty-something volunteers and staff, we'd gravitated toward one another. I admit I'd initially been put off by her styled platinum hair, lavish makeup, and the elegant clothes she wore even for her shelter shifts, but once we got talking, I found we had much in common. Underneath her picture-perfect exterior, she and I were sisters.

Frannie had never lied to me, and there was no reason to think she was lying now, but...

"Fun?" I grumbled. "They're going to throw me out on my ear."

"No, they're not. Why would you say that?" Frannie turned and stared at me with those blue-shadowed eyes.

"What's wrong with you today, Lynley? You're usually up for anything."

"I don't know," I sighed. "Sometimes I feel so old, like I'm never going to be able to learn anything new."

"You're not old!" Frannie clipped back at me. "Why, you just turned sixty."

"It's been a while," I put in.

"Sixty is the new forty, Lynley, but twenty years wiser. Now come on. You're going in there if I have to drag you."

Frannie was right. I was only as old as I felt, but for the past month, I'd been feeling my age and more. I needed new glasses but was hesitant to make that expensive appointment. I had a funny pain in my shoulder that didn't used to be there. My yearly wellness check was coming up, and though I had no reason to fear, getting poked and prodded, quizzed and questioned, only to sit like a naughty child awaiting the final verdict from my doctor was always a bit unnerving. These were things that never crossed my mind a decade ago.

"Frannie, I really don't feel like doing this right now. Can't I just drop you off and pick you up when you're done?"

"Absolutely not. Now get out of the car and come with me."

Begrudgingly I did what I was told, lagging behind Frannie as she crossed the sidewalk and climbed the steps to a screened front porch where a sign read, *Closed For Class—Ring Bell for Service.* I was about to balk again when I saw something that changed my mind.

Or more accurately, *someone.*

Sitting regally as a queen on a shelf beside the screen door was a cat. Her black fur was long and silky. Her green eyes were trained directly on me. Around her neck she wore a matching green collar.

"That's Mewella," Frannie related with a grin. "She and her brother Ridley own the place."

Frannie moved forward and rang a bell which was quickly answered by a blockish woman wearing a prim white blouse and a long, quilted skirt of a botanical design. Her hair, an unlikely shade of auburn, was piled on her head in a haphazard knot. Through the knot was stuck a pencil and a pair of long, purple-handled scissors.

"Frannie! Come in, come in!" the woman expounded as she scooped Mewella into her arms and unlatched the screen. "And this must be Lynley," she said to me. "I'm Pauleen. Welcome to House of Quilts."

Mewella allowed herself to be cuddled in Pauleen's substantial embrace, but as soon as the door was safely latched, she launched away to resume her vigil.

"She never tries to get out," Pauleen explained, "but please keep watch anyway. It would be tragic if she were to escape."

Pauleen led Frannie and me across the wide porch and into the house chattering about quilting things, much of which I didn't understand. The foyer had been turned into a shop room where bolts of fabric and piles of colorful cut yardage lined the walls. In one corner was a display of sewing machines and rolling cases and a shelf of oversized books. On tables sat baskets of threads, scissors and fabric cutters, markers, pins and needles, a smattering of homemade pincushions, and other sewing sundries that I was hard-pressed to name.

As I stared around with something between awe and confusion, a tiny woman in a yellow jacket ran up to us, an odd look on her face. If everything else about the environment hadn't seemed so serene, I would have marked it as fright.

It turned out my assumption wasn't far off. The little woman grasped Pauleen by the arm and gave a whimper.

"I can't find him anywhere, Pauleen! I've looked all through the house—the upstairs parlor and even the bedrooms."

Pauleen frowned. "Calm down, Dora. I'm sure he's here somewhere. Have you checked outside?"

Dora hesitated. "I did, yes, but I'll try again."

"Good girl. You know how he can disappear when he doesn't want to be found."

Dora fled away, shaking her hands in despair. Pauleen turned to me. "That was my dear friend Dora. She's always got my back. Now it seems we have a missing cat, Ridley, Mewella's twin brother."

"Oh, dear," I commented. "And you think he may have got outside?"

"We have an outdoor catio beyond the sunroom with lots of built-in shelves and perches and places for a cat to hide. He's asleep somewhere. Most likely," she added with a forced laugh that ended in a frown. "Give me a minute, please? Frannie, why don't you take Lynley into the sewing room and introduce her to everyone? I'll be right back."

And with that, she was gone.

Chapter 2

I hear owners lament when their cat doesn't return from their usual outdoor excursion, "but he's always come back before..."

I gave Frannie a questioning look. She blinked her eyes in a less than satisfactory reply.

"Well, you heard the lady," she said with a shrug. "Let me show you around."

Without waiting, she started for a wide archway through which I glimpsed the adjoining room. Once the old home's living room, the space was now dominated by a long, rectangular table. Rows of shelves ran along either side holding more sewing paraphernalia. The walls, where they weren't hidden by supplies, were of a rich, dark red. Through a bank of screened windows at the far end, a soft breeze carried the scent of a pear tree in bloom outside.

A frail, elderly lady reclined in an overstuffed chair by the window knitting something mauve and fuzzy. Three women and one man sat at the table working on various projects. All but one looked up at us as we came in.

"I thought you said this was a women's group," I whispered to Frannie as I studied the lanky young man with the sandy, close-cropped hair and beard. "You called them *gals*."

"Oh, sorry. That's Mark. He's new, but enthusiastic. We don't really think about his gender."

A friendly-looking matron in pink slacks and a

flowered shirt touched the arm of a woman busily running a sewing machine.

"We have a guest, Gilda."

Gilda paused the machine and looked around as if coming out of a trance. "What's that, Ruth?"

"We have a newbie. Stop your work and say hello."

"This is Lynley, everyone," Frannie announced. "She volunteers with me at Friends of Felines. Lynley, this is Ruth, Gilda, and Mark. Mrs. Paula Hart is the knitter by the window. That's Pauleen's mom. The gal at the head of the table is Pauleen's daughter Paulette."

The younger woman gave a gracious smile. "Call me Pet—Paulette gets confusing, what with all the other Paul-names in the family. Welcome to House of Quilts."

In that moment, she sounded exactly like her mom, and I saw the family resemblance. Pet tended to the same squarish build as her mother, but on the younger woman, it seemed more voluptuous than husky. The deep red of her hair was natural, the color Pauleen might have once had herself and was going for with the dye job. Pet wore a simple blue smock with a cat embroidered on the lapel. I instantly recognized the fluffy depiction as their beautiful Mewella.

My attention moved from the proprietress to the grand room with its vintage moldings and gas-lamp-era lights. "You have a lovely house."

"Thank you," Pet gushed. "It's been in our family for generations. Isn't that right, Gran? You grew up here."

"A long, long time ago," Paula Hart said. Her voice may have been reedy with age, but the sparkle in her eyes was timeless.

"Grab a seat," said the lady in pink, Ruth. She pushed aside a pile of quilt squares from the place next to her.

"What sort of quilting do you do?"

I glanced at Frannie. "To be honest, I don't quilt at all, and I barely sew. But the idea of making something to help cats appeals to me. Hopefully I can learn."

Ruth gave a gracious, if somewhat sympathetic smile. Mark nodded vigorously. Pet looked like she was holding back laughter. Only Gilda, whose default expression seemed to be a frown, was put off by my honest admission, emitting a harrumph and returning her attention to her project on the sewing machine.

Pet rose and came around the table. Tossing an exasperated glance at Gilda and the noisy machine, she took my arm. "Come with me. We'll go somewhere we can talk."

I shot a look to Frannie, but she was already rooting around the shelves. Grabbing a turquoise-lidded storage box, she took it to the table where she seated herself in the vacant chair.

"You go ahead, Lynley," she said. "I'm going to get started on my mini-quilt." She held up a square of fabric with a trio of stylized cats appliqued on the front.

Okay, why not? I told myself. If anyone could convince me I had a place at that sewing table, it was Pet.

"Never mind Gilda," Pet said as we walked into the shop room. "She considers herself a professional quilter because she's won prizes at the county fair. Don't get me wrong—her work is exceptional, but her attitude leaves something to be desired. She loves cats though, so you two do have that in common."

"My reputation precedes me?"

"Little bit," Pet laughed, and I liked the young woman instantly. The verdict was still out on the grumpy Gilda.

Pet continued across the shop area and through a set of

open pocket doors into a glass-walled sunroom. The sun had warmed the small space to a summertime temperature, while an open door let in the fresh April breeze. Beyond was the catio Pauleen had spoken of, and past that, a lush garden just beginning to come to life. I could see clumps of yellow-headed daffodils dotting the grass and tulips in an array of colors running along the border. A sprinkling of petals drifted like snowflakes from a flowering plum tree. The scent of hyacinth infused the air, and I found myself smiling. For the first time in too long I felt happy and at peace. Maybe things weren't so dire after all.

Then Dora rushed in once more, followed by Pauleen who had a crazed look on her face.

"He's gone!" Dora moaned. "Ridley's gone."

Pauleen swung on the smaller woman. "He's not gone, Dora," she burst out. "He's been taken. And there's no question in my mind as to who did it."

Dora took the distraught woman into her arms. Pauleen let her friend console her briefly, then turned to stare blackly out across the catio to the house next door. Pet followed her gaze.

"Oh, no!" Pet intoned. "Not again!"

Chapter 3

If you think your cat has been stolen, immediately file a report with your local police, sheriff, and/or animal control agency. Theft of a pet is illegal.

Pauleen grasped her daughter by the arm and led her aside. I watched their low, hurried discourse, then turned to Dora.

"Taken? Their cat's been taken? What does that mean?"

Dora's eyes grew wide, but then she shook it off. "Things," she replied ambiguously. "Stuff."

Pauleen and Pet had wound up their discussion, and Pauleen headed outside while Pet came back to me.

"Let's go into the sewing room," Pet said as if nothing had happened, "and get you started on a project."

"But..." I began, though Pet was already walking away. Dora shot me a sorrowful look, then traipsed after her. I glanced out to the garden, but Pauleen was nowhere to be seen.

Pet cast a backward glance. "Come on, don't be shy. Everyone has to start somewhere."

This time I did as bid.

She motioned to the chair by Frannie who, hard at work hand-sewing cat-shaped cutouts together in an Escher-like design, had completely missed the strange exchange in the shop.

"Look around." Pet leaned over my shoulder as I took the seat like a good little girl. "Check out what other people are doing. Here's an album of the pieces we've sent to auction so far."

She slipped a binder in front of me, open to the image of a gorgeous multi-colored quilt with a repeating design of sleeping cats. In the photo, a middle-aged woman with a fancy blonde coif stood proudly before the full-sized piece. It took me a moment to recognize her as Gilda whose hair was currently done in a straw-colored blunt cut.

I gave a huff. "Well, I'd better quit right now if that's what you're expecting of me."

"Oh, no," Pet apologized. "Most of ours are smaller, décor appliques or mini-quilts like the one Frannie's working on. It's for charity—no one is fussy as long as the theme is cats."

As if in agreement, Mewella chose that moment to hop onto the table. She surveyed the group with her deep green gaze, then picked her way demurely between the clutter to settle in a green poof bed on the end near Mrs. Hart. I noticed there was a vacant blue one next to it and wondered if it belonged to the absent Ridley.

* * *

There was no more mention of the missing cat, and though I was curious about anything feline, I soon became distracted by the work going on around the table. After looking through the album and taking note of other people's undertakings, I'd decided to revive an old talent from my hippie days—embroidery. Pet hunted down a tray of cotton floss, a hoop, and an assortment of large-eyed needles. She also retrieved a well-used paperback booklet of design templates with a whole section on cats. I chose a flouncy calico with simple proportions and traced it onto my fabric. Assuming I completed the piece, it could be incorporated into a quilt as an appliqué.

The creative effort was fun, just as Frannie had promised. The gentle rhythm of the needle passing in and out of the material forming lines and spots of color, and the simple talk among the group whose favored topic was of a sewing nature felt relaxing. When the session was over and people began to putting things away, I'd come to a whole new outlook on needlework.

"So you think you'll want to try this again?" Frannie asked, neatly folding her piece and placing it back into the turquoise box along with the unfinished cutouts.

"I have to," I replied, adjusting my glasses and holding up my half-calico. "Poor sweetie needs a tail."

"She needs a little more than a tail," Frannie pointed to the entire missing back end. "But it's a great start. I didn't know you embroidered."

"Not for years, but I used to enjoy it. There are so many different stitches. I love the texture, and the vibrant colors make it come alive."

Pet was clearing off the table, placing scissors, rotary cutters, and pinking shears in their sheaths and gathering the leftover scraps and threads into a little cloth bag. When she saw me watching she smiled.

"We give the remnants to a local recycling company. They clean them thoroughly, shred them into fibers, then re-spin them into new textiles for rags, garments, insulation, and other things."

"That's wonderful," I applauded, a staunch proponent of the ever-growing movement to recycle instead of tossing stuff into the garbage.

"It was nice to meet you, Lynley," said Ruth, slipping on a loose-weave sweater.

"I second that," said Mark. "Always good to see new faces." He gave me a tentative smile which noticeably broadened as he turned it on Pet. "Need any help with the cleanup, Pet?"

Pet grinned indulgently. "I'm good, Mark. You run along. I know you have things to do."

The smile faded. "Not really," the man said glumly. "See you next time then."

Mark turned to go but tripped on his feet which, in his Birkenstocks, seemed too small for someone so tall. For a moment, embarrassment painted his face an angry red, then he and Ruth headed through the shop room and out the front door. Gilda, who had packed her sewing machine into a rolling case and put on a puffy coat that seemed much too warm for the season, was quick to follow.

"Gilda, you forgot your scarf," came a thin voice from across the room.

Gilda stopped and turned to glare at Mrs. Hart.

"Your scarf, the one with those rude colors." Pursing her lips, Mrs. Hart nodded to the back of the chair Gilda had been occupying.

Gilda returned to snatch the red and hot green muffler, then stamped out the door.

"Goodbye, Gilda," Pet called after.

There was no response, and Pet gave a sigh. "I keep trying to break through to her. It hasn't worked yet, but maybe someday..."

"Your grandmother doesn't seem to care for her much," I said aside, eyeing the elderly Mrs. Hart who, still knitting by feel, had her gaze fixed on something outside the window.

"You noticed?" Pet flipped.

"Kind of hard not to. Why does Gilda come if she's so antisocial?"

"Cats," both Frannie and Pet said at the same time.

"She loves them and appreciates what we're doing for them here. Last year our efforts brought in thousands of dollars for various shelters, and her offerings were a big part of it. Everyone wants a quilt by Gilda, even if it's only one-foot square. And she and Mom get along well, so she's not a complete elitist."

"Maybe she's shy," I offered, knowing that bashfulness can manifest in what others perceive as snobbery.

Pet shrugged, then handed me a small floral-printed storage box. "Here's for your project. Or would you rather take it home with you?"

I realized I was still holding the half-finished embroidery. "Oh, no. It would just get lost at my house. Or a cat would decide the threads would be fun to tear into and bite." Taking the container, I placed the piece inside, along with the floss I'd been using—orange, white, and black for the calico colors. I handed it back to Pet, and she set it on the shelf beside Frannie's.

I shot a look at Mrs. Hart, who now seemed to be dozing in her chair, the knitting forgotten. "I didn't get much of a chance to talk to your grandmother."

Pet looked over fondly. "She's pretty quiet, except when she's chewing out Gilda. She can't quilt anymore because of her macular degeneration makes it hard for her to see the small stitches, but she can knit just fine. She makes squares for cat carriers and bed inserts."

"Did she establish House of Quilts?"

Pet nodded. "She sure did. She used to be the driving force and still insists on doing her part."

Pet launched into a history of the quilt shop—how the young Mrs. Hart, a quilter from way back, formed a quilt guild, then repurposed the downstairs floor of her home into the shop and meeting room. I was interested, of course, House of Quilts having been a cornerstone of the neighborhood for as long as I'd lived in the area, but basically I was stalling, hoping Pauleen would return with news on the missing cat. It looked like I'd have to put my questions on hold however, since Frannie was ready to go.

"Say goodbye to your mom for me," I finally told Pet, "wherever she's got to." I gave a farewell scritch to Mewella who had come to see us off, for which I received a purr. "I hope you find your other kitty."

Frannie was silent until we got into the car. "What was that you said about finding their kitty? Is Ridley lost?"

"I'm... not sure."

Frannie gave me a puzzled look.

"Really, I don't know. Pauleen and Dora were running around saying Ridley had been taken by someone. I never did get a coherent story out of them."

"Taken? As in stolen? Then they didn't find him in the catio after all?"

"I guess not."

"Pet didn't seem worried during the session, so it can't be too dire. Ridley is her baby."

"That's good to know. My imagination gets the better of me sometimes."

"It's that cat-like curiosity of yours," Frannie said. "If it's not satisfied, it makes up its own stories which sometimes tilt to the darker side. I wouldn't worry if I were you."

"I guess you're right. You know those people better than I do."

Frannie pulled a compact mirror out of her purse and checked her look. Blinking her mascaraed eyes, she smacked her lips, then dug around for a tube of lipstick while I started the car.

"Oh, gosh! Is that the time?" she exclaimed, catching the readout on the dash clock. "We really need to get going. I'm meeting Martha at the dress shop up the street in a few minutes. Can you drop me there?"

I slipped out of my parking spot, turned at the first corner, and joined the Hawthorne Boulevard traffic heading east for the twenty-block drive to the local clothing store. Frannie chattered about her friend who needed an outfit for a special occasion, but my mind was still on the missing Ridley. Sadly, cats who were allowed outside got lost all the time, but rarely were they stolen. It did happen, usually with breed cats the thief thought he could sell or with especially cute kitties that someone without boundaries took a liking to. If Ridley was a twin to his gorgeous sister, he might fit into that second category.

I pulled into a loading zone in front of the boutique. Frannie hustled her things together and jumped out.

"There's Martha just going in now," she shot back to me. "See you at the shelter?"

"Tomorrow, morning shift. I'll be there."

The door shut with a clunk, and I watched Frannie hurry away, making sure she got safely to her destination, an old-fashioned courtesy that I still practiced. Once I saw her meet up with the blue-haired Martha, I checked my rearview mirror and swerved back onto the street, heading for destinations of my own.

Chapter 4

Therapy animals play an important role in raising the spirits of people with disabilities. If the animals themselves have their own physical challenge such as a neurological condition or a missing limb or eye, the connection becomes even more personal.

Pulling over in front of my home, I gazed up at the classic Old Victorian. Even after all these years, I am still in awe that it is mine. Before I bought it, I'd only lived in apartments and duplexes. The fourteen-room house was everything I could have dreamed of. Lots of space for hobbies, for guests, and for cats.

As a widowed older lady on a fixed income, I'd managed to keep it in reasonably good condition, and its care was reflected in its friendly façade, but with a place of that era, there was always something. I frowned, noting the bushes needed trimming and the porch begged for a new coat of paint. The former was inevitable this time of year; the latter would require work and money.

It seemed like everyone in the neighborhood was enjoying the beautiful day. Amy Allen, the multi-media artist who lived across the street, was poking at a planter box of fat green sprouts, possibly hyacinths. Seamus Ferris was mowing his lawn, a first run over the scraggly winter tufts. Patty and Jim from the apartments next door were out on their little porch having a sun bath. Patty looked up and waved, then went back to her magazine while her husband seemed to be napping. Down the street, I spied a group of step-walkers led by a spare woman in a purple jogging suit, the elderly but indomitable Olive. I couldn't help but smile. Those outdoor activities, like the crocuses and daffodils, were sure signs of the coming of spring.

As I climbed my front steps, I smiled again. Through the window I could see Little, my faithful one-cat welcoming committee, perched in her spot on the entrance table. I'd never quite decided if the little panther parked herself there to wait out my absence from the moment I left the house, or if some feline intuition alerted her to the time of my return. Either way, nine times out of ten, she was there, skewering me with her golden eyes as if to say, *Home at last*, or maybe, *Why did you leave?* Since today I was late with their snack, it was likely her rapt attention had to do with food.

Once inside, I shed my coat and dropped it on the chair—no point hanging it up since I was on a quick turnaround and would be leaving again shortly.

"Hello, sweetheart," I said to the watch cat. "Snacks will be up in a jiffy."

A few more of the greeting brigade came sauntering into the hallway, my other two black-as-night felines Emilio and Tinkerbelle along with beautiful Hermione. Hermione smoothed my ankles with her striped sideburns, then strutted toward the kitchen flourishing her luxurious tail. Mab, the petite lilac-point Siamese who at three years old still thought she was a kitten, zoomed in, made a mad dash around my legs, then zoomed out again. Mab was followed at a more sedate pace by large Violet. The gray and white fourteen-pound shorthair and the tawny, fleet Siamese had little in common, but they loved each other greatly.

I made it into the living room, avoiding a near collision with Elizabeth, who as far as I could tell, had intended to go left but instead had swung right and into my path. The silver tabby with the cornflower blue eyes had been born with a condition that made her wobbly, which could be cute and funny or sad and tragic depending on how one looked at it. Elizabeth felt no sorrow for herself, however, and behaved the same as any other cat.

Because of her ability to work through her shortcomings, I'd been training Elizabeth to be a registered therapy cat. Humans, especially those with troubles of their own, found such tenaciousness uplifting. It was that way with Tinkerbelle who had been my certified pet partner for many years, but Tink was getting up in age, and since so many therapy animals were dogs, a new cat on the team was always welcome.

I passed through the living room and into the farmhouse-style kitchen, acquiring two more stragglers as I went. Big Red, as shy as he was substantial, waited until he was sure there weren't going to be any surprises, such as a visitor or a monster from outer space. Dirty Harry lingered on his perch until he heard the crackle of the treat package. The elder of the crew, Harry wasn't about to interrupt his rest for a false alarm.

Once I'd distributed everyone's diet-appropriate treat and watched to make sure they didn't eat each other's, I went to gather the things I'd need for my next outing. It was just a short trip to the pet store, but Elizabeth would be going along with me.

The first step for Elizabeth to get registered was for her to pass an assessment test. In preparation, I'd been taking her all sorts of places—the park, the mall, Home Depot, and anywhere else that allowed pets. It was important for her to become comfortable in a wide range of circumstances, because even though most of the facilities we would be calling on were quiet, one never knew. Something might get dropped; someone might talk loudly or cry out; there might be other animals present. A therapy cat needed to be unflappable. Tinkerbelle was such a cat, and I was hoping Elizabeth would turn out to be as well.

Maybe I should take her to the quilting group, I thought suddenly. Since dealing with unfamiliar cats was also part of her training, I could evaluate her reaction to Mewella and Ridley. The next session was a few days away. I'd ask Pauleen then.

I finished with cat snacks and was headed for the front hall to grab Elizabeth's leash and harness when my phone rang. I'd recently changed the ring tone from the flowery waltz that I loved but could barely hear in noisy settings to a basic *brrring brrring brrring*. I managed to make it back to the kitchen before the voicemail came on.

"Hello, Halle," I said after clicking on the speaker.

"Hi there, hon. How's it going?" came a familiar husky voice from the other end of the line.

"Not bad." I plunked down in a chair for a more relaxing chat. I hadn't heard from my old attorney friend for a while and figured it might take some time.

I was wrong.

"I can't chat, hon. I've got a deposition in a few minutes, but I'm free tonight. Want to grab something to eat?"

"Tonight? Ooh, sorry, I've already got plans. Seleia is bringing Mum over for dinner and a movie. How about lunch tomorrow instead?"

There was a pause. *"Nope, won't work. I'm booked through next week."*

I noted a catch in Halle's usually upbeat voice. "I can

put off my family thing if it's important."

Again the hesitation. *"No, that's okay. I've got a little issue I need to talk out with someone, but it can wait."*

"I'm sorry," I apologized again. "Do you want to plan a date?"

I heard the clacking of a keyboard. *"Saturday, noonish at the Pub and Pony?"*

"Sure," I said, trying to picture the little square in my date book—yes, a paper one with a cat picture on the cover. I couldn't recall a conflict, but if there was one, I'd cancel it. Something was going on with my friend, and that took precedence.

"What's up?" I began, but Halle cut me off.

"Gotta run. See you Saturday."

The line shut off with a ding-dong sound. I put the phone down on the table, but I didn't move from the chair.

I'd originally met Halle Mackay Pratt through our shared Scottish heritage. My mother Carol Mackay had married my father Collin Mackey, awarding me a double clan affiliation which Carol never let me forget. Halle also took great pride in her birthright, often quoting the Mackay motto *Manu Forti*. It translated to *With a Strong Hand*, and no one was stronger than Halle Pratt.

Halle brought in good earnings as one of Portland's top attorneys which allowed her and her wife Barb to live comfortably in one of Southwest Portland's nicer neighborhoods. It may be true that money can't fix everything, but it can fix a lot. Between Halle's wealth, intellect, and inherited Scots vigor, I'd rarely seen her in a bind. I had a feeling that the thing she wanted to *talk out* with me might be that exception.

I found myself wondering if I should just scrub my evening plans and take Halle up on her dinner offer. Mum would understand, and as for my granddaughter Seleia, as a sophomore in college with a boyfriend and a full social life, I was sure she could find something else to do besides hang out with her elders.

Retrieving my phone, I touched the icon for Halle, a tiny photo of her in her great kilt trying to look like that fellow from *Outlander*. With her flame-red spike of hair and beach ball figure, she cut an impressive image, though in a far different way than the hunky TV highlander.

After one ring, it cut to voicemail. I didn't bother to leave a message. It hadn't been a well-thought-out plan to begin with, and the more I considered, the more the idea of calling off my family night because I sensed something off with Halle seemed extreme. I was probably reading too much into that brief conversation. She was one tough cookie and could handle anything that was thrown at her without my help.

Besides, time was running short. If I were going to make it to the pet store with Elizabeth and be back to feed the cats their supper before Seleia and Carol arrived, I'd better get moving. I thought of the red pack-like pouch I'd previously used for Elizabeth's outings. With the bag strapped to my front, she could sit quietly and watch the world go by as we wandered. That wouldn't work for her Pet Partners certification, however. For that group, cats needed to be in a harness and carried in their partner's arms.

I chose a special wraparound vest-style harness and a matching dark green leash. Elizabeth must have known what was coming because just as I was about to go look for her, she appeared, wobbling over and flopping down on my foot.

I scooped her up. "There you are, sweetheart. Want to

go on an adventure?"

She blinked her blue eyes and gave the smallest of *purrumphs*. I took that to mean yes.

Slipping on the vest and fastening the Velcro flaps around her neck and torso, I hefted her onto my shoulder and went to check on the other cats. Elizabeth liked the closeness of being held, and as I toured the big house, she watched eagerly from her high vantage point. Her mobility issue made it difficult for her to climb like the other cats, and though she had her own special cat tree, it was really more of a *bush*, no taller than would be safe for her to drop if she accidentally flipped over the edge of a perch.

When I was assured the other eight felines were present and accounted for, a ritual I faithfully maintained when I left the house, I transferred Elizabeth into her fancy round carrier and put on my coat. Grabbing my bag, I slung the carrier's strap over my shoulder, and we were on our way.

After arming the alarm and locking the front door, I glanced to the side window. I fully expected to see Little staring back at me from her watch post, but she was oddly absent. I felt a rush of disappointment accompanied by the sudden impression I was forgetting something. Though I paused for a full minute trying to recall what it might be, I could not put a finger on it. Finally I gave up and continued to my car, trying to ignore a vague feeling that all was not right with the world.

Chapter 5

It's fun to see someone with a cat in a public place such as the store or the park, but always ask permission before reaching out or petting.

The Pet Pantry was the absolute downright best pet supply store in town, at least in my opinion. In this day of big-box retailers and business chains, the single-older-woman-owned shop was as unique as its owner. Harlene Meadows, along with her cat Scout and her assistant Danny, ran the little place with a mixture of efficiency and humor. Her shelves boasted nearly everything one would find at a larger outfitter as well as many locally made and one-of-a-kind items the others didn't have. That's where I'd bought Elizabeth's special-needs cat tree, hand crafted to my specifications by a young woman right here in Portland.

    The bell over the door jingled my arrival, or I should say *our* arrival, since I'd taken Elizabeth from her carrier and had her draped across my shoulder like a silver-striped shawl. Seeing no one upon entering, I called out a hello. A pouf of short blonde hair popped out from behind an endcap, followed by a body of round proportions garbed in a muumuu-like dress under a peach-colored *Pet Pantry* apron that seemed to be made of pockets. Already smiling, the gnome-like face brightened at the sight of me, or more likely at the sight of Elizabeth. Who can resist a cat?

"Lynley, welcome! What can I do for you today?"

"Nothing really. I'm training Elizabeth here to be a therapy cat, and taking her out and about is the best way to prepare her for her certification assessment."

Harlene approached in a few brisk steps. "Hello, sweet one," she said to the cat. "May I touch her?" she said to me.

"Yes, of course. But thank you for asking. So many people don't understand that simple common courtesy."

"I know. It's the same with Scout." She nodded to a small seal-colored kitty lounging in a cat bed on the checkout counter. "People just walk up and begin petting her willy-nilly."

"It's for their own good," I furthered, "as much as for the good of the pet. Some pets react badly to a stranger's hand coming at them from out of the blue."

"Not this one though," Harlene commented as she scratched Elizabeth's cheek. "This one is all love and kisses."

I turned so Elizabeth was facing Harlene and listened while they purred and crooned.

"She's beautiful. Such lovely blue eyes. And just look at those white mittens! Very striking on a silver tabby." Harlene came back around. "A bit of a head tilt I see."

"She's a CH kitty—cerebellar hypoplasia. It's not a bad case though. We've been exercising to strengthen her muscles which improves her control. She's only two, still young enough to make some progress."

The sound of boxes toppling followed by a muffled swear brought Harlene's attention back to the store.

"Oh, dear. That must be Danny. I've got him stacking cartons of cat mats in the storeroom. Nothing breakable, but I'd better check it out." With a hurried, "You'll have to excuse me," Harlene rushed off down the middle aisle.

Besides the sleeping Scout, Elizabeth and I seemed to be the only patrons in the place, so I decided to browse a bit. I didn't need anything, having just picked up my standing order of cat supplies the week before, but it was always fun to look. I chose an aisle of cat toys, since one could never have too many of those, and was poring over a display of catnip *Pop Tarts* handmade by a local woman when I heard the tinkle of the entrance bell.

Harlene was still busy in the stockroom, so I made my way up to greet the newcomer. Though her back was turned to me, I instantly recognized the yellow jacket. That color, though pretty and bright, wasn't something one saw on a regular basis.

"Dora?"

The small woman turned and looked confused. Then recognition hit and she smiled.

"Lynley. Fancy meeting you here. And with such a delightful companion!"

We went through a similar exchange as I'd done with Harlene. While Dora fussed over the cat who lapped up the attention like cream, I had a chance to study the quilter I'd so recently met.

Dora—I'd never gotten a last name—must have been no more than a few inches over five foot tall and slim as a sapling. With her dark hair tied behind her neck and the absence of makeup, I'd taken her for an older woman, but now I saw she was likely nearer to her thirties. The agitation over the disappearance of Ridley had aged her. Here, petting sweet Elizabeth, the worry lines all but disappeared.

"Frannie mentioned you have several cats," Dora

commented, still smoothing Elizabeth's sideburns. "I think she said nine?"

"Something like that," I replied ambivalently.

"Wow!" Dora commented. "I love cats, but I don't have any of my own. Pets aren't allowed in my building. But I do a little cat sitting, so I get to spend time with other people's. And there are always Mewella and Ridley." At the mention of the Harts' black cats, a loving glow lit her face. "Pauleen is my best friend, so I'm over at the quilt house all the time. The family lives upstairs, you know — the three of them together. It's kind of sweet and old-fashioned — three generations of women, don't you think?"

No husbands? I wanted to say, but since that was none of my business, I steered my interest in a different direction.

"Did you find Ridley?" I asked, hoping I didn't sound like the busybody I was.

"Oh, yes. He turned up just after you left. He was hiding in a cubby in the catio, like Pet thought."

"Then he wasn't *taken* after all?"

"Not this time." Her look darkened, and I could see she was one of those people whose emotions were transparent on their face. "But it has happened, Lynley, so we're always on guard. You see, Pauleen's neighbors believe Ridley is their cat. It's a problem."

"That would be a problem. But whatever would make them think that Ridley is theirs?"

Dora peered up at me, then took my arm and guided me to a back aisle. Her grip was surprisingly strong.

"I'm not one to gossip, but I know I can trust you. Anyone with so many cats..." Her voice tapered, and she seemed to be gathering her thoughts. "It's not the parents — only the girl, Veronica, but they indulge her.

When she did it the first time, climbed over the back gate and plucked Ridley straight out of the catio, Pauleen and Pet went to talk to them. Pauleen said it was like talking to a brick wall."

Dora paused for a breath since she was becoming visibly agitated by the memory.

"It was awful! Ridley had been gone for two days. The Harts were at their wit's end. They couldn't help thinking the worst, that Ridley was lost on the street, and with Hawthorne just around the corner... It's not safe for a cat, not by a long shot. Then Pet spied Veronica playing with him through the window, and they discovered he'd been right next door the whole time."

I cringed, knowing firsthand what it was like to fear your beloved cat was in danger. Then I frowned as a deeper meaning of the tale sank in.

"So the girl brought home a cat who clearly wasn't a stray, and her parents did nothing to seek out the owner?"

"Nothing!" Dora harrumphed. "In fact, quite the opposite. They told Veronica she could keep the cat for herself."

"Doesn't Ridley have a collar?"

"Of course he does. They replaced it with one of their own. But Ridley has a little scar on his shoulder underneath all his fur. Pauleen easily identified him. The girl threw a tantrum when Pet took him away."

"You said Veronica grabbed him out of the catio?"

"Yes, there's a door from the catio into the garden. The garden is completely fenced with a latched gate to the back alley, but Veronica's a kid—she gets in anyway."

"It's happened more than once?"

"Twice now. Pet thinks they should call in an animal cop from Northwest Humane Society, but Pauleen wants to keep it hush-hush so as not to upset the neighbors."

"Stealing cats is a crime," I commented. The reference to NHS's humane investigators made me think of the team's lead agent, my good friend Denny Paris. He would be the one to call, and I almost said something but decided to file it for a later date. My help might not be needed or wanted since Dora had indicated that Pet and Pauleen preferred the Ridley conundrum remain a private matter.

"I think Pet might be right about getting the authorities involved," Dora went on. She leaned close and whispered. "I think that girl's a little off. She goes nuts when she doesn't get her way. Throws fits and lashes out. I've seen it—it's scary."

"Little girls do act out," I countered. "I was one once—I remember. Thankfully my mom and dad gave me guidance, but not all kids have such perceptive parents."

"Veronica isn't a little girl." Dora's eyes squinted. "She's fourteen."

Elizabeth gave a squirm, indicating she was growing tired of sitting on my shoulder. I put her down on the ground where she tipped to one side, then straightened and took off at a quick clip down the aisle, pulling me along with her.

"Here we go," I tossed back to Dora. "Elizabeth is a wobbly cat. If she doesn't walk fast, she'll fall over."

Dora rushed to catch up with us. "We had one of those at the shelter where I worked. She was a delight, and so friendly and loving! But I'd better be getting on. I just came in to get a few supplies for Pauleen. I like to help out wherever I can."

Elizabeth finished her sprint at the pet bed display where she proceeded to flop down in the middle of it, allowing Dora and me a less-hurried goodbye.

"It was nice talking to you, Lynley." Dora brushed down the sleeves of her coat. "Thank you for listening."

"Having the neighbor girl steal the Harts' cat is a puzzling predicament, that's for sure. If it happens again, let me know. I have a friend at the humane society who might be able to help."

"Thank you. I will."

I watched Dora shuffle off to find her items. Once again, her movements gave the impression of an older woman.

I thought about Pet and Pauleen. I thought about Mewella and her brother Ridley. I thought about a willful little girl who was not so little after all. A few hours before, I'd known none of them and nothing about their unfortunate situation. Trying to imagine what I would do in such a dilemma, I found the feelings of anger, confusion, and helplessness overwhelming.

"There you are," said Harlene as she came around the end cap. "I see Elizabeth got herself a comfy spot."

We both smiled indulgently at the little tabby who was lying like a queen in an oversized dog bed.

"I hope you don't mind her messing up your presentation."

"Not at all, though some doggie might get a surprise when their people bring home a new bed that smells of cat."

"Oh, dear," I remarked. "I am sorry."

"Just kidding. I'll get Daniel to give it a spritz of Anti-Icky-Poo." She leaned down to pet Elizabeth, then straightened. "Now come along and let me show you my latest line in locally-sourced Chinook salmon cat treats. And maybe a boingy-spring toy for Elizabeth."

Chapter 6

It's good to harness-train your cat from kittenhood, but it's never too late. Even if the first sessions are failures, gentle patience and perseverance often win out in the long run.

I'd barely got my coat off and Elizabeth extracted from her harness when there was a knock at my door. I opened it to see my mother Carol, granddaughter Seleia, and Seleia's boyfriend Fredric. Fredric was the all-around helper when it came to odd jobs for our little family, and today he was loaded up with two large cartons.

"We're here," Carol announced, giving me a hug, then pushing by me to proceed into the living room. "Dinner should be coming soon. DoorDash." Carol Mackey, a small woman with wispy white hair and laughing hazel eyes, may have been in her eighties, but her dynamic Scots spirit had not diminished with the years—if anything she had grown more resolute and self-assured.

"Come in, come in," I said to Seleia and the box-carrier who, unlike my mother, lingered politely in the entrance awaiting an invitation. With a smile that could light up a city, Seleia joined her great grandmother. Fredric shuffled in behind her, placing the cartons on the coffee table.

"I asked Fredric to help out, since he lives across the street. I hope you don't mind."

"Of course not. Thank you," I said to the young man.

"Are you sure you don't want to stay for the movie?"

Seleia asked Fredric, her voice betraying a slight wistfulness. "I'm sure it's okay with Lynley."

She glanced at me and I nodded yes.

"Thanks, but I need to get back home. It's Tarzan's feeding time, and he's rigorous about routine. Kittens are a lot of work."

"Yes, they are, but Tarzan is hardly a baby anymore," I remarked of the stray brown tabby who had scampered his way into the young man's life six months before.

Fredric gave a sheepish shrug.

"If you must," Seleia resignedly told her beau. "I'll walk you to the door."

The pair ambled into the hallway where they paused to talk in hushed and intimate tones.

"Cute couple," Carol stated, sinking down into an easy chair. "I wonder if they'll ever get married."

I turned and studied the paramours thoughtfully. Seleia Voxx with her soulful brown eyes and long chestnut tresses which she'd begun wearing in an updo twist, and Fredric Delarosa, a handsome natural redhead with an easy smile, did seem the perfect couple, but not just by way of their looks. Fredric had been with Seleia ever since they met on a film shoot where he was working as a production assistant. At the time, she was sixteen and he was nineteen. I'd had my concerns, but he treated her like a treasure, and she adored him back. They'd grown together, Seleia graduating high school, then heading to college to work toward a degree in astrophysics with a more recent minor in dramatic arts. Fredric was freshly promoted to lead production assistant for a Portland-based film company. Their relationship had experienced ups and downs, but they'd come out of the downs with a greater understanding of themselves and each other. Sometimes I felt a bit envious—as a young woman, my love life had never been that easy.

I was still considering my mother's conjugal comment, when Fredric departed for his duplex, and Seleia returned to the living room with a frown on her face.

"I don't know why he didn't want to stay," she grumbled, "or why he just couldn't come back after Tarzan had eaten. Sometimes I think he loves that cat more than me."

I said nothing, having often been accused of caring more for cats than for people.

Then Seleia perked up. "What about some tea, grandmother? I need a lift."

This was something I could do. "What kind would you like? I can make a pot, or we can have single serving bags if you prefer."

"Let's have a pot of that Genmai-cha you're so fond of," said Carol.

"Seleia?" I asked since I wasn't sure she'd go for Carol's unilateral decision, but the girl nodded.

"I'll help."

Seleia followed me into the kitchen where she began to gather tea things from the familiar cabinets. I filled the teapot with hot water from the faucet, then leaned against the counter to wait while it warmed.

"Mother says hi," said Seleia. "She and daddy are off on a cruise again."

"Oh? Where's Lisa gone this time?" I said a little too brusquely. My relationship with my daughter, Seleia's mother, was complicated. Though we loved each other, I thought she cared too much about superficial things like cruises, and she thought I had too many cats. I gave up a silent thanks to the Powers that Be that my granddaughter had chosen to follow my philosophy of life, one that placed kindness and compassion above material things.

"Why do you do that, Grandmother?" Seleia asked.

"Preheat the teapot? A prewarmed pot is supposed to help keep the brewed tea warm. And that's how Carol taught me to do it," I added. Then it was my turn for questions. "You know I have to ask. What's in the boxes?"

Seleia examined my collection of cat print mugs, then set three cups on a floral melamine tray. "You'll have to corner Granna about that. She wouldn't tell me. When I went to pick her up at her condo, she had one of the caregivers bring them out and put them in my trunk. I asked then, but she said I had to wait."

I dumped the tap water from the pot and added a scoop of loose tea leaves mixed with puffs of roasted brown rice. "Hmmm. Sounds mysterious."

"They're not very heavy. I lifted one. I could have carried them in myself, but Fredric saw us through his window and offered..." She gave a little smile. "Who am I to refuse?"

"Good man. And knowing Carol, we'll find out soon enough. She's never been able to keep a secret for long."

I set the teapot on the tray along with an old-fashioned silver strainer. Since Genmai-cha is customarily drunk without flavorings, I didn't bother with milk, sugar, or lemon.

The cats had heard the rattle of dishes in the kitchen, and decided it was suppertime—which it was. Suddenly surrounded by a meowing horde, I handed Seleia the tray.

"Take this in for Carol and get the movie set up while I give the cats their evening meal. I'll be along in a minute."

It took more than a minute to serve up individual nibbles to nine cats and make sure they ate their own and not someone else's. I was still working on it when I heard the doorbell ring. The front door opened, and after a short deliberation, closed again as the scents of exotic spices wafted through the air.

"Soup's on," Carol yelled.

"Do we need anything?" I called back. "Forks? Knives?"

"No, I think they included all that," said Seleia.

"Movie's ready, and so am I," Carol declared. "If you're done indulging that clowder of yours, come in and we can get started."

"Why so grumpy?" I asked my mother as I sat down next to Seleia on the couch. The cartons had been shifted to the floor, and the coffee table was now spread with brown paper take-out boxes labeled with different combinations of foods.

"I'm always grumpy when I'm hungry," Carol said, choosing a box from the assortment. "You should know that."

"Then by all means dig in. But first, aren't you going to tell us what you brought? My curiosity is killing me."

"Quilts," Carol mumbled around her mouthful of butter chicken.

"Kilts?" I replied, not quite understanding the garbled word. Knowing my mother's penchant for all things Scottish, a box of kilts was not out of the question.

Carol swallowed and cleared her throat. "No, *quilts*. You said you were joining Frannie's quilting guild. I thought I'd show you some of my endeavors from back in the day."

"I didn't know you were a quilter, Granna," Seleia commented between forkfuls of spicy vindaloo.

"Never a faithful one," Carol replied. "It was just

something people did before we had televisions."

I could see that got Seleia thinking. She likely couldn't remember a world before smartphones, let alone imagine the dark ages when Carol was growing up.

"Can we see them?" I was interested.

"Let's eat and start the movie first," she said, taking a big bite of saffron rice. "We can peruse during intermission."

I looked up in surprise. "There's an intermission? How long is this movie? Wait—what movie is it?"

"*The Tragedy of Hamlet, Prince of Denmark*, the 1996 version," said Seleia. "It's four hours."

"Four hours?" I gasped. "Then I hope it has more than one intermission."

"That's why we're watching it on DVD," said Carol. "We can pause it any time we want to."

"Humph," I grunted. "I know you've become a fan of Shakespeare now that you've discovered your acting muse, Seleia, but four hours? Really?"

"I need to watch it for one of my drama classes. I can do it at the apartment, but my roommates are always coming in and out which makes it hard to concentrate, and if I play it on my laptop in my room, it doesn't give the full effect of the magnificent sets."

"We'll try it, dear." Carol pulled a DVD out of her purse. "And I brought an option, just in case." She wiggled it temptingly, but I could still read the title running across the image of a handsome dark-haired man in the checkered polyester jacket, circa 1970s.

"*The Rockford Files*. I should have known."

Carol giggled like a schoolgirl. "Gotta love Rockford."

I, too, enjoyed the now-dated detective series and was thinking it might be more entertaining than Seleia's long

Shakespeare play, but the night wasn't about what we viewed—it was about family. With Seleia busier than ever in her second year at Portland State and Carol getting up in years, these moments were precious.

I wrangled my collection of remote controls, turning on all the necessary media components to play the DVD. Seleia had already slipped the disc into the slot, so in a blare of dark fanfare, the screen jumped to life. As the three of us finished the last of our marsalas and curries, we turned our attention to the Bard.

* * *

"I'm not saying it isn't good," said Carol. "It is. But I need to stretch my legs."

I paused the disk and began loading empty takeout boxes onto the tea tray. "I'm just going to run these into the kitchen."

"That's okay," Seleia sighed, smoothing a hand across Dirty Harry's sleek black back. The old tuxedo cat had decided her lap was the place to be and was now snoring softly. "I can watch the rest of it with Fredric or someone from school."

"It is very good," Carol repeated. "We can come back to it after we have a break. Or maybe, if you'd rather..." Her hand edged toward the *Rockford* DVD.

"How about you show us what's in your boxes," I called from the kitchen, "and then we'll decide about the movie."

"I think someone else likes that idea," said Seleia.

"Pardon? Oh." I returned to see Emilio vigorously rubbing his sideburns along the edge of the larger carton, then sinking his sharp teeth into the cardboard side.

"That one?" Seleia asked the cat. "Granna, can I open

it, or do you want to do the honors?"

"You go ahead dear. I'll supervise from here."

I took a nearby chair, and Seleia knelt on the carpet. As she carefully flipped open the top flaps, I was reminded of Christmases when she was a little girl. Unlike most children her age, she wasn't one to rip and tear at the wrapping, then toss the present aside to retrieve another. Seleia opened each package slowly, as if the anticipation and wonder were part of the gift. She was doing the same thing now, and it took all my restraint not to tell her to hurry it up.

Pulling out a gorgeous hand-sewn quilt, Seleia and I both drew our breath.

"It's beautiful, Granna! You made it yourself?"

Carol nodded proudly. "Yes, with the help of some friends. That sort of quilt is crafted by a group, each person sewing blocks for the top layer, then stitching them together and hand-stitching the completed cover onto the backing on a big wooden frame. We called it a quilting bee."

Seleia passed me the blanket, and I laid it out carefully on the sofa so we could get the full effect.

"That pattern is called the Inner Cat. See the little cat shape inside the bigger one? We liked cats even back in the olden days."

Seleia extracted another piece, smaller in size and made up of fabric bits sewn together.

"That's a lap quilt I made on the sewing machine, probably around the late sixties," Carol narrated. "Crazy quilts, as they were termed, were very popular at the time. With the advent of the zigzag stitch on the newer machines, you could put one of these together quite easily, and since no one ever threw away the extra fabric after making a dress or blouse, there were plenty of scraps to work with."

I zoned in on an oblong of red calico print in the center of the random design. "Is that from my pinafore?"

"You remember?" Carol exclaimed. "You were only a toddler when I made you that frock to go with your little white shirt. It was for some girl's party, if I recall correctly."

"I loved that dress and was heartbroken when I got too big for it! Wow, that brings back memories."

The activity on the floor had roused a few cats from their after-dinner repose. Emilio had been joined by Little and Tinkerbelle, and the three black cats leapt around the alien box like dancing shadows. As I watched them, I suddenly had a feeling they were trying to tell me something.

"What else have you got in there, Carol?"

Not waiting for an answer, I bent over the carton and pawed through the quilts. Emilio jumped on my lap for a better look, then gave a definitive *me-rrow*. There, nestled in among the soft fabric was a cloisonné dresser box. As I drew it out, Little grabbed my hand with her paws, trying to wrestle the item away from me.

"Mine," I said, pulling back. "Give it up, you guys!" I looked at Carol. "What's in here, Mum? Catnip?"

"No, dear, nothing like that. Go ahead and open it."

Not without trepidation, I did as she bid. It took a little effort to wrest the long-shut lid from the body, but finally it swung up on its hinges to reveal a second box. This one was brown and square with a tiny crest embossed in one corner. Upon opening it, I found there was a scent, not of catnip but of—

"Roses!" I exclaimed, peering at a trio of shriveled

brown buds tied up with a blue lace ribbon.

Carefully, I lifted the spray from its satin-lined bed and held it up to my mother. "A corsage? There must be a story here."

"A love story, perhaps?" Seleia teased.

Carol smiled. "Nothing so romantic, I'm afraid. The corsages were given to us at our high school graduation. My mamma put it in the fancy container. I'd not have bothered with it myself, but she was proud of her daughter's achievement since she never had the opportunity to make it past eighth grade."

Seleia was already digging out another quilted coverlet, this one in a pattern I recognized as Log Cabin. I replaced the corsage box in the cloisonné chest and set it aside. Busy with the new find, I didn't notice Little reach up to softly paw the glassy enamelwork surface.

Chapter 7

The Rainbow Bridge is a (mythical) link between Earth and the afterlife where humans reunite with their departed furry friends.

The rest of the week flew by as it does for us retirees who find we are busier now that we've left our regular job than ever before. When Friday rolled around, I was looking forward to the session at House of Quilts and picking up where I left off with my little embroidery. Maybe I'd be able to finish it this time.

I was also looking forward to the chat around the sewing table. As with most groups working toward a common goal, people got to talking. Last time, the topics mainly centered around the projects and their final destination at the upcoming ShadowCat Rescue's charity auction, but other subjects crept in as well: family, the weather, and cats.

I'm not one to gossip per se, but if I could nudge today's discussion in a certain direction, maybe I'd be able to find out a bit more about the Harts' neighbors who had allowed their little girl to steal a cat. *Not so little*, I reminded myself. At fourteen, Veronica should have been developing the moral compass that would guide her into adulthood. Teenagers had issues of their own, complicated by a conflicted world, but as far as I could tell, she had two loving parents that would help her through that difficult time. Maybe the parents had issues of their own.

Frannie was driving herself to the quilt shop this time, so I didn't have to run across town to pick her up at her apartment. That meant instead of a thirty-minute drive, it would be nearer to ten. I gave myself fifteen and got there five minutes early. I found the perfect parking place right out front, pulled in, and turned off the engine. Setting the brake, I picked up my bag, but I didn't get out right away.

I was looking at the house. Looking at the *houses*, I should say, because now I noticed that the homes to either side of House of Quilts were of similar design. It was common in the early nineteen-hundreds for landowners to sell off lots to contractors who would then put up twin or even triplet buildings, utilizing a single architectural plan. My own house, built in 1904, was one of three of the same construct.

The place to the right had a *For Sale* sign in its front yard, so the one on the left had to be the home of the wayward Veronica. A gray exterior with white trim contrasted with the House of Quilts' bright colors like night and day. The yard was as spare as the monotone exterior, a boxwood bush to either side of the porch steps and what looked like the beginning of a primrose edging that had yet to be completed. One lone clump of daffodils bloomed brightly in the lawn, making the place look even duller by comparison.

I turned to the for-sale house. It hadn't fared much better in the way of a color palette. I didn't understand how, in a locale that boasted the most days of cloud cover in the Pacific Northwest, gray could be in such fashion, but it was. Slate, charcoal, battleship, and flat black were all the trend, likely promoted by some famous designer from Los Angeles where the sun shone on a regular basis.

This house was more of the bluish gray they called

gunmetal and looked to have been recently painted. Other signs of a pre-sale fix-up were the black-shingled roof, perfect and moss-free; the sparkling clean windows; and the blanket of red cedar chips beneath the newly-planted shrubberies. For no good reason, I got out my phone and snapped a photo of the yard sign with the number of the realtor. Curiosity, I supposed. What was the going rate for a house off Hawthorne Boulevard these days?

I noticed Mark coming up the street and turning in the walkway to House of Quilts. I glanced once more at the three single-family homes deciding hands-down I preferred the quilt shop's wild forest garden and colorful exterior to its lackluster companions, then I got out of my car and followed the one male quilter up the steps.

* * *

Everyone arrived and took their places at the table within minutes of each other, indicating an enthusiasm that I admired. Pet and Pauleen gathered sundries, then started on projects of their own. Mewella oversaw everyone's efforts from her pink bed. Mrs. Hart was in her easy chair by the window as though she had never left, but she wasn't knitting this time since a second black cat—Ridley I assumed—lay curled up in her lap.

Frannie and I sat next to each other catching up on the week's adventures which mostly involved the goings-on at Friends of Felines. There had been a surprise intake of cats from a California town that had recently suffered flooding. All able volunteers had been called to assist. Intakes like that were arduous, but with the expert supervision of the FOF emergency team, thirty-five cats were checked in, examined, and dispersed into kennels to eat, rest, and await the next step in their new, safe life.

"I really fell in love with the little snaggletoothed tabby," said Frannie. "I hope they don't have to remove her funny fang. It gives her character."

"She seemed healthy," I replied, "but you never know when it comes to dental issues."

"We had a cat with a snaggletooth at my shelter," commented Dora.

"Oh? What shelter was that?" I asked, fascinated by anything having to do with cat rescue. It was the second time Dora had mentioned her former volunteering efforts to me, which I took to mean she was quite proud of them. So why wasn't she still doing it?

"That was the Blue River Cat Shelter in Blue River, before my husband and I moved here. You wouldn't have heard of it. It was small but served the entire community."

"Friends of Felines is always looking for experienced volunteers, if you're interested."

Dora's eyes lit, then the spark died. "I'll think about it," was all she said.

"Rats!" I exclaimed suddenly. I'd been trying to thread the orange embroidery floss through my needle, while it stubbornly refused to comply.

"A rat?" Ruth screamed, jumping out of her chair. "Where?"

"Oh, no, I'm sorry, Ruth," I exclaimed. "It's not a real rat—just an expression I use in place of a stronger swear word." I straightened my glasses, inspecting the frayed end of the thread. "In this case, I was expressing frustration."

"Whew." Ruth reseated herself and adjusted her skirt. She was wearing pink again today, a spring dress and sweater set with a cat pin on the collar. "I'm the one who should be sorry for acting out. But I'm deathly afraid of rats, you see. I know there would never be a rat in this house."

I caught Ruth's eye, and we exchanged a look of understanding. I had a few phobias myself.

Gilda was working away on her sewing machine, piecing together a complicated pattern of little squares. I decided it was time to face the dragon.

"What are you making, Gilda?" I asked in my most innocuous tone.

For a moment, I thought she was going to ignore me, but finally she stopped her machine and gave me a glare. Still, she held up the edge of her project so I could see the design.

"Why, it's beautiful!" I exclaimed as all the separate parts came together in the image of a cat sitting tall.

"Thank you," she said politely as she returned her attention to her work.

"Is it your cat?" I blurted before she had a chance to run the machine.

She looked startled, then pensive. "We no longer have a cat," she said finally.

"Gilda's puss crossed the Rainbow Bridge a few months ago," Mark explained softly.

"Oh, I'm so sorry," I offered from my heart. "That's so hard."

"Thank you, Lynley," Gilda said. "Yes, it has been. Fritz was with us for all of his twenty years. I never knew I could feel such loss."

Suddenly it was as if all Gilda's gruff pretense had fallen away. A tear slipped down her cheek, but she was smiling.

"He was such a joy! I'm trying to remember all the good times, like the grief counselor told us to."

"Good for you. I'm sure you have some wonderful memories."

"We do. Now if you'll excuse me…" The smile faded as she pushed her quilt away and got up from her chair. Skirting the table, she headed out of the room, her shoulders sagging.

So much for happy memories, I thought to myself, but I understood. I'd lost many a cat throughout the years, and it never got easier. Grateful that all nine of my clowder were currently in good health, I sent up a little thank you to the Heavens along with a prayer that they would stay that way for a very long time.

"She's really broken up about it," said Frannie.

"I can imagine."

"We've all been worried," said Ruth, "but she doesn't want to talk about it. I get that, but it makes it hard. Working with her has been like working with a statue."

"A statue with attitude," Dora harrumphed.

Pet gave Dora a look of admonishment. "Now Dora, be nice."

"Maybe you could talk to her, Lynley," said Pauleen. "That was the most positive reaction I've seen from her since it happened. She was actually smiling for a bit there."

"And admitted to seeing a counselor," Frannie furthered. "Yes, Lynley, why don't you try. She's obviously in pain."

"Good luck," Dora murmured, then added, "I'm sorry. I just have a hard time with…"

I waited for her to finish, but she turned her attention back to her mini-quilt. It seemed apparent there were bad feelings between her and Gilda, but whether it was something specific or a general dislike was yet to be seen.

I was ready for a break—maybe when I came back, my

needle and floss would be more cooperative. Putting the little embroidery work in its box, I rose and went after Gilda. I didn't know what I could say that would soften her loss, but maybe just reaching out and letting her guide the conversation would be enough.

When she wasn't in the shop, I moved on to the sunroom. Since I hadn't heard the bell over the front door, I could only assume that she'd gone out the back. But the sunroom was vacant as well, which left only the catio and the garden beyond.

It was a lovely spring day—I figured a trip outside wouldn't do me any harm. As I slipped through the catio, I took in the layered platforms, cat trees, and bits of grass and plantings the Harts had assembled for Mewella and Ridley. There were lawn chairs and a bench around a table for human visitors. It was a nice place for either humans or cats but was currently bereft of either.

I stepped out to the garden through a sturdy door with a knob-style latch. The garden itself was larger than I'd expected, with a horse chestnut tree to one side and a tall oak to the other. Spikes from last year's flowers stood black among mats of violets, clumps of bluebells, and mounds of forget-me-nots.

Sprays of climbing roses were just beginning to leaf green and red along the cedar fencing. Nearby was a nice set of outdoor furniture, including an old-fashioned table with a hole in its center for an umbrella and a covered backyard swing. What wasn't in that pretty patch of greenery was Gilda.

I homed in on a gate in the center of the fence, a whimsical design with the tops of the individual boards cut into the shape of cats' heads. It was open a crack. Gilda must have gone through there. I started for it, then hesitated, wondering if it was time to curtail my search for the melancholy quilter. Would following her into the alley be an invasion of her privacy? If she went to such lengths to be alone, would she be open to my company?

I headed for the gate anyway. Something else was on my mind, circling back to Veronica and her pursuit of Ridley. I was curious—curious to see the route the girl might have taken for her thievery; curious to see how hard it would be to slip into the Harts' garden and nab the cat. With the catio door unlocked as it was now, there seemed to be little issue.

When I reached the gate, I spent a moment checking out the brass latch. I jiggled it, latched it, then unlatched it again. It seemed substantial enough to keep trespassers out and was set low on the frame so as not to be reached from the outside. But Dora said Veronica had climbed up and over. Though I knew I could never make it, it wouldn't be difficult for someone small and agile, like a kid.

I decided since I'd got that far, I might as well continue. Making sure the gate remained ajar behind me, I stepped into the alley, a quiet little lane that time had forgotten. Looking left, I saw where it sloped down to meet the street. On my right was a green wooden bench.

To my surprise, I found the bench to be occupied, not by Gilda but by an elderly man in a gray-green cardigan sweater and a jaunty moss-colored Gatsby that perched atop his head like a mushroom cap. Propped next to him was a burl-handled cane. In the shade of the old horse chestnut boughs, he could have been a woodsman from fairy lore.

Chapter 8

Is your cat a lap-sitter? One of the most frequent questions we get at the shelter from potential adopters is whether the cat sits on laps. Unfortunately there is no way to tell until the cat gets settled and safe into a home.

The man in the green cap saw me and smiled.

"Good afternoon. I've been standing guard, if you're wondering." He gave a conspiratorial wink. "Or to be more accurate, *sitting* guard."

"Oh?" was all I could think of to say.

"I'm Colin. I live over there."

He waved a weathered hand toward a yellow house across the block, a big home of original Portland design. Its façade was partially hidden by a tall Douglas fir that loomed over a wrought iron gate and a row of mature birches standing tall along the parking strip.

"I stop here to rest on my walks. Not so young as I used to be," he confided with a chuckle.

"None of us are," I sighed. "I'm Lynley. Did you happen to see a woman come out a few minutes ago?"

"How do you do, Lynley? Yes, Gilda came through just before you. She went down the lane and turned onto the street."

"You know Gilda?" I asked in surprise.

"Sure, I know everybody. Comes from living here some fifty years. That, and being a friendly sort."

I peered down the vacant alleyway and made the snap decision I was done with the chase. Hopefully Gilda's stroll had cleared her head, and she would return to the quilt shop in a better mood. I felt bad for triggering her grief, but I hadn't done it on purpose. Just the opposite, I'd started up the conversation in hopes of breaking through her surliness. How was I to know that beneath that gruff exterior she had a vulnerable side?

I realized I should probably rejoin the group as well, but the sun felt so warm on my face, and the air was fresh and clear. My project could wait another couple of minutes. Besides, I wanted to know more about Colin and his self-appointed guard duty.

I seated myself on the green bench and peered at the man. "What did you mean when you said you're standing guard? What are you guarding against?"

The sparse white eyebrows rose. "You are a direct one, Miss Lynley."

I laughed. "So I've been told."

I turned my gaze to a budding azalea and waited for an answer. I figured anyone who made such enigmatic statements would be compelled to expound on them eventually. It didn't take long.

"Firstly," he began as if tutoring a child, "I must preface with the fact that this is a nice, quiet neighborhood. As I mentioned, I have lived here a long time. I've watched families come and go, children born, the old folks passing on. Portland has changed, but by some miracle, this little quarter has managed to remain the same."

He paused for a breath, then frowned. "There are a few troubling concerns, however."

He turned to stare at the gray house beside the quilt shop. I followed his gaze. What I could see of its backside behind the chain-link fence was as featureless as its front. On the covered flagstone patio was a barbeque and a couple of folded lawn chairs. The blinds in the windows were drawn which I thought sad on such a perfect day.

"Is the girl in that house one of those concerns?" I ventured.

The brown eyes moved to me, and he nodded his head. "That poor child tries to sneak into the Harts' place every chance she gets. She's even stolen their cat on a few occasions. It drives Miss Paulette crazy. I can't be here all the time, of course," he made known, "but when I am…"

"I've only recently joined the Harts' quilting group, but I heard about the cat abductions. Apparently, Veronica's parents told her she could keep Ridley, even though he was plainly someone else's cat."

"The Naylors are…" He paused. "They are broad-minded when it comes to their daughter," he finished, though I felt that wasn't what he'd originally meant to say. *Indulgent, lenient,* or even *loose* might have been more to the point.

"They moved into the house a few years ago. The couple are pleasant though not overly friendly. Middle-aged, quiet. There's an uncle of advanced years, but he rarely comes out, at least not during the day. Maybe he has a nightlife?" Colin gave a laugh. "You never know with us old codgers."

"And Veronica? What's she like?"

Colin shrugged. "Adolescents these days… Not the same as when I was a young man."

His gaze drifted away, back to his own home across the block. "I'd better be getting on now, or Mary will worry I've gotten lost. She doesn't like me to be gone too long."

He hefted himself up off the bench with the help of the cane, then turned and held out his hand. "Nice to meet you, Miss Lynley. Maybe I'll see you here again sometime."

I took the proffered hand, warm and calloused. "Nice to meet you too, Colin. And thanks for *sitting guard*."

He gave a short nod, then began to amble off down the alley, his eyes fixed on home.

* * *

I sat on the green bench for a bit more, enjoying the freshness of the afternoon and thinking how thankful I was to have survived another long, gray Portland winter. No matter what was going on with the world of humans, nature celebrates the growing season the same way every year. It's a small miracle and one worth acknowledging.

But despite the sun, the temperature was hanging in the low fifties. I'd rushed off after Gilda without a coat and felt myself beginning to chill. Giving the Naylors' house one last glance, I rose and retraced my steps through the gate, through the garden, through the catio, the sunroom, and the shop to retake my place at the quilting table. To note, when I got there, Gilda still hadn't returned.

"She's not back yet?" I asked, picking up my orange floss to give another try at threading my needle.

"Who, Gilda?" Mark glanced over at her vacant chair. "Haven't seen her."

"Did you catch up with her?" Frannie asked. "You were gone for some time."

"No, but I did meet someone. A man who was sitting on the bench in the alley."

"Colin?" Pet smiled as she carefully pinned a cutout of red fabric onto her square. "He's quite a character, that one."

"Colin is a neighborhood institution," explained Pauleen. "A sweet old guy. He knows this area like the back of his hand. But he's got beginning Alzheimer's, so don't take what he says too seriously."

"Really?" I remarked in surprise. "He seemed lucid to me." But now that I thought back, there were clues. Colin, himself, had revealed his wife's concern over his getting lost. I'd taken it as a quip, but maybe it had really happened.

Pauleen drove her needle through her block, making tiny, precise stitches. "He has good days and bad."

"I'm sorry," I said. "Dementia is such a hardship for everyone involved." Taking a conversational turn, I went on, "He did tell me a bit about your neighbors, the Naylors."

Pet frowned. "Did he mention that thieving little girl who thinks Ridley is her cat?"

"His comments were on the polite side, but yes, he found her behavior disturbing. It seemed like he's made it his business to try to thwart her attempts. Ah!" I added, finally maneuvering the floss through the eye of the needle.

"I wish he could be there all the time," Pet grumbled. "Veronica wouldn't dare climb the fence with someone looking on."

"The Naylor parents, George and Jan, are nice enough," Pauleen said. "Veronica runs roughshod over them. They don't know how to say no to her."

"I understand that, and it's good to let kids that age test their wings, but it's not an excuse for letting her get away with theft." Pet stabbed a pin into her square with more force than necessary, then dropped the fabric onto the table. "Oh, I know—we got Ridley back, but really? What a way to raise a kid!"

"You wait until you have children of your own," Pauleen commented. "Setting them straight, especially during the teenage years, isn't as easy as you might think."

Pet looked aghast at her mother. "You're not comparing me to that little brat, are you?"

"No, never, sweetheart. You were a veritable angel at fourteen." She turned and gave a wink to the rest of the group. "No, really. You had your foibles—remember when you had a crush on that English musician and began to talk like a Brit? And the Goth phase, where all your clothes had to be black? And..."

"Please stop! I remember," Pet said sheepishly.

"You grew out of them, and I'm sure Veronica will too."

"Not if she doesn't get some guidance," Dora muttered. "Things could go very badly for her if she continues to think her choices don't have consequences."

"I heard there was an uncle," I mentioned. "Does he help out with the girl?"

"Christian Naylor?" Pet scoffed. "Christian Naylor is an enigma unto himself."

I expected her to elaborate, but she shut her mouth, her lips firmly pressed together in a frown. I waited, but she took up her quilt square again and busied herself with her work, marking the subject as closed.

Then my attention slipped beyond Pet to Mrs. Hart. The old woman was staring owl-like at the back of Pet's head. I hadn't realized how dark her eyes were, like onyx marbles set in the ivory of her face. Grasping the chair arms, she made to rise, dumping poor Ridley on the floor. For a moment, she half-stood, her mouth open as if she were about to speak; then she folded back down, took up her knitting, and turned her gaze to the window, working the needles back and forth in a rhythm all her own.

Chapter 9

Though cats spend much of their waking time grooming themselves, keeping their environment clean falls to us, their human companions.

It was Saturday morning, and though I hadn't held a real, go-to-the-office job for years, the day still had a routine of its own. After feeding the cats, I washed their various water cups and bowls, deep-cleaned the litter boxes, and vacuumed. I did things that had nothing to do with cats as well, like catching up on my email and social media, plus a good amount of spontaneous surfing of the web.

As I scrolled through the news, an article concerning a spate of housing market scams being run by unethical realty companies caught my eye. The exposé roused my curiosity, and I picked up my phone to find the yard sign photo I'd snapped by House of Quilts. It had been an impulse shot at the time, but something about the name of the realtor had nagged at me. Now I knew what that was. According to the commentary, the company, *Holmes Homes*, was not to be trusted.

The piece which originated at a local news station didn't come right out and accuse Holmes Homes of committing fraud, but they did mention in their roundabout journalist way that, along with several others, the group was under investigation. That could point to innocence, guilt, and anything in between.

I was still studying the photo when my phone rang, making me jump.

"Hello?" I said unsteadily as my blood pressure returned to normal.

"Hey, Lynley," came Halle's basso voice over the line. *"Did I catch you napping? You sound strange."*

"No, I'm fine. Just concentrating on something else. Is this about lunch?"

"Yeah. I wanted to make sure you were still on."

"Definitely. Noon?" I looked at the clock on the shelf next to my computer—a bit before eleven.

"Right. I might be a few minutes late. Grab us a table and order me a beer."

"I'll get us a table, but you'll have to order your own beer. They have—what? Fifty different kinds?"

Halle laughed. *"Sorry. Don't know what I was thinking. I know you don't drink anymore."*

"Other people's drinking doesn't bother me—unless it makes them boring or obnoxious."

"Is that a hint?"

"Halle, you could never be boring, and I know you reserve your innate obnoxiousness for the courtroom."

"I call it confidence, but yeah, I think you're safe on both counts. See you in a few."

I heard a ping as the phone icon at the bottom of the screen turned from green to red. The Pub and Pony was only a short walk from my house. I still had plenty of time, but I'd seen enough of the news, so I bookmarked the real estate scam article and closed the window. Briefly I admired my wall photo, a black and white cat in a summer garden. It was not one of mine, but a pretty scene all the same.

I found myself lingering over the picture though I

wasn't sure why. I felt like I'd missed something and needed to stay put until I figured out what it was. Then, as my eyes traced the flowing lines of the tuxie and sank into the colorful floral background, I remembered. Didn't Halle have a friend in the real estate business?

* * *

The Pub and Pony, a popular English-style eating and drinking establishment, was predictably busy, but I managed to snag a small table by a window toward the back. I'd barely got my coat off when Halle arrived, not late after all.

She stowed her Hawk leather briefcase under her chair and sat down with a sigh. In her tailored men's suit that fit snugly around her beach ball figure, she looked every bit the conservative attorney, until one got to her hair which was colored an impossible shade of fire orange and coaxed straight up like a match flame.

"Oh, hon! What a day! What a week! I swear, one of these times I'm going to take a vacation."

"Vacations are good, but what about retirement?" I proposed. "You are due, you know."

"Retirement?" she shot back at me as if I'd uttered a dirty word. "Never! Well, someday," she amended, "but not anytime soon. You know I love my job."

And I did know. Halle was a brilliant lawyer, one of the good ones who fought for right, not might. She wouldn't take a case unless she believed in her client. As she'd told me many times, there were lots of other attorneys who could represent the apathetics and the sociopaths. If you were innocent, or even guilty but with extenuating circumstances, Halle was your man.

Picking up the menu sheet and putting it down again,

she loosened her blush-pink necktie. "I don't know why I even look," she said. "I always order the same thing."

"Burger with HP Sauce and cider vinegar fries."

"Yup. Do you know what you're going to have? I'll call the server."

I nodded, and she waved down a girl in a white apron over a red print dress.

"Have you decided?" the server asked with just a hint of a British accent.

"I'll have your number four burger with a side of kale slaw and a Mackeson Stout. Lynley?"

"Veggie burger with yam chips, please."

The girl punched our order into her handheld device. "Anything to drink besides water?"

"Ginger ale."

Both Halle and I uttered thank-yous as she spun off to the kitchen. In record time she returned to drop off our beverages.

Halle had been silent since giving her order. If it had been a comfortable silence between old friends, I would have let it go, but I felt it was something more.

"Do you want to talk about it?" I softly pressed.

She raised an eyebrow. "Not mincing words today, are we?"

"You implied something was wrong when you called me the other day. Now you look as jumpy as a cat on the Fourth of July. If there's a problem, I want to help."

Halle hesitated, spinning her bottle of stout with her fingers though she had yet to take a drink out of it.

"Yeah," she said finally, uttering another sigh. "I'm just not used to asking for advice. I'm the one who solves everyone else's problems, right?"

"No one can be the hero all the time. Tell me what's

going on."

"It's nothing, really."

"It's something," I pressed, "or you wouldn't be worried about it."

Now she took a swig of beer directly from the bottle as was her style. "It's my wife's brother Alex. He's staying with us..."

"And?" I encouraged.

"He's staying with us because he lost his job and subsequently his apartment. He's a drinker, a heavy drinker. Doesn't seem to care about much else." She put down the beer bottle, giving it a black look as if it were the cause of all her ills. In a way it was.

"An alcoholic?"

"I guess, though he won't admit it. But all he does is lie around the house drinking our booze. It's really getting to Barb. She hates seeing him like that."

"I can't imagine you like it very much either," I commented. "Unfortunately it's hard to help someone until they admit they have a problem."

"I'm at the end of my rope, Lynley. I don't want to kick him out onto the streets, and I'm not sure Barb would forgive me if I did, but it's weighing on us both. He caterwauls all night long, and we barely get any sleep. I've taken to spending nights at the office. This can't go on!"

"No, it can't," I agreed.

"You know about alcoholism, Lyn. Tell me what I should do."

"I know about my own battle with booze," I confessed. "I can't speak for others. But I do have something that might help." I rummaged in my purse, brought out a ragged address book, and thumbed through it until I found what I was looking for. Retrieving a *Hello Kitty* notepad and a pen, I copied the name and number. "Here's a guy who will come and talk to your brother-in-law. He won't preach or push, he'll just tell his own story and then see if Alex wants to go to a meeting of men who have had similar experiences."

"You mean AA?"

I nodded. "Alcoholics Anonymous still has the best track record for getting people sober and keeping them that way."

I handed her the note. She took it, gave it a once over, then tucked it in her pocket.

"You really think this guy could help?"

"I can't promise anything, but it's the only solution I know of."

"Thanks Lynley. We'll give it a try. It's got to be better than sleeping on the office couch."

"Now I've got a question for you," I said. "What do you know about the real estate scams that are going on around town?"

Halle looked up in surprise. "Why? Have you been approached by someone who wants you to sell your house?"

"No, nothing like that. But I was reading an article about some iffy companies who are bilking both buyers and sellers for money, personal information, and whatnot. One in particular is called Holmes Homes. Have you heard of them?"

"Not personally, but Arden would know... Arden Caplin. She is on the board of the local chapter of NAR, the National Association of Realtors. I'll give you her number." Halle pulled her phone from her inside pocket and punched at it. I heard a ping from my own phone which was still in my purse. "There you go, hon. But may I ask why?"

I frowned. "There's a house for sale off Hawthorne next to the place where I've been attending quilting sessions."

Halle gave a snicker of disbelief. "You're quilting?"

"Right now I'm embroidering a patch for someone else to appliqué onto their project. The group is making donations for a cat shelter charity auction."

"Ah, I should have known it had something to do with cats. But I didn't mean to interrupt. What about this house for sale?"

"I'm not sure." I paused, trying to retrieve the apprehension I'd felt when I was there. Now those suspicions seemed farfetched, but through the years I'd learned to trust my instincts. "It's listed with this Holmes Homes. I don't know anything else about it. But if they are doing something illegal, it could affect the neighborhood. It could affect the nice people at House of Quilts."

Chapter 10

Using treats and rewards, you can train your cat to come when you call. Did I mention treats?

The days after my lunch date with Halle had been hectic. Along with the new cats from the emergency intake came extra shelter shifts. That, on top of my own cats' care, social engagements, housework, and spring yardwork, had made the time fly by.

I'd also spent more than a few hours running internet searches to find out more about Holmes Homes. I called the number Halle had given me for her real estate contact Arden Caplin, but I'd yet to hear back. I wasn't sure what I would tell her. Sometimes there was a fine line between being a concerned citizen and being a nosy parker.

Elizabeth and I had been working extra hard in preparation for her therapy cat certification assessment test scheduled for next week. So far, she'd taken everything in stride—the walks in the park, the visits to stores and the houses of friends. Whenever I called her with the two-word summons, *Elizabeth—leash*, she'd hobble and wobble out from wherever she'd been resting with a purring meow as if to say, "I'm ready!"

That's how she was when it came time to go to the quilt shop. She'd been following me around all morning, staring up at me with those beautiful blue eyes. Did she have a hunch something exciting was about to happen? I wasn't totally convinced taking her to today's quilting session was the best idea, but I'd cleared it with Pauleen who said both Mewella and Ridley would be, if not enthusiastic about a visit from another cat, at least tolerant. Elizabeth clearly wanted the outing. I could almost swear she meowed the word, *leash*.

When I arrived at House of Quilts, I felt some trepidation, but Pet was all smiles, eager for me to bring her in. Setting her carrier on the sewing table, I zipped off the removable top and put it aside. Elizabeth blinked as she took in her new surroundings, her gaze finally coming to rest on the two cats at the far end of the table. The black siblings stared back with mild interest, then Mewella turned her head toward a shaft of sunlight beaming through the window, and Ridley settled into his blue plush bed for a nap. Elizabeth watched a little longer, then cocked her head nearly sideways and uttered a small chirp. So much for my fear of a clash.

That had been an hour ago, and now all three cats were sleeping. The quilters worked quietly on their various projects, while I concentrated on my embroidery. Frannie had decided she could incorporate my patch into her mini-quilt, so I was hurrying to finish up the tail.

"There!" I announced as I tied off the last bit of orange thread. "Cali the Calico is ready to move on to greater things."

"You named your piece?" Ruth pondered.

"She names everything," said Frannie. "It comes from having to name the stray cats who arrive nameless at the shelter."

"I named my cats when I adopted them," said Dora. "Frisbie and Simeon. The names they came with were silly."

Sillier than Frisbie and Simeon? I wondered briefly but kept my opinions to myself.

"Cali the Calico it is then," said Frannie, spreading her little quilt on the table. "I think she'll be perfect right about there."

I laid the embroidery on the spot she indicated. The bright calico colors on their natural linen backing contrasted nicely with the blue and black cat shapes in Frannie's design.

"I'd bid on it," I proclaimed.

Frannie chuckled. "I would too, if I do say so myself!"

Frannie pinned the Cali square in place with long, pearl-headed pins. Smiling with satisfaction, she held it up for the others to see.

There was a round of favorable nods and murmurs. Even Gilda managed a brief glance and a thumbs up.

"I love it!" said Pet. "We haven't had anything with embroidery before. It really makes the whole thing pop."

"Are you going to do more?" Mark asked me. "Because this could use something." He offered the runner he'd been working on, scratching his beard thoughtfully. The cat print fabric at either end was the only relief to an otherwise plain collection of rectangles.

"How about a white cat for that dark colored patch in the center?" Dora suggested.

Mark studied the piece, then looked at me. "What do you think, Lynley?"

"I can try." I got up and went to the bookshelf for the design book where I'd found the Cali template. Leafing through, a pattern for a perfectly round sleeping kitty caught my eye.

I showed it to Mark. "The picture gives it in black, but I can do it in white or another color if you like."

Mark turned a wistful gaze to Pet. "What do you think, white or colors?"

"Sure," the girl replied distractedly, her concentration solely on the difficult topper she was piecing together. It was obvious Mark adored the young quilter, and equally obvious she didn't return his adoration. Was she indifferent, or were Mark's advances merely too subtle for her to notice?

Ah, youth, I thought to myself. *Such a lot of work.*

My mind drifted to Seleia and her boyfriend Fredric. My granddaughter and her beau enjoyed a comfortable relationship that had weathered a few storms and become stronger for it. But relationships can't stay static forever. Eventually the couple would either drift apart or feel the need to take things to the next level. As Seleia's devoted grandmother, I was unsure which seemed the scarier.

"Lynley?"

"Huh?" I grunted, my reflections returning from petal-strewn aisles and white lace dresses.

"Lynley," Dora repeated. "Did you see? Your little cat just headed for the door."

"What?" I leapt up. I hadn't even noticed her get down from the table. Despite her disability, she was a young cat with lots of ingenuity and spunk, and the vacant chair next to me had made for an easy jump. Now she was halfway across the room and moving fast.

Elizabeth could cover ground when she had a mind to. Watching her tail disappear around the corner, I shot back a quick, "Excuse me," and rushed after her.

When I got into the shop, I paused. Elizabeth was nowhere in sight. I gasped, thinking she'd gone through to the sunroom. I knew she couldn't go outside even if the door to the catio was open, but she could still get in trouble. That beautiful cat-space had been designed for cats who could climb without fear of falling. Elizabeth's feline enthusiasm often exceeded her physical limitations. It had taken much trial and error to make my big home Elizabeth-proof.

Then I heard a meow from above and realized she must have gone upstairs to the personal rooms. My heart fell. I didn't feel comfortable entering the Harts' private space without permission and was about to go back to ask when I heard a crash. Imagining Elizabeth inadvertently destroying valuable antiques or precious mementos, I decided to skip permission and ask forgiveness once I confirmed the Hart's belongings were safe.

The carpeted steps ran straight up from the back of the shop, then made a left turn at a small landing with a window that looked down onto a strip of side yard. That was where I found Elizabeth, happily rolling around on the rug, a crocheted banana clasped tightly in her claws. A ceramic bowl lay upside down nearby, along with two more of the handspun fruit.

I knelt and returned the bowl to its place on the bottom shelf of an antique tea table. "What do you think you're doing?" I asked the mischievous cat. She blinked innocently as I unhooked her from the banana, then placed it and its mates in the bowl. "No," I told her sternly with absolutely no hope she would cooperate.

I was right about that—it took less than a second for her to go after the target once more. At least that time she snagged only the banana and didn't topple the whole bowl.

"I said no," I admonished as I again retrieved the poor fruit.

Scooping the cat into my arms, I was about to head

back downstairs when I heard voices. The screened window was open a crack, and the voices were coming from there.

I paused to glance outside at the house next door, the one that was on the market. A high cedar fence separated it from the Harts' property, concealing the talkers who must have been directly on the other side. I might not have been so keen to listen except the people were shouting at a decibel that was impossible to ignore.

To be more accurate, one person was shouting, a woman with a voice that could break glass.

"You can't be here," she screeched. "How many times do I have to tell you?"

I couldn't catch the gravelly words of the other speaker, but it seemed to be a man.

"I don't care about your grandfather. He could have come over on the Mayflower, and that still wouldn't give you the right to prowl around..."

Another unintelligible response.

"I'd call the police if it wouldn't turn into such a hassle. Still, if I catch you one more time..."

Her voice had risen to a strangled scream, then cut off abruptly. I listened a few moments more, but now all I heard was the tweet of a robin in a nearby tree. The argument seemed to be over.

Elizabeth had eyes on the banana again and was beginning to squirm, so I gave up on my snooping and proceeded downstairs to rejoin the others while making a mental note to work on the small cat's patience before her assessment test—and to be sure there weren't any crocheted bananas around the testing area to distract her.

Once back at the sewing table, I set the rebellious cat in her bed. I wondered if, now that she'd had a taste of freedom in the big house, she would try to escape again, but she curled up with a kitty sigh and closed her eyes. Apparently, the excursion to the upstairs banana landing had tuckered her out. I was relieved. I had no intention of chasing her all around the place, and if she'd insisted on roaming, we would have had to leave.

I picked out a skein of white floss from the embroidery tin in readiness for my new project. Those first stitches were always the most exciting, and I was eager to start.

"You found her," Frannie remarked.

"I did. Silly girl. She was trying to go upstairs."

"She must have had fun," said Dora, reaching over to stroke the silky fur. "Look, the poor thing's exhausted."

"There was a vigorous tussle with some crocheted fruit. No casualties, I'm thankful to report," I added to Pauleen in case she was concerned about her still life arrangement, but she just smiled and shrugged.

"Cats will be cats," she said brightly.

I chose two more shades of white floss and a light blue accent for the shading. The room slipped into silence as the quilters applied themselves to their individual work. The hum of Gilda's sewing machine and a soft conversation between Ruth and Mark mingled with the birdsong coming through the window, a robin's melodious chirps.

"That reminds me," I said thoughtfully as I began tracing the cat design on the linen with a square blue chalk. "When I went to get Elizabeth, I overheard people arguing next door at the house that's for sale. They were on the other side of the fence so I couldn't see them, and I couldn't really hear the man, but the woman was quite unhappy about something or other. It sounded like the man might have been trespassing. Do you get much of that around here?"

"Trespassing?" Pauleen answered. "No, not really."

"We're too close to the main street," Pet furthered. "And that big fence they put in—I'd be surprised if anyone could climb it. But it is an unoccupied property. I suppose it could happen."

Pet and Pauleen turned their attention back to their sewing, and the conversation lapsed. Frannie was nearly done stitching on the Cali applique. Gilda finished her hem, pulled her piece out of the machine and clipped the threads. Mark fiddled with two squares of a nearly identical color, trying to decide between them. Elizabeth snuffled in her bed, as did Mewella on the other end of the table. Ridley had gone off somewhere, and apparently so had Mrs. Hart.

Chapter 11

A cats' point of view is one of living in the here and now, something we humans can learn from.

It was the day of Elizabeth's therapy cat evaluation! Today my sweet cat would go up in front of a panel of peers to be judged on her ability to stay calm in unfamiliar surroundings, to be friendly with total strangers, to tolerate unusual noises and movements, and to generally be unflappable in the face of whatever might occur in a nursing home, hospital, library, school, or other public or private environment. She was excited. I was scared to death.

Not that I didn't have faith she could pass the test—I did. But if there happened to be a mishap or snafu, it wouldn't be Elizabeth's fault—it would be mine. I reminded myself that we'd been training hard and had covered all the testing elements. Besides, this wasn't my first rodeo—Tinkerbelle and I had been a pet partners team for some years now. Still, I'd be glad to put the assessment behind us and get on to the fun part, the client visits.

I had combed Elizabeth's silvery fur until her stripes shone, and I'd brushed her little teeth. Her cornflower blue eyes glittered with anticipation as I put on her harness and brought out the carrier. A few other cats gathered around to see what was going on, but for the most part, they avoided the scene, glad it was Elizabeth going off in the *magic transporter* and not them.

It didn't take any persuasion for her to bumble into the comfy plush carrier and settle down for the trip. I was just about to attach the black mesh dome top when my phone rang. Since I was essentially out the door, the instrument was stashed in my purse, and I had to rummage for it. The call was from Frannie.

"Hi, Frannie. What's up?"

"I'm at the quilt shop."

I sighed. "I'm sorry, I'm not going to make it today. Elizabeth has her evaluation. I told Pauleen. I thought I told you too."

"You did. This is something else." There was a hesitation on the other end. "Something's happened," she finally said, her tone ambiguous.

"Can it wait? We were just leaving."

Frannie's voice lowered. "No, it's not that kind of thing."

I suddenly felt cold. "What?" I uttered through clenched teeth. I knew without words that the *something* Frannie had referred to wasn't going to be good.

A sigh, another pause, then, "Mrs. Hart is dead."

Slumping into a chair, I let my purse drop onto the carpet. My mind was going through the laundry list of possible causes for someone of her advanced age. Heart attack? Stroke? A fall? Those old stairs were carpeted and had a double banister on either side, but accidents happened.

"How...?"

This time Frannie didn't hesitate. "She was murdered."

Frannie's statement crashed into my brain, only to be instantly expunged. *Murdered? That couldn't be.* Who would want to do in a sweet old lady like Mrs. Hart?

"Somebody killed her," Frannie reiterated. "The police have taken a suspect for questioning."

"Anyone we know?" I stammered, though I was afraid to ask.

"Yes, Gilda. They have reason to believe Gilda is the killer."

I could hear someone crying on the other end of the line. Pauleen? Pet? Probably both. Heck, I could feel my own chest tighten for the elderly knitter I barely knew.

For a few moments neither Frannie nor I spoke. Then, as the sorrow settled, the questions began to bubble to the surface and come out in one big rush.

"How did it happen? Where was she? Why do they suspect Gilda? Are Pet and Pauleen all right?"

My bluster was greeted with silence. Even the background sobs had stopped. Then I heard someone talking, and Frannie's muffled reply. When she came back on the line, she was calm and surprisingly unemotional.

"Lynley, I know you're busy, and I know Elizabeth's appointment is important, but is there any way you could come by the quilt shop when you're done? Mrs. Hart's death has been a terrible shock, and we could really use your unique skills."

Skills. I knew what that meant. Frannie must have been blabbing to the Harts about my previous brushes with violent crime. I was the first to admit, whether because of my insatiable curiosity or some *Murder-She-Wrote* curse, I'd had more experience than most. But just because I'd helped crack a few cases and one of the homicide detectives knew me by name didn't mean I could solve mysteries. Besides, it sounded like the police already had their killer.

Gilda. The sulking, scowling Gilda. She and Mrs. Hart had definitely displayed some animosity toward each other, but that was a far cry from murder. It made no sense to me. Of course I'd just met the people involved and knew next to nothing about their true natures. Maybe the rift between Gilda and Paula Hart went deeper than I'd guessed. Maybe there was some terrible backstory. Or maybe Gilda was a sociopath. Maybe there were extenuating circumstances. Maybe...

"Lynley, are you still there?"

"Yes, sorry, Frannie. Just thinking."

"Could you possibly come to the shop and do your thinking here?" Frannie's voice sank to a whisper. "Pauleen is being stoic, but I know she's devastated, and Pet's about out of her mind. You don't have to resolve anything, but if you could shed some light on the criminal process, tell them what to expect from the police, etcetera, I know it would make them feel better. It would make me feel better too."

I considered, then made a snap decision. "Tell them I'll be there in a few minutes."

"But what about Elizabeth's appointment?"

"I can reschedule. This is more important—the panel will understand. And I doubt Elizabeth will mind staying put for the afternoon." I glanced at the little cat all curled up in her carrier bed fast asleep. "Go put on water for tea if you haven't done that already. Tell Pet and Pauleen I'll see them soon."

* * *

With adrenaline pounding in my veins, I kissed Elizabeth goodbye, made a quick check on the other eight, and hotfooted it to the car. The short distance from my house to the quilt shop seemed interminable. Every red light, every jaywalking pedestrian, every slow vehicle seemed to be personally thwarting my mission of good will. I knew it wasn't the case, but as the blood pulsed in my ears, it hardly mattered. Delay was delay, and whether it was coincidence or conspiracy, my impatience had me about to boil.

The spring weather had taken a turn, and now the city was back to good old Portland rain. The persistent drizzle and dark, wet gloom did nothing to aid my attitude. The news of Mrs. Hart's death was hitting me hard. Despite the fact I'd barely exchanged more than two words with the quilt shop matron, I felt an acute loss. She hadn't merely died—the frail old girl had been murdered! Who does that sort of thing?

Apparently, Gilda, the champion quilter who mourned a cat named Fritz. At least that was what the police seemed to think. But I had a problem with that. I just couldn't see it. Murder requires a motive, and no matter what sequence of events I ran through my mind, nothing added up to Gilda versus Paula Hart.

I grunted with relief when I finally pulled up to House of Quilts and parked behind a police cruiser. Locking the car, I dashed up the front steps. The sign read closed, but even before I could raise my hand to knock, Frannie was there to let me in. As she hustled me through the empty shop, I glanced toward the workroom. Projects were still scattered across the table as if everyone just dropped what they were doing and left, which they probably had.

"Pet and Pauleen are in the sunroom," Frannie said in lieu of a hello. Turning, she grasped my arm. "Thank you so much for coming, Lynley. I didn't know what else to do."

"Where are the police?"

"Been and gone—for now," Frannie whispered.

The sunroom was far from sunny as I stood in the doorway studying the scene. Though brighter than the house interior, the dense clouds seemed to hover bare inches above the skylights like impending doom. There was a chill from the uninsulated windows, almost painful in its intensity, and I kept my coat on as I came to sit in a wicker chair across from the Hart women.

"I'm so sorry for your loss," I offered, hating the cliché but not coming up with anything better for the sad occasion.

"Thank you, dear," said Pauleen, who looked like a deflated balloon. Her auburn upsweep lay flat on her head, wisps falling in her face though she seemed not to notice. Her sunken eyes were ringed by deep shadows. It never ceased to amaze me the toll tragedy took on the human body. I wished we could be more like cats and accept whatever came at us in stride.

Pet, whose appearance had fared only slightly better than her mother's, attempted a half smile before she broke down in sobs. "How could this happen? Everyone loved my grandmother. She never hurt anyone in her whole entire life."

I found that an odd statement from someone so much younger—did Pet really know all the ins and outs of Mrs. Hart's lengthy lifetime? But that was a rhetorical question. There were more important things to resolve here and now.

"Did you make tea?" I asked Frannie aside.

"Yes, it should be ready now. I'll fetch it while you stay with Pet and Pauleen."

I nodded, then turned back to the distraught mom and

daughter. "Do you want to talk about what happened?"

"No," and "yes," rang out simultaneously.

Pauleen, who had been the yes vote, looked at her daughter. "It's good to get it out in the open. Frannie said Lynley has been around this sort of thing before. Maybe she can help."

"I know," said Pet. She turned to me. "I'm sorry."

"Nothing to be sorry for," I quickly assured. "You've had a terrible shock and you're grieving. Everyone experiences grief in their own way. But your mother is right—it's often good to talk it out. I'm sure you had to go over everything with the police."

Pauleen sighed. "Yes, they were here for hours. A detective named Croft, I think it was."

"Marsha Croft?" I asked, though I knew there was only one homicide detective in the Portland Police Force with that surname. She happened to be the very one with whom I'd had several previous encounters.

"I think so. She asked lots of questions and gave us exactly zero answers. But I suppose that's what they do."

"She probably doesn't have any answers yet," I replied.

"So then why did they arrest Gilda?" Pet shot back.

"They didn't arrest her," Pauleen corrected. "They just wanted her to go with them so they could ask her some questions."

"They weren't taking no for an answer. And I'm sure I heard the word, *suspicion*, when they were escorting her out." Pet turned to me. "That's almost like being arrested, isn't it?"

"Not necessarily," I put in. Now that I had real details on which to concentrate my energy, my agitation began to ease.

I was about to gently push for more information on the death itself when Dora came rushing through the catio. Her clothes were soaked, and her face was drawn. She stumbled into the sunroom and shook off her wet spring coat, then cast baleful eyes at the Harts.

Pauleen stared back, her face going pale. Pet took one look at Dora's sad expression and burst out weeping once more.

I glanced questioningly at Frannie who was standing in the doorway with a tray of mugs.

"Mrs. Hart's passing isn't the only awful thing that's happened today," Frannie said in a somber tone. "Ridley's missing again. He's been gone since last night."

"There's no one home at the Naylors'," Dora panted. "At least nobody answered the door when I rang the bell."

Pet jumped to her feet and turned in frantic circles.

"He's dead," she cried out, her expression a paradox of anger and fear. "He's dead. Just like my gran!"

Chapter 12

Do you know where your cat is right now? Cats are excellent at hiding when they do not want to be found, such as when you bring out that carrier for a trip to the vet.

"He's not dead!" Pauleen snapped. "Don't say that. I couldn't stand it if he were gone too."

Pet choked back a sob and turned her tear-stained face away from her mother. Dora came up behind Pauleen to lay her hands gently on her shoulders, then turned to Pet.

"Your mom's right, dear," she consoled. "There's no reason to think the worst. Why, I bet when the Naylors get home, we'll find Veronica's the culprit. And whatever else one can say about her, at least we know she'll keep him safe and sound."

"If that little scamp took him again," Pet hissed, "I swear I'm going to call the police on her. I'll have her arrested for stealing! I'll press charges, make them put her in one of those jails for kid criminals!"

With that, Pet vaulted from her chair and flounced out of the sunroom. A moment later, I heard her stomp up the stairs.

"She's on edge," Pauleen explained.

"Of course she is," I agreed. "It's understandable."

"Should I take her a cup of tea?" asked Frannie who was still standing by with the tray.

"No, let her work through it." Pauleen ventured a

weak smile. "She'll be back once she has some time to reflect. This thing with her grandmother has both of us in shock." She shot a look at Frannie. "I could use a cuppa though."

Frannie came and set the tray on a low wicker table, then handed a mug to Pauleen and took one for herself.

"Dora?" She held out a third mug.

"No thanks, Frannie. I've got to take off. Dental visit. Unless you need me," she added to Pauleen.

"No, you run along. Thanks for looking for Ridley. I just couldn't…"

"Perfectly fine, dear. I'll pop back after my appointment. Can I bring you some dinner?"

"I can't imagine eating, but yes, Pet will need something, and I doubt either of us will feel like cooking." Pauleen gave her friend a soft blink reminiscent of a friendly cat. Dora blinked back, collected her coat and purse, and was off.

Frannie passed the mug to me. "Lynley?"

I took it thankfully, the heat on my hands helping to ground my thoughts.

"So Lynley," said Pauleen. "Can you make me understand what's happening?"

"I'd like to try. Would you mind if I ask a few questions?"

At first, she looked surprised, but then she nodded.

"This may not be easy. Just stop me if it becomes uncomfortable."

Again the nod, this time with a bit more conviction. "Whatever it takes. Thank you."

"Let's start with where your mother passed away." I said gently. "Not here, or this would be marked as a crime scene."

"Next door, in that horrible house for sale. The real estate agent found her when she went in this morning to get ready for a client. We didn't even realize..." Pauleen paused, eyes going round with guilt. "We didn't even know she was gone."

I gave what I hoped was a reassuring smile, appreciating how tough this admission was for her.

"Paula sleeps late sometimes," Pauleen hurried on. "I did look in on her before coming down for breakfast. It was early, barely light. The blankets were all in a bunch—I swear, I thought she was there." She pressed her eyes closed. "Maybe if I'd noticed... if I'd taken more time, I could have stopped it. Maybe this whole thing is my fault."

I reached out to touch Pauleen's hand. "None of this is your fault. It's the killer's fault and his alone. Or hers," I added, thinking of Gilda.

"But if I'd known, I might have done something, kept Paula from going out."

The quandary of *what-ifs* was a rabbit hole it didn't pay to go down, so I took things in another direction.

"Do you have any idea why your mother would go next door at that hour?"

"Not a clue. With Paula's declining eyesight, I don't know why she would even attempt it on her own." Pauleen wrinkled her brows. "Though Paula has been guarded of late."

That was the second time Pauleen had used the incorrect tense in relation to her deceased mother, but I overlooked it. "Guarded? How so?"

Pauleen brushed a faux-auburn lock from her eyes. "I don't know. Paula was never a big talker, even when I was growing up. She was raised in the era of *don't speak unless you have something to say*. But recently she seemed quieter than ever. I thought she was content, happy with the way things were. She loved the quilt guild and enjoyed connecting with the members."

"So she hadn't quit communicating completely."

"She let them do most of the talking, but you're right," Pauleen sighed. "Her silence was mostly aimed at me."

Tears rose in Pauleen's eyes, but she blinked them back.

"Do you have any idea why that might be?" I pursued. "Did you have a disagreement or a fight?"

"No! We always got along. Always! We were closer than mother and daughter. Paula was my best friend."

"Maybe she was keeping a secret," Frannie said out of the blue.

We both looked at her in surprise.

"Maybe Mrs. Hart had a secret," Frannie reiterated. "Something personal she didn't want you to know."

"No way!" Pauleen burst out, her face flushing. "My mother told me everything!"

"Or maybe she didn't," I mused out loud. "Frannie has a point, Pauleen. I know it may be hard to accept, but you've got to admit something odd was going on with your mother, and whatever it was may have got her killed. Unless her death was random—which seems doubtful since the police are talking to a suspect—there's more to this story."

From somewhere in the house I heard the chime of a clock, three resonant bongs. A few seconds later, Pet appeared in the doorway, accompanied by Mewella. She had taken some time to pull herself together, brush her hair, wash her face, and apply a bit of makeup.

She resumed her seat by Pauleen on the wicker bench,

and the black cat hopped into her lap with a *mumph*. Smoothing her hand down Mewella's long back, she turned to Frannie and me.

"I'm sorry for running out like that. I think worrying about Ridley keeps me from thinking about losing Gran. And from being anxious about the fact her killer is still out there somewhere."

"Then you don't think Gilda did it?" I asked.

"No," Pet scoffed. "Why would she?"

I shrugged. "The police must have had some reason to question her."

"I guess, but I don't know what it would be. They don't know Gilda. She can be grumpy, sure, but a killer?" Pet shook her head.

"I'm not so certain," Pauleen mused.

"What? Mom?"

"Gilda and your Gran go back a long way—a really long way. Before you were born, during my last year at college, Paula had a bad fall and broke both wrists. I offered to come home, but she wouldn't hear of it. Instead she hired Gilda from an agency. Gilda took care of her, did all the things two-handed beings never think about."

Pet turned an incredulous glare on her mother. "Why didn't I know about this?"

"Paula never spoke of it. By the time summer break came around and I returned to Portland, her wrists were healed, and Gilda had moved on. I never heard of her again until she suddenly showed up at the shop a few months ago. During the intervening years, she had become a master quilter. That, and being a cat lover, brought her to join our little guild."

This was an unexpected backstory. In the few sessions I'd attended at House of Quilts, I'd rarely seen Gilda utter a word to Mrs. Hart. In fact, she seemed to make a point of sitting as far away from the old woman as possible.

"The two must have formed some sort of relationship while Gilda was Mrs. Hart's caregiver," I said. "How did they get along after the reunion?"

"Not well, and I always wondered about that." Pauleen cocked her head. "I never saw them fight or anything, but when they weren't ignoring each other, they were snippy. Now that I think back, it was about the time Gilda arrived on the scene that Paula stopped talking to me. Oh, goodness! Could Gilda have something to do with her death after all?"

The conversation lapsed as everyone followed their own musings. My brain was clicking a mile a minute, but it wasn't about Gilda von Gluck. Frannie's comment had stuck in my mind.

A secret Paula couldn't tell her daughter? Sneaking out in the middle of the night? Those actions pointed to a rendezvous. People—younger people, that is—assumed persons over a certain age became indifferent to intimacy, but I knew better. Love happened at all stages of life. How that love manifested itself was entirely up to the individuals involved.

But if Mrs. Hart had ventured into a relationship, who would be the paramour? I doubted she would have set up a Tinder account for herself. On the other hand, secrecy and roaming were both common signs of dementia. Mrs. Hart's actions could be motivated by a change in her mental cognition and have nothing at all to do with emotions.

Where did the not-so-friendly reunification with Gilda fit into the mix? I thought about approaching Detective Croft for a bit more insight as to why Gilda had been apprehended. I told myself I'd be asking in the Harts' interest, but in the back of my mind, I knew the curiosity sat firmly on my own shoulders.

Suddenly Mewella's head lifted, and her ears shot forward. A moment later, there came a knock on the front door. Pet and Pauleen looked at each other though neither made a move.

"I'll get it," said Frannie, jumping up and rushing away before anyone could object.

I heard the rattle of the latch as Frannie opened the screen door. A brief and muffled conversation ensued, then the door closed again, and two sets of footsteps approached the sunroom.

Mewella took a flying leap off Pet's lap, but instead of running away as a cat might do when a stranger called, she dashed right up to the woman behind Frannie. When Frannie stepped out of the way, I instantly saw why.

Then Pet was up and running as well. In the woman's arms lay a complacent but wide-eyed Ridley.

Chapter 13

I know you want to pet that kitten, but baby cats have yet to fully develop their immune systems, so it is extra important to limit touching and holding until they get a bit older.

The woman in the prim business pantsuit and hummingbird-patterned scarf held Ridley out to Pet. "The cops were just leaving when this animal showed up. The tag says it's yours."

"He sure is!" Pauleen had risen as well, a look of vast relief erasing some of her worry lines.

Pet took the cat and embraced him tightly. "Where did you find him? Not outside, I hope."

"It was in the house." The woman smoothed the tight brown bun atop her head and frowned. "I haven't looked to see if it made any messes, but if it did…"

"Thank you for bringing back the Harts' *beloved* cat since they've been so worried about *him*," I broke in, emphasizing both *beloved* and *him* to make it clear Ridley wasn't a stray, or an *it*. "And you are…?"

The woman's scowl morphed into a well-rehearsed smiley face. "I'm Josie Brimm, real estate agent."

She held out her hand. I took it and ran through quick introductions.

"I'm handling the house next door," she went on. "Stasha, my partner, was here earlier, but she went home after she found that horrible dead body. Man, she took it hard."

Again I intervened. "I assume you don't know, but the deceased was a member of Pauleen and Pet's family."

Josie Brimm looked momentarily nonplussed, then her face resumed its plastic smile. "I'm sorry for your loss."

"How did Ridley get into your house?" Pet asked, still clinging onto the wayward cat.

"It... *he*," she corrected. A fast learner, I acknowledged. "I don't know. I suppose he coulda got in when the police were there. Or wait, no," she exclaimed. "Stasha said something about a cat being there when she arrived. I didn't think anything of it at the time because... you know... the murder and everything. Kinda preoccupied."

"Your partner saw Ridley when she discovered Mrs. Hart?" I asked to confirm.

Josie nodded. "I guess. Like I said, I wasn't really paying attention. And I didn't see him myself 'til later. Oh, sheesh," she remarked. "If he was inside all night long there's sure to be a mess somewhere."

She whipped out her phone, punched a single number, then held it flat. "Joe, get over to the Hawthorne house right now and check around for cat crap. Yeah, that's what I said, c-a-t."

Josie wandered into the shop room, still talking to her associate. I looked at Frannie. "If Ridley was there when the real estate lady came this morning..."

"...then he must have gone into the house with Mrs. Hart," she finished.

I nodded. "Exactly."

"But what does that mean?" asked Pauleen. "Ridley should never have been out at all."

"No, of course not. But it might help us to figure what time your mum went next door. When did you notice

Ridley was missing?"

Ridley squirmed in Pet's arms, eager to join his sister on the floor. Pet bent to let him down, then straightened. "About eleven o'clock. He's usually on my pillow when I go to bed, but last night he wasn't there. I wasn't really worried then, but when he still hadn't come a few hours later, I got up to look for him. I even woke Momma up."

"Then what did you do?" I asked.

"We searched some more but no luck," said Pet.

"I didn't think much of it," said Pauleen. "Sometimes the cats get in the attic. They love it because of all the storage and hidey places, and unless they choose to answer when we call, there's just about no way to find them."

The women watched the two black cats smooth each other's long, silky fur. Though Pauleen and Pet differed in age, shape, and stature, their grief-ravaged expressions were identical.

Suddenly Pauleen winced as if hurt. "Oh, no," she moaned. "I looked everywhere for Ridley but never even noticed my mother was missing! What..." she choked. "What does that say about me as a daughter?"

I felt it had been coming, but now Pauleen broke down, crumpling in on herself as the tsunami of grief crashed over her. Pet grabbed her shoulders to steady her, then turned to Frannie and me.

"That's enough for now," Pet said stoically. "Thank you for coming, for being here. And Lynley, call us if you have any thoughts on how we can get through this. I know the hard part is just beginning."

"I wish I could say otherwise, but you're not wrong," I confessed. "There will be more investigations and interviews with the police, and until the crime is solved, I doubt you'll feel much relief. But do be gentle with yourselves."

"Call us anytime," Frannie added. "We're here for you."

As Pet guided Pauleen into the house and up the stairs to their private rooms, Frannie and I went through to the shop where Josie was still talking a mile a minute on her phone.

Frannie took her arm. "We're leaving now."

The agent looked up in surprise but allowed herself to be hustled out the door. Once Frannie made sure the lock was set, we descended the steps to pause on the sidewalk. The rain had stopped for the time being, but the streets still shimmered with recent wet. I noticed the police cruiser was gone, but a strip of yellow tape had been strung across the front walk of the sale house. The house itself seemed closed up tight.

Josie ended her call and put the phone in her personalized tote. "It was nice meeting you," she said in a practiced tone.

Frannie and I looked at each other. Nice wasn't exactly the word I would have chosen to describe an encounter at a murder site, but she probably didn't know what else to say. Dead bodies likely weren't part of her job description.

I mumbled a reply, and she headed off to the house next door. For a moment, she stood out front, then glancing from side to side, she lifted the crime scene tape and ducked under. With another furtive glance, she scurried up the steps, undid a length of tape that had been placed across the doorway, and disappeared into the house.

"Should she be doing that?" Frannie asked dubiously.

"Of course not," I replied. "But since she did, I have an

idea."

"What is it, or would I rather not know?"

I gave a mischievous smile. "Nothing dangerous and only slightly illegal."

Frannie sighed. "I should have guessed when I asked you to help Pet and Pauleen that you wouldn't be able to resist sleuthing. But be careful. I don't know about you, but I haven't a clue what's going on here."

"Neither do I, but I've got the feeling there's a lot more to it than a random death. I need to find out what that is. It's the only way I can help the Harts."

Frannie let the subject go. "Will you be at the shelter later?"

"Tomorrow. I've signed up for the early shift in the behavior unit. You?"

"Cleaning this afternoon and socializing tomorrow morning."

"Too bad those litter boxes don't clean themselves," I pondered.

"I sort of like it. It's the only time volunteers get to play with the kittens, since they're off limits due to their sensitive little immune systems."

"Give them an extra pet for me. I'll see you tomorrow."

I watched Frannie get in her car and drive away, then turned back to the sale house just as a small SUV swooped into the vacated space. A slightly overweight man of about twenty lumbered out but paused to stare at the ribbon of crime tape.

Josie appeared on the porch. "Get on up here, Joe."

Joe gave her an incredulous look. "But Mom, what about...?" He plucked at the yellow plastic.

"Just go under," she called back. "What can they do? Arrest us for being on our own property?"

"No," I said, stepping up beside Joe, "but you can get in trouble for entering an active crime scene."

"Doesn't look active to me." Josie adjusted her hummingbird-print scarf and gave her bun a pat. "Besides, the cop said they were done here. Come on, son. It shouldn't take long. I just need you to make sure that horrid animal didn't do its business on the brand-new carpet."

I noticed she'd reverted to her original ailurophobic disdain of Ridley. It was plain to see this woman disliked cats, and in my humble opinion, such views were often indicative of other unpleasant traits.

I might not trust her, but she could have her uses just the same. Pasting a smile on my face, I called after.

"Hey, Josie, can I come too? I've been looking for a house like this one." It was a lie, pure and simple, but I didn't feel a lick of remorse because, in my eyes, her speciesism made her fair game. Besides, giving me a quick tour of the place Paula was killed wouldn't do her any personal harm.

She hesitated less than a millisecond. "Sure, come on up. Joe, hold that tape for the nice lady."

Joe complied, and together he and I proceeded to commit criminal trespass.

"Wipe your feet," she instructed, looking daggers at a muddy stain that could have been a smallish footprint on the white carpeting near the threshold. The smear was marked by a yellow evidence tent, and once I'd scuffed the rain off my shoes, I made a point of avoiding it.

Josie went right into her spiel. Taking only a moment to send her son off in search of cat messes, she guided me through the place recounting stats, delivering details, and cracking the odd joke intended to make the sucker—I mean, *client*—feel at ease. I only half listened. I was looking for something that wasn't on her list. I had no idea what it was but hoped I would know it when I saw it.

Josie paused when we came to the archway leading into a large room where a smattering of the yellow numbered evidence markers had been placed around the carpet. "And that's the morning room," she was saying. "We'd better not go in there 'cuz that's where it happened. The, you know, death."

I took her reticence as a sign she had some restraint when it came to stomping all over the scene of crime, however that was the very place I wanted to see.

I brushed past her, steering clear of the markers. The big, airy room had been staged with trendy furniture that looked out of place in a house of that period. The walls, painted a bilious orange by some interior decorator, were hung with large, framed posters of high contrast scenes. A few token knickknacks had been placed around on various surfaces.

On the coffee table sat a box of expensive bonbons, presumably an empty prop, and a glass bowl filled with something resembling scraps of indigo blue fabric. The arrangement seemed so ludicrous, I found myself looking closer. Sure enough, the bowl held a collection of denim strips tied into knots and bows.

I was trying to process the purpose of this flotsam when I noticed something else—a sudden sparkle where, by rights, none should be. Bending closer, I glimpsed a small, glittery stone set in a gold claw—a woman's diamond engagement ring. I was tempted to pluck it out and examine it, but I didn't dare. Since I was reasonably certain it wasn't part of the silly display, that meant it had to be an anomaly. Someone had put it, dropped it, or flung it there, and I doubted that someone had anything to do with the staging team.

Josie was standing in the arch, shuffling her Sarah Jessica Parkers. "Wanna see the upstairs now?"

"No, I think I'm good. Thanks for the tour."

I pulled out my phone, snapped a quick closeup of the ring, then headed for the door.

"Ya sure?" she said, trundling after me.

I smiled at the agent. "I'm sure."

Whipping out a business card, she shoved it into my palm. "Well, thank you, Lynley. May I follow up? Just give me your email, or would you prefer text?" She started to pull a notebook from her tote.

I waved her card in the air. "I'll get back to you."

The poor woman couldn't hide her disappointment. "Oh, okay. Let me know though. I imagine the owner would offer you a better deal now that..."

"Now that it's a murder house?" I filled in.

She cast her gaze to her silver-toed shoes.

Then I had a new thought. "This house must be quite old. What's its history, do you know?"

She was about to answer when Joe trundled down the stairs. "Second story is clean. Maybe the cat didn't go up there. But there's no stuff in the downstairs either. Must have been a very polite kitty."

Josie harrumphed, but Joe gave a sweet smile. Unlike his mother, he seemed to have a fondness for cats.

Suddenly the young man turned toward the front door. Then I heard it too, the sound of heavy footfalls and a commotion on the porch outside.

Joe peeked through the curtains. "It's the police!" he hissed. "Mom, what do we do?"

"Quick, this way," Josie whispered as she ushered us

through the kitchen and out the back door. *Not quite so flippant about the police after all*, I thought to myself.

I flew down the steps into the landscaped yard with Joe on my heels. Quickly locking up behind her, Josie pushed past us and made for the gate that led into the alley. We followed, tumbling through like characters in an old slapstick comedy. Once on the other side, Joe began to giggle and so did I.

Josie took a more serious stance, tugging her jacket into place and patting at her hair. "Well, that was close."

"I thought you didn't care about getting caught."

"No one needs trouble," she shrugged.

Pulling a shiny brochure from her tote, she handed it to me as if nothing had happened. "This has a bit of the house's history. Call me and we'll talk. Come on, Joe."

I watched the two saunter down the alley toward the street, then turned my attention to the pamphlet. A big picture of the house, retouched to make it look far grander than it was, took up most of the front panel. Then my eyes slipped down to the caption in its curly cursive font:

For Sale—Hawthorne Neighborhood
Built 1904
The Naylor Historic House.

Chapter 14

Many cats are afraid of thunder and will run and hide even before we humans know the storm is coming. It's not magic — cats have heightened senses and can detect changes in the atmosphere.

The rain had fled, leaving the sky a luminous white. The hedges that backed up against the alley glistened with tiny droplets, and the unimproved roadway was slick with puddles. I hadn't planned on doing any outdoor trekking when I'd run out of my house to join Frannie and the bereaved Harts, and my canvas TOMS had already begun to wick water. Even without the drizzle, the light coat I'd chosen for Elizabeth's assessment did little to hold off the persistent wind. All in all, I was ill-prepared to be out in the weather.

Someone else in the alley had done a much better job of planning. On the green bench under the cover of the chestnut tree sat Colin, appropriately garbed in a yellow slicker, duck boots, and a jaunty fedora-like rain hat. His eyes were closed, and for an instant, a sunray pierced the blanket of clouds to touch his upturned face.

Hearing my footsteps crunch on the gravel, he opened his eyes and glanced over.

"Lynley Cannon. Beautiful day, isn't it?"

I gave a huff. "If you don't mind the cold and damp," I retorted, but his expression held no mockery. He really did think the day beautiful. "I suppose it could be worse," I capitulated.

"Never dwell on worst case scenarios," he advised, making me feel like a youngster being tutored by the wise old sage. At my age, that doesn't happen often. Or ever.

"What brings you to my place of solitude?" he asked with a smile.

I didn't think running from the police would be the best admission, so instead I mumbled something generic about how nice it was to see him again. Strangely enough, it was true. I'd felt a rush of tranquility the moment I spied him, as if, in the sea of troubled waters that was currently my life, this old man was a boat.

"And you too, my dear," he answered. "But I hear there's been a tragic event," he went on. "The death of Mrs. Hart? And murdered—how terrible. You must give my condolences to the family."

"Oh. Yes, of course." There went that lovely wisp of serenity. "It's awful. They're coping as best they can, but it will be a long road for them, what with the investigations and all." I paused. "But how did you know? The police only just came a few hours ago."

"A little birdie told me," he said, an impish twinkle in his eyes. Then he sobered. "I'm sorry. This is no time for tomfoolery. I ran into the constabulary out front on my walk, and a kindly young officer gave me far more information than he should have. I suppose he assumed from my appearance I was harmless. Which I am," the old man added with a guileless grin.

Suddenly I had a thought. "Colin, little birdie informants aside, you get around the neighborhood a lot, right?"

He laughed, pulling off his hat and spilling the

accumulated droplets onto the wet ground. "A fair bit, yes."

"And you know all the neighbors."

A nod.

"Do you have any idea who might want Mrs. Hart dead?"

Colin's eyebrows rose. "Not mincing words, are you, Lynley?"

"Well... no, I'm really not. I've never found it a useful form of communication."

"That's very American of you," he replied. "Where I was born, people hemmed and hawed and commenced long discussions on the weather before finally coming around to the matter at hand."

"But we did touch upon the weather," I teased, "and how it could be worse."

"That's fair. So, to answer your question, no, I have no idea who killed Paula Hart."

I let go a small sigh of disappointment. Of course he wouldn't have known. Why would he? The image of the know-all neighborhood guru was my fantasy and mine alone.

"I do know something though, Lynley. Paula Hart had been keeping a secret or two. My hunch is that secret led, if not to her death, then to her undoing."

My heart gave a little jump, and I thought of Frannie's similar guess. "I only met Mrs. Hart a few weeks ago. I don't think I ever saw her out of her rocking chair," I mused. "She was so quiet. She didn't seem bothered by anything. What do you think she was hiding?"

Colin scrunched his brows. "I don't know. But ask yourself, Lynley, what was she doing out in the middle of the night? How did she get into the house next door? Did she have a key, and if so, why? Also to the point, was this her first time, or had she done it before?

"If these outings were a routine thing for her," I expanded, "another question would be why hadn't anybody noticed."

"Oh, pfft," Colin scoffed. "I can answer that one, and at your age, you should be able to as well. It's simply that we elderly are invisible to the younger folk. No one sees us. No one pays attention to what we do. We are passed off, over the hill, waiting to die."

Colin's fingers tightened on the brim of his hat, crushing the oilskin. "It's not so, of course. Old people are just young souls stuck in an aging body. We have lives and aspirations. We've learned to let go of society's expectations. We know what we want and how to get it."

The grip let up, and he turned to me. "So now, ask yourself what a woman like Mrs. Hart most wanted. If you can answer that, everything else should fall into place."

I inadvertently shivered. The clouds had crept lower, and a good old Scottish mist was rolling in.

Colin replaced his hat on his head and took up his cane. "Brrr. Best be heading home before the storm breaks."

"Storm?"

He rose and pointed to the western sky where the horizon had turned near-black. "Thunder, lightning, the whole onslaught. You'd better get yourself inside where it's warm and safe, my dear."

With that proclamation, he began to shuffle away down the alley, turning when he got to the street. He vanished behind the houses, then reappeared a block down. I watched him cross the intersection and stride up the sidewalk to the gate beneath the big fir. There, he paused to glance back before heading in. I could almost swear his look had been aimed at me.

A raindrop hit my face, stinging with both cold and force. It was followed by another and a dozen more. Though often short-lived, these spring storms could be fierce while they lasted. Colin had warned of thunder and lightning. Though lightning storms weren't common in the area, they did occur. In this case, I believed him.

The sky above me had deepened to the color of dirty oil as the squall moved in. Driving rain hit full force, and I was drenched within seconds. Then came the flashes, one upon the next, the thunder only moments behind.

Suddenly a bolt of lightning snaked from the heavens, striking a tall tree not half a block away from me. I stared in stunned silence as a blaze coursed down the trunk with the boom of a salvo. The next moment, the whole top of the tree burst apart, sending torched twigs into the air like fiery confetti.

Springing into action, I ran for the Harts' gate and wrenched the brass handle. It didn't open, locked from the inside.

"Rats!" I cried into the wind. "Rats, rats, help!"

The rain was coming in torrents now, beating down the tulips and ripping blossoms from the azalea bushes. The wind had intensified as well, and I heard a loud crack as a limb of the cherry tree fractured and broke, crashing to the ground in a flurry of pink petals.

Then I heard something else. Someone was yelling. I stared around, pulling off my glasses which were creating more of a blur than my poor eyesight. On the back porch of the house next to the Harts', a woman was waving at me. I couldn't hear her words, but when she made an exaggerated beckoning motion with her arm, I understood.

Running through her open gate, I dashed across the lawn to the safety of her covered deck, dripping like a wet cat.

"Thank you!" I yelled over the squall.

She nodded furiously. "Get yourself inside now," she shouted back. "No point trying to talk in this."

Ushering me into a linoleum-floored mudroom, she wrestled the door shut. The clamor cut off, leaving only a residual pounding in my ears.

The woman turned to me and smiled. "You poor thing, you look like a drowned rabbit. I'm Jan."

"I'm Lynley Cannon. Thank you so much! But I'm getting water all over your floor."

"No bother." She waved a hand in a dismissive gesture. "It'll dry."

I took a moment to study my savior, a plain woman who looked to be on the near side of forty. She was dressed for home in a printed top and jeans that had seen much wear. Her black hair was tied in a short ponytail with a purple scrunchie. On her feet, she wore brown bunny slippers.

"It came on so fast!" I commented. "One minute it was drizzle, and the next..." I pointed to the window where huge raindrops pelted the glass like rubber bullets. "The quilt shop's gate was latched, and I couldn't get in."

She raised an eyebrow. "Oh? You're one of the Harts' people?"

"Why, yes..." My voice petered out as I abruptly realized whose house I'd taken refuge in—the dreaded Naylors.

But Jan didn't seem bothered by the connection, already helping me pull off my soaked coat. "Come on into the living room. My husband's got a fire going. You can warm up there."

I slipped off my muddy TOMS and followed. The cozy room was furnished in an unpretentious style that bordered on dull but in a nice way. I beelined for the fireplace, relishing its heat. Amazing how fire could produce such polar opposite effects, I mused. A minute ago, the lightning had scared the living daylights out of me. Now its little sister, safely corralled in its gray brick box, was restoring my wellbeing.

My gaze drifted from the friendly yellow flames to the white-tiled surround, then to the mantelpiece where framed studio photos of the family had been lined up like soldiers. A staged trio of Jan, a man, and a little girl. A vintage sepia-toned shot of a young man in an army uniform. Another of the girl whom I guessed to be a more recent Veronica looking sweet in her pretty dress and nothing like the little klepto-terror Pet and Pauleen had described. But photos can lie, I reminded myself, or at least not tell the whole story.

Then I saw something that stopped me in my tracks. Hanging in the place of prominence above the mantle was a large gilt-framed painting of a black cat. I felt a soft tickle against my bare foot, and upon looking down, I found said cat staring up at me with luminous green eyes.

"Ridley!" I exclaimed.

"No, dear," said Jan as she came up beside me. "That's not Ridley. It's Clarice, Ridley's and Mewella's mama."

Chapter 15

Cats, like people, develop particular tastes when it comes to their food. If you have multiple cats, likely you, their meal provider, are sometimes left scrambling to find what the little highnesses agree to eat today.

Thanking Jan Naylor profusely for saving me from being struck by lightning, I grabbed my sodden coat, squelched into my shoes, and went back outside. As I'd predicted, the storm had passed quickly, the sun breaking through the clouds to transform the lingering droplets into rainbow sparks. With only the slightest nod to such visual splendor, I started my car, flipped on the heater, and headed for home with only one thing in mind — getting dry.

Once that goal was achieved and I was comfy in my bathrobe with a cat on my lap, my thoughts moved on to other things. Mrs. Hart's murder; Gilda's arrest; Colin's proposal of a secret; the cast-off ring and the footprint at the scene of crime.

Then there was the Naylors' black cat Clarice. Cats were important to me, and the revelation that Mewella and Ridley were Clarice's kittens cast a whole new light on the Veronica-stealing-Ridley situation. It by no means justified what she'd done, but depending on how the adoption had been arranged, it might explain why she still thought Ridley was hers. What it didn't explain was why she had no similar feelings for Mewella. The answer might not have meant much in the grand scheme of things, but it was a puzzle, and puzzles tended to stick in my mind until I solved them.

The bit about the house for sale turning out to be the Naylor Historic House—not to be confused with the Naylors' house, residence of Jan, George, Veronica, and Clarice—was another surprise. Naylor wasn't a common name, so there had to be a link. What was the connection?

It was getting on toward dinnertime, at least that's what my clowder was telling me, so with great reluctance I swapped my fuzzy robe for real clothes, a pair of comfortable drawstring pants and a sweater, and got busy with the kitty buffet.

Feeding the nifty nine their supper was no fast matter. Most ate the same high quality wet food, but where Little was a dainty eater, Big Red scarfed his meal, then moved on to hers if not intercepted. Elizabeth had trouble keeping her head from wobbling, and the result was messy, so she was fed in an easy-to-clean cubby. Violet, who was slowly losing weight with her special diet, wasn't enthused about her new prescription food and needed to be secluded in the bathroom without distractions. Emilio and Hermione were patient and polite, but Tinkerbelle growled at anyone who came too near when she was eating.

It was my routine to make myself a cup of tea—or coffee during the morning feed—and sit at the antique mission oak table which dominated my farmhouse kitchen to supervise the cats until they were done. I'd catch up on Facebook or read an article in *Catster*, my favorite cat magazine. As the diners finished, I'd pick up their bowls, one by one. I was just washing up the last of them when there came a knock on my back door.

I smiled as I dried my hands, recognizing that little tap

tap tap.

"Seleia!" I greeted my granddaughter, pulling the door wide, then closing it fast once she was in since the weather had turned nasty again.

"Lynley," she returned, giving me a damp hug.

I shivered when a droplet fell down my back. "Ugh! Come in! Take off that wet jacket."

"The rain is terrible," she blurted as she peeled off the sodden garment. Pulling the pretty quilted bucket hat from her head, she patted her chestnut updo back into place. "It was nice when I left the apartment. At least I thought to wear a hat."

"Cup of tea? I just made a pot."

"Feeding the cats, eh?" She knew me well.

"I was just about to make some dinner for myself. Are you hungry?"

"I could be." She picked a cat-print cup out of the cupboard, the one with the round black kitty face on it, and sat down at the table. Pouring herself a cup of steaming beverage and adding a large dollop of honey, she gave me a sly smile. "What are you making?"

"I have some taco bowls in the freezer. Easy to microwave."

"Vegan?"

I nodded. Though for years I'd preferred meatless dishes, I'd only recently come to veganism. At first, I worried I'd find the fare limiting, but in fact it was just the opposite. By choosing interesting recipes and shopping at vegan-oriented stores, I discovered I could make almost anything.

"Or I could whip up a salad. I've got an avocado, and I think there are some artichoke hearts in the fridge."

Seleia, who was not a vegan, let her eyes drift around

the kitchen. Her gaze lit on the fruit bowl in the middle of the table.

"Banana pancakes," she said assertively. "And I'll make them. You can sit back and relax. Okay?"

I gave my answer by plopping myself down across from her and spreading my hands. "Have at it. I trust you know where everything is."

She grinned from ear to ear, pancakes being her meal *du jour*.

Leaping up with the weightless energy enjoyed only by the young, she pulled the cast-iron frying pan from a hook above the stove and put it on a low flame to warm. Grabbing the organic pancake mix from the cupboard, she mixed in the water, then cut two bananas into oblong slices.

She seemed happy with her work, so I let her be and checked a text on my phone. I hadn't noticed it come in, but then I often missed that little announcing ping when I was busy. It was from Halle. *Be in your area around seven. Got time to talk?*

I glanced up at the Kit-Kat clock on the wall. It was now six-fifteen, but Halle was one of those friends whose visits required no effort—no frantic clean up or proper dressing. I texted her back, *Sure. See you soon.*

Seleia ladled spoonfuls of batter into the hot pan, poked in the banana, then covered the slices with a drizzle more batter. As she watched them sizzle, her back to me, I sensed something was off.

"You're quiet tonight."

She sighed and turned. I was shocked to see she was crying.

Leaping up, I took her in my arms. "What is it, sweetheart? Has something happened?"

She pulled away and dried her eyes with a tissue from a box on the table. "No!" she barked, suddenly sounding angered. "No, nothing's happened, and that's the problem."

Casting an eye on the pancakes to make sure they weren't going to burn, I led her to a chair and bade her sit. "I'll watch these while you tell me what's upsetting you."

She gazed at the floor, collecting her thoughts. When she finally looked up, she seemed neither angry nor weepy but merely a little sad.

"It's Fredric. I just don't know what's going on with him."

I felt my own anger begin to bubble up inside me. *If that man has done anything to hurt my precious granddaughter, why, I'll...* But instead of blurting something half-baked that I couldn't take back, I flipped the pancakes and posed with ultimate restraint, "Do you want to tell me about it?"

"I do. I do want to," she said hurriedly. "That's why I came over. I need your advice, grandmother. I don't know what to do."

I waited but again she'd gone silent. Not wanting to spook her, I checked out the pancakes which were perfectly brown with the banana slices nicely caramelized. Sliding the batch onto a plate, I fetched a bottle of real maple syrup and a tub of coconut yoghurt and set them in front of her.

"Go on, dig in. These will be done in no time."

I finished a second batch, moved the frypan off the burner, then joined her at the table. Wiping the sticky from her mouth with a paper napkin, she smiled.

"That's better. I love food. Food is always reliable, even if men are not."

I was done waiting for her to beat around the bush and

figured a little prompting was in order. "So what's going on with Fredric? Did he do something to hurt you?"

"No, it's nothing like that. Actually I don't know what it is."

"He seemed the same old Fredric when he brought in Carol's boxes on movie night." I took a bite of pancake and crisp-fried banana.

"Yeah, I guess. But the old Fredric would have stayed and watched the movie with us... with me."

"He had to feed Tarzan. Being dad to a rambunctious kitten is a big job."

"He could have come back once Tarzan was fed. Or he could have brought the kitten with him—I know he's done that before and you didn't mind. He could have asked me to come over after. Carol would have got a taxi—she's used to making her way around the city without a car. But he didn't do any of those things. He barely even said goodbye."

"Have you seen him since then?"

"No, and that's another thing. I've called, but he always says he's busy or doesn't pick up at all. And he hasn't replied to any of my texts."

I was beginning to get the idea. I think the kids called it ghosting. As opposed to being hostile, someone merely ignores the other person as if they didn't exist. The practice may not have been openly aggressive, but it was definitely cruel.

But Fredric? He was a kind young man, liked cats, did favors, was polite and friendly. It just didn't seem in his nature for him to ghost anyone, let alone Seleia, the girl he had been in love with for the past few years.

Two things came to mind. Either Fredric was having some sort of difficulty in his life that he wasn't ready to talk about, or he'd met someone else."

Seleia was looking at me, her brown eyes wide. I put down my fork and transformed into grandmother mode.

"Well, the first thing you need to do is to talk to him. It's hard when he's not willing to take your calls, but he can't avoid you forever. Back in my day, we would write the person a letter."

"This has happened to you?" she said in surprise. "Someone you cared about, that you thought cared about you, suddenly turned their back on you?"

"It did," I said, trying my best not to think of Tom and that crazy summer of 1982.

"And you wrote them a letter? Did it work?"

"Yes and no. Let's just say he got the message, and I got my answers."

Her face fell. "But you didn't get back together?"

"He was nothing like Fredric," I said ambiguously. "Whether you write a letter, send a text, or tackle him somewhere you can talk privately, at least you will find out what's going on. Anything is better than not knowing."

"But what if he wants to break up?" she said in a whisper.

I sighed. "Then you'll deal with it, Seleia. If that does turn out to be the case, which I personally doubt, you'll come to terms with it and decide what's next."

"I can't imagine my life without Fredric." She hung her head.

"Cross that bridge if you have to, but first find out what's bothering him. It could be something quite different. You won't know unless you ask."

Seleia leapt to her feet, nearly knocking over the chair. She caught it and set it straight. "Lynley, I'm going to do it!"

Grabbing her jacket and hat, she made for the door.

"What? Now?"

"He's home. I saw shadows on the curtain when I came in. No time like the present, right?"

"Right but... what about your pancakes?" I said to thin air since she was already gone.

A moment later I heard a voice from the living room.

"Hey, hon," barked Halle. "Seleia let me in. Where was she off to in such a dither?"

"Boyfriend issue," I called back.

Halle stepped into the kitchen and surveyed our half-eaten dinners. "Smells good."

"Banana pancakes. Seleia made them. Comfort food."

"Does she need comforting?"

"A little. Potential trouble. I'm hoping for the best."

"The handsome, red haired Fredric? I don't know him well, but he seems nice enough. Then again, one never can tell."

"He's been avoiding her lately."

"Oh, dear. Think he's got a roving eye?" Halle took off her coat and set her briefcase on the floor by the table. "I never felt like settling down until I met Barb. Then suddenly all my bachelor fantasies disappeared, poof, and I couldn't imagine myself with anyone else. Seleia's probably due for another beau or two before she makes the big commitment."

"I suppose. Still, some couples hit it off right from the start. I was hoping... But you didn't come over to talk about Seleia's love life. What's up?"

"Can't a friend just drop by to visit?"

"Of course you can. Want some tea? A pancake?"

"Actually..." She swung her leg across the straight

back chair and plunked down. "There is something on my mind. I needed to thank you for connecting me, and by me I mean my brother-in-law, with your AA contact. It worked! Alex has decided to go into a treatment facility and try that route. Your friend is a miracle worker."

"It's the program that's the miracle, but I'm glad Rob could help. Recovery isn't an easy road. It's really true what they say, it's one day at a time."

"So did you get any information from Arden about your iffy real estate people?" Halle asked.

"I haven't been able to connect with her yet. But there has been a development with the house I was telling you about."

Halle picked a strawberry from the fruit bowl and plucked off the stem. "Oh, yeah? What's that?"

"Last night someone got murdered."

Chapter 16

No robot toy can take the place of interactive play between you and your cat.

"No kidding," Halle exhaled when I finished telling her the details of Paula Hart's murder, or at least the ones I'd been privy to. There were still a lot of holes, but the case was young. "You're not thinking of getting involved, are you?"

"Of course not," I retorted, though I'd been thinking just that. "It's none of my business. I barely know the people. Frannie just asked if I could help them understand the process of a murder investigation, what they could expect."

"Because you've had so much experience," Halle said sarcastically.

I ignored her. "Pauleen and her daughter have just had their world turned upside down. Not only did a beloved family member die unexpectedly, but it wasn't by natural causes—someone killed her. Now, along with the arrangements, notices, and personal grief that comes with losing a loved one, they will be questioned by police, their home will be searched—they may even be harassed by the news media. There will be no peace until the murderer is caught."

"It doesn't end then," put in the seasoned attorney. "After the arrest, there's still the arraignment, the preliminary hearing, then the trial itself and possibly an appeal if the killer has a good lawyer. Those things can draw out for years. And that's assuming the police find the perpetrator in the first place and the case doesn't go cold."

"Exactly. All I want to do is to guide the family through the hard parts, let them know they're not alone."

"Very commendable of you," Halle commented. "Now tell me what you've got so far."

Halle wasn't just a savvy lawyer, she was amazingly intuitive. But it didn't take a psychic to know my cat-like mind would be cogitating on who killed Paula Hart. Still, I'd promised myself I was going to stay out of it. Why, I hadn't even called Detective Croft to press her for info… *yet*.

Halle had accepted a soda, and we'd taken our drinks into the living room where various cats were enjoying their after-dinner grooming sessions. The minute I touched down on the couch, Tinkerbelle crawled into my lap, curled into a black, floofy circle, and promptly fell asleep. I ran my hand down her sleek fur as I thought how to reply to Halle's query.

"Nothing," I finally answered. "I've got nothing. Nothing but questions, that is. For instance, what was an octogenarian doing running around in the middle of the night? And not merely heading to the kitchen for a snack but going next door to a vacant house? Also, why did no one know she was gone? Were they not paying attention, or was she actively trying to deceive them?"

Halle made a *hmmm* sound. "Alzheimer's? Wandering is a symptom."

"I thought about that, but wouldn't there be other signs as well? You'd think her family would have noticed if she was in a mental decline."

"Denial. It's common for family members to overlook those strange behaviors and little lapses in memory for as long as they can. No one wants to think their auntie or grandma or husband is going down that dark dead-end road."

I took a sip of my tea and grimaced. It was the same cup I'd poured when Seleia was there an hour before and was now stone cold. "Okay, that would answer the wandering and possibly the sneaking, but why would Mrs. Hart go to the empty house? Since the place was locked up tight by the real estate agents, she must have had a key, which implies she knew what she was doing."

"Either that or someone coerced her. Someone let her in."

There was a pause while we considered the implications, then we both said at once, "The killer!"

"But then how did the killer get the key?" I pursued.

"They wouldn't need a key if they broke in to rob the place. Maybe your Mrs. Hart strayed in and surprised them so they killed her."

That made me think. No one had mentioned if the house was burglarized. It hadn't looked it, unless they were very tidy burglars. Besides, there was little among the staging for anyone to steal unless you counted the bowl of Levi scraps.

"It's possible, but I doubt it. There was a woman's ring stuck in the potpourri bowl, and it looked expensive. A thief would have grabbed it up in a heartbeat."

"Then someone seeking shelter? A houseless person? Or kids doing it for kicks?"

I shook my head. "It had been raining, but the white carpet was spotless except for one stray footprint. I doubt squatters would bother to wipe their feet. Kids either.

More likely it was one of the estate agents."

"Why would they kill someone in their own listing? For heaven's sake, Lynley. You really got something against those guys, don't you?"

My hand rested on Tink's back while I reflected. "That article I read about the companies that are being investigated was extremely accusatory, alleging the group had been doing all sorts of illegal things."

"Sure, like overcharging clients for extra services they didn't need or bumping up their commission. The old bait and switch, where they offer a place at a bargain price, then when someone calls, they say it's sold but they just happen to have other properties, which turn out to be vastly overpriced. None of those come close to committing murder. What would they hope to gain?"

"Maybe they're *connected*. You know — to the mob."

I looked Halle in the eyes. She blinked in disbelief, then we both broke out laughing.

"You got some imagination, sister," Halle guffawed.

"I know. It's a curse, but it can be entertaining at times."

"I bet it can."

There was a long meow as Big Red sauntered into the room. The meow was especially loud and slightly garbled because in his mouth he carried a bright red sparkly ball. Dropping it at my feet, he meowed again in a more normal tone.

"Look at that!" Halle exclaimed. "He wants you to play with him."

I picked up the ball, thanked him and told him he was a good kitty, then tossed it across the room. The red tabby flew after it, his well-toned muscles taut as he rolled to capture the object in his jaws once more. He lay for a few seconds to catch his breath, then rose with the grace of a dancer. Bringing it back, he again dropped in on the floor in front of me.

"That's amazing," Halle commented. "Can I try?"

She scooped up the little ball, shifting Big Red's attention from me to her. For a moment, she held it up where he could see it, then she let it fly. Red watched the high arc, his head moving in concert with the sweeping curve. The instant it landed, he was on it. This time, though, he made no attempt to return it, instead flopping onto his side with the sparkly ball tucked neatly under his paw.

"Think he'll do it again?" Halle asked.

"Maybe, maybe not. He's not a dog, you know."

Halle gave me a look of mock incredulity. "He's not?"

Red had tired of the game and was settling in for a nap. "Cats!" I mused.

The two of us were silent for a spell, contemplating the wondrousness of the feline species, then I thought of something.

"Speaking of the real estate agents, before the murder, I overheard one of them chewing someone out for coming into the yard. She said a strange thing, something about a grandfather—that she didn't care who his grandfather was, he still wasn't allowed to prowl around the property."

"Prowl around? What does that mean?"

"That's what I was wondering."

"Or did it mean anything at all?"

I shrugged. "I didn't think much of it at the time, but now… The man she was speaking to was obviously trespassing. Maybe he came back. Maybe he was the one who killed Mrs. Hart."

"And maybe you have just enough fragments to drive yourself crazy." She reached out and put a hand on my knee. "Lynley, with all due respect, the case will sort itself out without your help. That's on the police. Give the family comfort and guidance, be present for your poor granddaughter and her boyfriend problem, go volunteer at your shelter, pet your cats, but leave the murders to those who are trained—*and paid*—to deal with them. Okay?"

"No promises," I grumbled, "but I know you're right. And speaking of the shelter, I have an early shift tomorrow morning."

"What is it this time? Litter boxes or crazy cats?"

"Crazy cats, but they're not, of course. Most are just shy and fearful. They need reassurance and socializing to restore their faith in us humans."

"Then I'd better let you get your rest. That's important work you do, and I'm not being facetious."

Halle rose and took her empty soda can into the kitchen where she set it on the counter by the sink like the polite guest she was. Returning with her coat and case, she gave me a kiss on the cheek, then started for the door.

"My morning won't be nearly as interesting or fur-filled as yours," she tossed back, "but I do have early sessions. Thanks again for helping Alex. You wouldn't believe what a relief it is to know he's safe."

I followed her into the hallway and was about to say goodbye when she went pensive. "You know what I'm going to do? I'm going to call Arden myself and make sure she gets back to you. If there is something going on with Holmes Homes realty, it would be good to know."

I raised an eyebrow. "That would be great. I have this feeling..."

Halle gave a laugh. "Yeah, I know all about your

feelings. Thing is," she continued, her voice taking on a somber tone, "they are usually right."

Chapter 17

In Oregon, when a cat bites a human and breaks the skin, the cat must be quarantined and observed for ten days. This quarantine period eliminates the need to euthanize the cat in order to test for rabies.

The Friends of Felines Behavior Modification Unit, BMod for short, was housed in a small outbuilding across the rose garden and down from the main shelter. Away from the noise of cars and people, the cats resided in quiet comfort. Each cat had their own floor-to-ceiling kennel with a window so they could look out over the hillside to the mountains beyond. In the office area, a large flat screen ran Bird TV on a loop. The lights were low, and aside from the chirping and chattering, the only sounds to be heard were a few soft meows.

The cats that came into the little sanctuary had issues that affected their adoptability to the general public. Signs on their glass doors stated things like *Fearful*, *Needs socializing*, or *Lashes out when approached*. A few had red signs indicating they were in quarantine for biting someone, though oftentimes it was more the fault of the human than the cat. Fear was at the root of most feline behavior problems, and it was the job of the BMod staff and volunteers to help them overcome those fears with the use of play, treats, and gentle perseverance. Most of the cats graduated into loving homes with flying colors. The others were placed with people who could handle their special natures.

I had been working with Romeo, a big orange tabby who didn't look like he should be scared of anything, but something had happened to the poor boy, and by the time he was brought in to FOF, he'd entirely shut down. Our cat-savvy director Oakleigh assessed his behavior and formulated a program that she hoped would bring him out of his shell and teach him to trust. It was still early days, and the current strategy was simply for the volunteer to sit and talk to him while he hunkered on his window perch like a lump of red-striped bread dough.

I had just finished reading my emails out loud—cats don't much care about the subject matter, reacting solely to the tone of voice—when I heard someone open the outer door. Twisting from my spot on the floor, I saw Frannie. She panned the room until she found me, then gave a wave as she came over.

"How's our Romeo?" she whispered.

"About the same," I sighed. "He let me give him a treat without flinching away, so that's progress. Are you done with your cleaning shift?"

"Yes. Now I'm heading over to the Harts. I've asked Denny to meet me there."

I looked up in surprise. "Veronica again?"

Frannie nodded. "They're still having trouble with her. This time she banged on the front door and demanded they hand Ridley over. She's a big girl, and Pet said she felt quite threatened. I thought maybe an intervention by an official humane investigator might do the trick."

"Scare her straight?"

"Something like that. He could explain that she could get herself and her family in real trouble if she continues to do what she's doing. Threatening someone, even verbally, can be a crime, and stealing certainly is. And none of that behavior is good for poor Ridley."

Grunting, I pulled myself up with the help of a cat tree. It was getting harder and harder for me to rise from the floor, and I suddenly wondered how much longer I'd be able to do this job. The thought of losing my ability to volunteer broke my heart, and once again I found myself lamenting the advancement of age.

Pushing the wave of self-pity aside, I placed another crunchy treat on the window shelf beside Romeo. "There you go, big boy. I'll see you soon."

The cat's eyes darted mistrustfully between me and the treat, but as I turned to leave, he gave the briefest of blinks, a tiny but significant sign he was coming around.

Letting myself out of the kennel, I crossed to where Frannie was playing with Maxie, a brown-black female, in the common area. Maxie had a tendency to morph from friendly to feisty with little or no warning, but Frannie knew all about Maxie's predispositions and was bobbing the string toy ever so lightly, allowing the young cat to play at her own rate.

"I found out something interesting about Ridley," I teased. "And Mewella, for that matter."

Frannie turned, perfect eyebrows raised and kohl-lined eyes wide.

"Did you know..." I leaned against the counter and let the words draw out mischievously. "Did you know that Ridley and Mewella's momma lives with Veronica and her parents?"

Frannie's eyes opened even wider, if that were possible. "Really? How did you..."

"That's a story in itself. Yesterday after you left the

quilt shop, I got caught in the back alley in that horrible rainstorm. The Harts' gate was latched, so Jan Naylor invited me to wait it out in her house. While I was there, I saw they had a black cat. At first, I thought Veronica had been up to her tricks with Ridley, but this one was older and thinner. Turns out her name is Clarice, and she's the mom."

"Wow, Lynley!" Frannie exclaimed. "That was a terrible storm. What were you doing out in it?"

I laughed. "That's what you got from my tale? Not the maternal relationship between Clarice and the Harts' cats, but how come I was outside?"

"Yes... No... I don't know. Go on, then. I'll save my questions for the end."

"That's about it. The rain stopped and I left. But isn't that a surprise? If the kittens were born at the Naylors', that could be why Veronica insists upon thinking Ridley is hers."

Maxie had tired of playing and retreated to her cubby, so Frannie began wiggling the ribbon in front of a small tuxedo cat who was peeking out from behind the open door of his kennel. The cat stared at the tempting object but remained undercover.

"Wouldn't her parents have explained about the adoption process? Made it clear that Pet and Pauleen were taking the kits to be their own?"

"One would hope so, but who knows?"

Frannie flicked the toy, enticing the tiny cat a few inches from its hideout. "And," she furthered, "if that's what's motivating Veronica's behavior, why doesn't she go after Mewella the same way?"

"I wondered that too." I shook my head. "There must be more to it. I'm glad you've got Denny in on it now. He may be able to shed some light on the conundrum."

"I hope so. Pet and Pauleen have enough to worry about, what with Mrs. Hart's death and all." I noted Frannie avoided the word, murder. "The cats give them solace. They shouldn't have some badly behaved kid messing that up for them."

"Veronica needs to learn about boundaries. If she accepted that Ridley was their cat and not hers, I bet the Harts would let her come visit him in a respectful manner."

The little tuxie dashed from his refuge, gave the fluttering ribbons a mighty bat, then scampered back into his kennel and slipped under his bed. Frannie rolled up the wand and returned it to the shelf. "I'd better get going. I told Denny I'd be there by noon, and it's already eleven-thirty. If you're done here, would you want to come by?"

I was quick to make up my mind. "I need to look in on Pearl, a new cat from a hoarding situation, to make sure she's eaten her breakfast, and then write up my visit notes for Oakleigh. It shouldn't take long."

Frannie pulled off her volunteer apron and stuffed it in her bag. Straightening her cable-knit Aran sweater, she grabbed a lipstick from her purse, and in a swash of berry red, transformed herself from a shelter volunteer to a stylish *grande dame*. Shrugging her feet into a pair of kitten heel booties, she stowed her sneakers in a shoe bag and headed out the door.

* * *

I arrived at House of Quilts to find the official Multnomah County Humane Society Investigators truck parked out front. It must have been a busy day in the neighborhood because the spots to either side were filled all the way down the block. I finally found a space across from Colin's house. As I got out of the car, I paused to stare up at the old Portland home with its stately fir tree overhanging the gate. An upstairs window was half open, and I could hear classical music floating out on the breeze though I saw no sign of the old man or his wife Mary.

I enjoyed the short walk since the day was as gorgeous as they come. I thought about all those parts of the country where winter lingered and was glad I lived in Portland. I knew I'd reassess that opinion when the May rains set in and we didn't glimpse the sun again until the fourth of July, but for the moment, I was content.

When I reached the shop, I found a sign tacked to the screen door, *Closed for Family Matters*. Underneath there was a phone number in case someone had a quilting emergency. How hard it must be, I thought to myself, for the Harts to continue running the family business now that Mrs. Hart was gone. To most of the shop's clientele, the place was just a store, somewhere to buy their supplies and take a class or two, but to anyone who knew the Harts, it was so much more. I didn't envy their struggle to maintain some balance in the coming days.

When I rang the bell, it was Dora who arrived at the door to let me in.

"He's here!" she said in an awestruck whisper. "Special Agent Paris. He's talking to them now."

She hustled me through to the sunroom where Denny sat holding court with Pet and Pauleen. The special agent spoke in a serious tone with the two women who were leaning in as if hanging on his every word. I had to smile — Denny Paris owned the room wherever he went.

I'd met the handsome six-foot-two animal cop ages ago when I first began volunteering at Friends of Felines, and over time our acquaintanceship had blossomed. His handsome, chiseled face had matured with the years, but his cat-green eyes had never lost their sparkle nor had he lost his zestful attitude toward life. Denny had a feline curiosity, which made him an excellent humane agent and was another reason we got along so well. I was also nosy by nature, but Denny had taken it to the next level, aiding those vulnerable souls who couldn't speak for themselves.

Denny believed there were at least two sides to every story, approaching each new case with an open mind. He did what he could to resolve issues with education and connection to services, and oftentimes that was all it took to turn a bad situation around, but when those tactics didn't work, Denny Paris and his two partners had little mercy. Animal abuse and neglect were crimes in the state of Oregon, and the three animal cops were known to pursue perpetrators with the relentlessness of cats on prey. Hopefully there would be no need for such heavy-handedness with Veronica Naylor.

Denny looked up as I entered the room. "Lynley, hey. Frannie said you were on your way."

Dora reseated herself on the bench beside Pauleen, while I took a chair off to the side. "Don't let me interrupt."

"Thanks for coming, Lynley," said Pet. "Agent Paris was just telling us we may have legal recourse against Veronica Naylor. Well, the parents, actually, since she's a minor."

"But that would require a lawyer," Pauleen put in. "I really don't want it to come to that."

Pet grunted. "I don't either, but I'm not sure how much more of this I can stand. Lynley, did Frannie tell you that little cat-thief came over and bullied me to my face?"

I nodded. "That's scary and awful. Do you suppose…" I paused, feeling I was about to dive into uncharted waters. "Do you think it's because she doesn't understand what happened? That when you adopted Ridley from her parents, he was no longer hers?"

Suddenly I had four sets of eyes pinned on me.

"Adopted from her parents?" Dora stuttered. "What do you mean?"

"Isn't it true?" I countered, turning to Pauleen. "Weren't Ridley and Mewella adopted as kittens from the Naylors?"

"Well, yes," Pauleen replied hesitantly. "Their cat Clarice had a litter before they could get her spayed."

Dora looked hurt. "You never said. I thought they came from the shelter."

"Well, no, we didn't make it known." Pauleen cast her eyes to the floor. "There was some concern about Veronica's attachment to the male even then, so we promised to keep quiet about the adoption and make sure the two kittens stayed out of her sight. I guess we messed that one up when we built the catio."

"But that still doesn't give Veronica the right…" Pet blurted.

"No, of course not," I said, "but maybe it's what triggered her belief that Ridley is hers. What do you think, Special Agent Paris?"

Though this was the first he'd heard of Ridley's lineage, he covered his surprise perfectly. "What if I go have a talk with your neighbors and their little girl? I can explain the adoption process and let them know that what they are doing is basically against the law. At the same time, I'll be able to assess their reactions. If they are willing to listen, that may be the end of it. If they're not, I can give you suggestions for further measures."

Pet dropped her hands in her lap, visibly relaxing at the special agent's offer. "That would be wonderful. Thank you so much."

Pauleen also relaxed a bit. "Yes, thank you. We have so many other things to worry about right now. I just can't take anymore of Veronica's shenanigans, not knowing what she will do next."

"No, of course you can't," soothed Dora, lightly touching Pauleen's shoulder. Pauleen cast her a grateful look, then turned back to Denny.

The discussion continued with Denny offering advice on how to keep Ridley safe until the problem was resolved and Pet asking questions about what they could do in case the olive branch wasn't enough, but my interest moved to something else. Mewella had come racing into the sunroom, but instead of seeking a comfy lap or a sunny spot by the window, she was pacing. Back and forth, back and forth, between the doorway and Pauleen's chair. Knowing cat behavior as I did, I was rapidly becoming convinced she had something on her little cat mind. When she began to yowl like a small banshee, I was certain of it.

Chapter 18

There are many reasons cats cry or howl. They may be bored or lonely, sounding off to another cat, or have a medical issue. Senior cats are often restless and feel they must tell you all about it.

Mewella's cries climbed to a volume that could not be ignored.

"What's wrong with her?" Dora exclaimed. "Is she sick?"

"Nothing to worry about," said Pet, though she didn't look completely convinced. "She does that sometimes when she wants attention."

Pauleen held out her hand. "What's up, sweetheart?" she asked the cat.

Mewella gave her a steely glare, then dashed out of the room as if she had a demon on her tail.

"Well, I guess that's over," Dora commented. "Whew, what a noise! I had no idea our little Mewella could scream with such gusto."

Denny and I exchanged looks. There were several reasons why cats cry. Fear, boredom, distress, discomfort, or just as Pauleen had said—Mewella wanted us to take notice of her.

Talk was just beginning to resume when Mewella started up again, this time from somewhere inside the house.

"Maybe she's hungry," Pet offered. "Did you feed them their snack?"

"Yes, of course," said Dora. "They got kibble and one of those little puddings-in-a-tub just before Agent Paris arrived."

Pet turned to Pauleen. "Do you want me to check on her, Momma?"

"No, I'll go. You stay and listen to what Agent Paris has to say. I'm so distracted I can't concentrate anyway."

As Pauleen got up to tend to her wailing cat, I made a snap decision. Just because Mewella had a history of vocalizing didn't mean this current outburst wasn't important..

Excusing myself from the group, I found Pauleen at the base of the stairs with Mewella prancing in place on the landing.

"Little one," Pauleen coaxed. She ascended a step, but Mewella retreated that much farther away.

"Darn it, Mewella!" Exhaling, Pauleen turned to me. Her eyes were ringed with tears and exhaustion. "What should I do, Lynley? I just can't think anymore."

Mewella had sprinted up a few more treads where she recommenced her yowls. She had quite a voice, and I could see why her pleading screeches would get on Pauleen's frayed nerves.

"She seems to want you to follow her. Mind if I come along?"

Pauleen made a helpless gesture. "Why not? Frannie says you're a cat behaviorist. Maybe you can figure out what she's doing."

"I'm just a volunteer," I corrected, "but I'm happy to help if I can." I came up to stand beside Pauleen. "She does seem agitated. Let's just see what happens next."

As if Mewella had understood, she turned and scampered the rest of the way up. Pauleen and I quietly pursued, pausing in the upstairs hallway. The cat had stopped by a door at the end. Silent now, her big eyes were fixed on us.

Rising onto her back legs, she stretched tall and pawed at the panels.

"What's in there?" I asked in a low tone.

"That's the stairs to the attic," Pauleen whispered back.

"Does Mewella like the attic?"

"Both she and Ridley love it. They enjoy prowling among all the old boxes and trunks."

Mewella was becoming more insistent with her scratching, and Pauleen gave me another searching look. "Do you think we should let her go?"

Mewella wasn't the only one who wanted to see the attic—inwardly I was jumping up and down yelling, *Yes, please!* Still, I managed a restrained, "It's your decision, but it might satisfy whatever whim is driving her."

Pauleen considered, then walked down the hall to the door. She'd barely had it cracked before Mewella slipped through and was gone.

"Watch yourself," Pauleen tossed back to me. "The steps are steep. And dusty," she added with a sneeze.

As I climbed the narrow flight, I caught the familiar attic scent, a nameless perfume of things packed away and forgotten. The only light came through a small, filmy window at the far end of the room. A single sun shaft filtered through the murk, illuminating an antique cedar hope chest. On top of the chest sat Mewella looking very pleased with herself.

The overhead light clicked on, revealing a rectangular room filled with packing boxes, old furniture, stacks of framed pictures turned to the wall, and the aforementioned steamer trunks that I knew from my days as an antiques and collectibles dealer dated back to the late 1800s.

"Excuse the mess," Pauleen sighed.

"It's an attic," I shrugged. "It's supposed to look like this."

Pauleen approached Mewella, hand out in a friendly overture. This time the black cat welcomed her pet with a purr. "Well, at least she's stopped running. I suppose this is where she wanted to be."

Mewella flopped down flat on the chest and began sniffing around the edges. I inched closer to where I could see the box's fine carving. Though indistinct with age, it looked like a row of cats.

"That's a beautiful trunk. And Mewella seems to like it. What's inside if you don't mind my asking?"

Pauleen stopped to stare at the piece, then her eyes softened. "It's my mother's. Was... I guess it's mine now. As to what's in it, I don't have any idea."

Mewella was becoming more aggressive with the box, curling upside-down and running her sideburns along the seam. With a brief glance at Pauleen, she opened her mouth to allow the tantalizing scent to pass across her vomeronasal organ.

"Should we take a look?" *Mewella says yes*, I wanted to add but wasn't sure a cat-to-English translation was what the woman was thinking of when she'd asked me for advice.

Pauleen started to reach for the latch but drew back with a cry. "You don't suppose it's mice? That she smells mice in there?"

I leaned over and inspected the outside of the chest. "I

doubt it. The box seems intact. Hope chests were designed to keep pests out, including moths and insects. That's why they were made with cedar. They were put together tightly and often double lined. Unless something's happened to the bottom where we can't see, there would be no way for a mouse to get in."

Pauleen seemed relieved by the assurance. "Okay, Mewella. Move so we can check out your find."

Mewella obediently hopped off. As Pauleen knelt on the floor and lifted the hinged lid, the cat turned a curious eye.

Opening a box or a trunk or in this case a hope chest always felt to me like Christmas morning. Until the contents were revealed, it could be anything in my wildest dreams. Often the reality was less than spectacular, but once in a while the wonder of the contents would meet my expectations and even exceed them. This was looking to be one of those times.

At first glance I picked out a vintage-era jewelry box and the edge of an antique quilt. Pauleen carefully drew the fabric aside to reveal even more treasures, a hardbound book of poems by Dylan Thomas, a round tin with a peacock painted on it, a little cluster of bird feathers. There was also a small brown box that instantly ignited my curiosity. I'd seen one like it before, though I couldn't recall where. Then Pauleen discovered something even more enticing, and I forgot all about the box.

Slowly, almost reverently, Pauleen drew out a packet of letters bound together with a faded pink ribbon. After a brief hesitation, she passed them to me.

"They must have been Paula's. I can't... Will you...?"

I took the bundle and ran my eye over the top envelope. The three-cent stamp in the upper right-hand corner dated back to the 1950s.

The stack was substantial, at least twenty pieces of mail. I brought it up to my nose for a sniff but could detect nothing other than the left-over pungency from the cedar chest where they had been housed for so long. *How long?* I couldn't help but wonder.

The letters themselves were small and regular, not like the hodgepodge of postal designs we have today. The ribbon holding them together was fastened in a simple overhand knot. I noticed the satin tails were crumpled as if it had at one time been tied in a bow. Someone had untied it and not bothered with the bow once they were finished, but whether that had been done recently or decades ago there was no way to guess.

I passed the batch back to Pauleen who eyed it with indecision. "You don't have to look at them now if you don't want to. After all, they were your mother's personal things."

Just then, Mewella jumped into Pauleen's lap and gave a purrumph. "No, I'm fine. And Mewella thinks I should open one."

She'd said it as a joke, but I didn't laugh. From the very beginning, it had been Mewella's show.

Pauleen undid the knot, and letting the ribbon slink to the floor, she extracted an envelope from the bunch. Bringing it close, she read the tiny ballpoint cursive, then with a gasp of surprise, she turned it over to study the backside.

Her eyes rose to meet mine.

"What? Who is it to?"

"It's to my mother—no surprise there. But you'll never guess who it's from."

With a shaky hand she offered me the letter. The front

was addressed to Miss Paula Hastings, Mrs. Hart's maiden name. I adjusted my glasses, then checked the sender's address which was written across the center top of the envelope's back side as was the custom.

The lines more resembled rat scratchings than words, and at first, I couldn't puzzle them out. Then all of a sudden, they came together. The letter, sent to Paula Hart sometime in the 1950s, was from someone named Christian Naylor.

Chapter 19

Can cats really see ghosts? If not ghosts, then what is it they stare at with such focused intensity?

Pauleen frantically riffled the stack of letters. "They're all from him... From Christian Naylor."

"Isn't that the elderly Naylor uncle who lives next door to you?"

"Yes, but why would Christian Naylor have sent my mother letters? And these are old. Look, this one's postmarked 1956 — she was just a kid." Pauleen gazed at the vaulted ceiling. "Let's see... She'd have been about sixteen. Not really a kid, I guess."

"What does it say?"

"It's hard to read, but this part is about some homecoming dance." She moved the page back and forth to get the right focus. "He's asking her to go with him!"

As Pauleen continued to read, sometimes out loud and sometimes to herself, I'd begun searching through the chest again.

"Here are some more." I picked out what looked to be a pair of greeting cards from the current era. No mail stamp; just the name, Paula, written across the front. Though shaky, the handwriting was the same.

"Pauleen...?" I held the cards out to her. She plucked one from its bright blue envelope, revealing a stylized watercolor of a lake in the woods. My heart skipped a beat as she opened it.

For a full minute, Pauleen stared at the interior of the card. Whether she was reading the paragraphs of small script or just pondering, there was no way to tell, but if my suspicions were true, this discovery was about to change everything.

"Is it from Christian Naylor too?" I asked when my curiosity bubbled over.

"Yes. Yes, it is. But how can it be? He's old! She was old. This stuff reads like a romance novel. And a steamy one at that."

She tucked the card back in its envelope and went on to the other one, a long, pink page with hearts and flowers.

"Valentine's Day!" she exclaimed. " 'You'll always be my sweetheart,' " she read out loud, then turned owl eyes on me. "Goodness, Lynley! How long has this thing been going on?"

"I'd say, for a very long time if those earlier letters are any indication. Paula would have been in high school. He must have been her first love."

"But I'd never heard of Christian Naylor until the Naylors bought the house next to us. Paula never mentioned him, not when I was a kid and not now. She married Percy Hart, my father. They were married for decades. They were happy..."

I could see the idea of her mother having a secret lover was taking a toll.

"That was a long time ago, Pauleen." I tapped the stack of old letters. "She probably hadn't even met your father then."

"But what about this? These look recent." She held up the Valentine, shaking it violently as if it had done something terrible. Perhaps it had, if one considers disillusionment a crime.

I had no answer for her, but I did have questions. Here was Paula Hart's secret, the one both the wise neighborhood codger and my insightful best friend had foreseen.

All evidence pointed to an intense relationship between Mrs. Hart and Christian Naylor when they were in their teens. Why had it ended? Why had it started up again?

Had she taken up with her childhood crush when the Naylors moved in next door? Mr. Hart had died years ago, so there was nothing stopping her from pursuing the new-old liaison.

Why had she kept her adolescent romance a secret, never even mentioning it to her daughter throughout the years? And then when she and Naylor rekindled their affair, why had she felt the need to sneak around behind her family's back like... well, like a couple of teenagers?

Then a new question came at me like a bolt of lightning, eclipsing all the others.

Had Mrs. Hart been sneaking out to meet Christian the night she died?

Had something gone terribly wrong?

Was he, not Gilda, the murderer?

"Oh, my!" Pauleen exclaimed. While I was ruminating, she had continued to rummage through the trunk and was now poring over a sheet of white paper, her breath coming in gasps.

I leaned closer, recognizing the now-familiar handwriting. "Another love letter?"

"Just the opposite," she burst out. "It's from Christian all right, but it's awful." She flung it at me. "This makes no sense at all."

I took up the page. It was dated at the top, April second, no year. "Do you think this is current? Because April second was only a few weeks ago."

When she didn't answer, I began to read. The first words jumped out at me like an attacking wolverine: *Paula, you shrew!* It didn't take much more for me to get the essence of the story.

"They broke up?" I refolded the page and handed it back to her.

"She broke it off. At least that's the impression I get. His handwriting is terrible, but there is no mistaking his intent."

Mewella, growing tired of the attic, stood, yawned, and headed for the stairs. I had the urge to follow, to get out of that place of faded memories and back to the present, but there was one other thing I wanted to check out first.

I'd remembered where I'd seen a little brown box matching the one in Mrs. Hart's hope chest. If I was right, it might indicate a way to get a bit more information about the formative years of Paula Hastings.

I picked up the box—sure enough, there was the embossed crest in the corner. "Do you mind if I open this?"

Pauleen had gone back to reading the letter, and it took her a moment to respond. "Probably some keepsake Paula saved all these years. Sure, why not?"

Carefully I lifted the lid from the base. I knew what I would find before I'd got it halfway off. The scent of old roses was a dead giveaway.

"You're right, it's a keepsake. Do you know anything about it?"

She peered into the box, then gave a shudder, as if it held snakes instead of flowers. "Not a clue."

I replaced the lid. "May I borrow it for a few days? There's someone I'd like to show it to."

"Have at it. The last thing I want to deal with right now is my mother's old... *stuff.*"

Dropping the angry page onto the stack of letters, Pauleen sighed. "What am I going to do, Lynley? This thing with Paula and Christian Naylor is all so sudden, such a shock. I wonder how close they really were?"

I assumed she would come around to it eventually, through all the same questions I'd asked myself. The accusatory letter would nail it, leading her to that final query: Could her mother's murder have been a crime of passion committed by the boy—now an old man—next door? The conclusion was inevitable, and I wanted her to have her support group with her when she reached it.

I shoved the box in my pocket. "Let's go back downstairs. Pet will be wondering where we got to."

"Yeah, okay," she said wearily. "My allergies are kicking up anyway. And I'm going to have to think about this."

"But not right now." I gathered the various correspondence and put them back in the hope chest. Closing the top, I pulled myself to my feet and held out a hand for Pauleen. Though the younger of us, at the moment she seemed the more fragile. Accepting my help, she rose awkwardly, sneezed, and proceeded back down the steep steps to the comfort of her friends and family.

When we got back to the sunroom, Mewella was already ensconced on a window shelf watching a robin pick at the grass for worms. Ridley had joined her, and to her annoyance, was attempting to groom her head. Denny had gone, leaving Pet, Frannie, and Dora. Everyone gave us *where-have-you-been* stares.

Dora fussed over Pauleen who sank down onto the bench, looking exhausted. "You have a cobweb in your hair. What have you been doing?"

"Following Mewella," she said ambiguously. "Up to the attic."

"Mewella, you scamp." Dora eyed the cat. "Why did she want up there?"

Pauleen brushed off the question. "Oh, you know how cats are."

"Maybe she saw a ghost," Dora replied, then gasped and covered her mouth. "I'm sorry, Pauleen. I didn't mean to insinuate... It wouldn't be... It couldn't..."

"No ghosts, Dora," I shot back, guessing what the woman was thinking, that if there were a ghost haunting the Harts' attic, it would likely be Mrs. Hart, an image Pauleen and Pet didn't need burned into their minds right now. As to the discovery of the hope chest and its significant contents, I would leave that story for Pauleen to tell or not as she chose.

Pauleen cast me a grateful look. "Mewella likes the attic. She just needed me to open the door for her."

"Denny took off?" I asked Frannie.

"The special agent went over to talk to the Naylors," Dora responded before Frannie had a chance to speak, "but no one was home. He said he'd try again later. Such a wonderful man!" she added, a beguiled glimmer in her eye.

I smiled. Denny had that effect on people. "I'm glad he could be of help."

"I do feel relieved," said Pet. "Worrying about Ridley on top of everything else was just too much."

The loud *brrring* of the doorbell cut through the conversation.

"Maybe Agent Paris connected with the Naylors after all," Pet said hopefully. "Maybe he has some news."

Pauleen looked at Dora. "Would you mind getting that? If it's not important, please ask them to come back at another time."

Dora leapt up and scurried through the shop room as if Pauleen's wish were her command. I heard the front door swing open, then muffled conversation. The exchange rose in pitch, though I couldn't make out the words. Then there was a little cry, the door slammed shut, and footsteps approached across the shop's wooden floor.

Everyone looked up to see Gilda von Gluck standing in the doorway. Her straw-colored hair was unkempt and her face was drawn. Her signature frown was more cheerless than ever.

Dora skirted around the incensed woman. "I'm so sorry, Pauleen. I couldn't stop her."

"That's fine, Dora. Gilda is always welcome. Come on in, dear. Perhaps you'd like a cup of tea?"

"Tea?" Dora burst out. "She killed your mother and you're offering her tea?"

"Gilda never killed Paula," Pauleen admonished. "The police wouldn't have let her go if she had." She turned to Gilda who was still looming on the threshold like a black cloud. "It never once crossed my mind that you were guilty. I'm sorry you had to go through that."

Gilda's righteous anger decreased a notch, and she consented to take a chair, though she remained perched stiffly on the edge. Hunched in her purple woolen coat, she very much resembled a grape, or an eggplant.

As I found myself dwelling upon food metaphors, I realized I was hungry. I thought about leaving but really wanted to hear what Gilda had to say.

"That," she began, her voice brittle, "was hands-down the worst experience of my life. I have never been so humiliated, so mortified. The whole thing was dreadful, just dreadful."

She reached into her pocket and pulled out an embroidered hankie. Wiping her face, she pressed on. "Besides questioning me till the cows came home, they made me fill out a written statement, took my fingerprints and a DNA sample. By the time they were done, it was nearly midnight. I went home and fell into bed. I was so mad I swore I'd never set foot in this place again. But I had to come. I needed to make sure you knew it wasn't me." She cast her eyes from Pet to Pauleen, skipping over Dora completely. "*It wasn't me.*"

"Then why ever…" Dora began.

"Shush, Dora," Pauleen commanded. "Let Gilda speak. Maybe she can tell us what's happening with the case."

"You'll have to talk to the detective about that. Why would you think they'd give me any information?"

"All right, all right," Pauleen sighed. "I can call her tomorrow. I think I have a number somewhere."

It looked like Pauleen was going to give Gilda a pass, but I wasn't feeling quite as magnanimous. There were still things I wanted to know.

"Gilda, you were at the police station for several hours," I put in quietly so as not to enrage the woman any further. "Why were they questioning you, if you don't mind me asking? Did it have to do with your role as Mrs. Hart's caregiver when she broke her wrists?"

All eyes turned to me in surprise. Gilda's face went red.

"Well, aren't you the little miss know-it-all?" Gilda shot back. "Not that it's anyone's business, Lynley, but yes,

Mrs. Hart and I had history. The police knew, and that lady detective wanted the full story." Her high color drained, and she slumped forward. "Seems it was my responsibility to tell them in case something I remembered might help reveal poor Paula's killer. I did my duty," she added with a grunt, "and now it's done."

For a few moments, the little group was silent, then Gilda rose. Facing Pauleen, she straightened her back.

"I'm going now. Let me know when the quilting sessions take up again. The auction is almost upon us, and we have obligations."

With that, she left the room. I heard her footsteps cross the shop and the front door open and close.

There was another silence, then Dora said out loud what everyone else was thinking.

"But if Gilda didn't murder Mrs. Hart, who did?"

I looked at Pauleen and she at me. Could it be we already knew the answer?

Chapter 20

No two tigers have the same stripes.

When my stomach growled like an angry tiger for a third time, I said my goodbyes to Frannie, Dora, and the Harts, but before setting out for home, I took Pauleen aside.

"You have to tell Detective Croft about the letters. They could be evidence."

"The police searched the house," Pauleen replied nervously. "Wouldn't they have taken them if they thought they were important?"

"Maybe they didn't find them. Did they go in the attic?"

"You'd have to ask Pet. She took care of that. I was hiding in my room trying to pretend none of it was happening."

Pauleen sighed. "You seem to know this Detective Croft. Would you call her for me? You have as much information as I do about what we found."

I mulled it over in my mind. "Sure, I can do that. But she will want to talk to you at some point, and I'm certain she'll need to see the letters."

"But you could give her the basics, Lynley. Right now I can't see up from down. And maybe those letters have nothing to do with it. Maybe it's not even what we think, that Paula and the Naylor uncle were… more than friends."

"Maybe," I conceded, though I sincerely doubted it was anything other than what it looked like, a romance gone bad. The big question, whether that relationship had led to Mrs. Hart's death, was as yet unanswerable. "Try to get some rest. I'll let you know what I find out."

As I slipped on my coat, I felt a bulge in my vest pocket and remembered the little brown box of old roses, another curious discovery from the Harts' attic. I was almost certain it was the same as the one I'd seen among my mother's things, which meant Carol had graduated from the same high school as Paula Hastings. The two women were close in age—could they have been in the same class? Portland was much smaller in those days so it was possible. A long shot, perhaps, but one worth pursuing.

I ducked out the front door and was halfway down the steps when I heard someone call.

"Yoohoo, Lynley!" Jan Naylor hollered from her porch. "Come on over. I've got something of yours."

My first thought as I circled around to her walkway was of Ridley, that Veronica had snatched him again, but of course it couldn't be the cat since I'd just left him grooming his sister on the window shelf of the Harts' sunroom. Still, if not him, then what?

"Yes?" I mumbled as I climbed the steps to the gray house.

"The other day when you were here all sopping wet, I think you must have left this."

Whisking a light green chiffon scarf from a side table, she held it out to me.

"Nope, not mine." I glanced at the hummingbird pattern. "But it looks like one I saw Josie Brimm wearing the other day."

"Who?"

"Josie Brimm, the real estate agent who's handling the sale of the house up the street."

"I've no idea who that is," said Jan.

"It might just be a similar pattern." I touched the delicate silk. "Hummingbirds are popular this spring."

Jan bent to scribble something on a plain white note pad, tore off the sheet, and passed it to me. "Here's my number. If you see your realtor friend again, have her call. It's an expensive piece. She's probably missing it."

"Actually..." I put the slip in my purse and climbed a step closer. The reference to Josie and the Naylor Historic House had given me an idea. It was a wild, spur-of-the-moment plan, but one I decided to run with. So far, Jan Naylor had been nothing but friendly and open with me. I was hoping what I was about to do wouldn't change that. "I wonder if I could talk to you about something."

"Of course," she replied without hesitation. "Do you want to come in? It's such a nice day—we could sit on the back deck. I'll make us some lemonade."

As I was saying, friendly.

We chatted small talk as she led me through the house to the kitchen. Retrieving a pair of tall glasses from a cupboard, she ladled in spoonfuls of bright pink powder, then added water and several cubes of ice. Opening a fancy box of chocolates that sat on the end of the counter, she held them out to me.

"Fruit bonbon? They're Uncle Christian's guilty pleasure, but he won't mind if we help ourselves to one."

Guessing the candies were unlikely to be vegan, I gave a no thank you. Jan shrugged and plucked up one of the brown confections for herself. "Yum, but I could just eat the whole box!"

Passing me one of the drinks, she led me outside where

we settled under the awning in gray canvas chairs. Raising her glass, she toasted, "Good health."

"Good health," I replied. Who couldn't drink to that?

Then her face grew sober. "Is this about Veronica? Because when we got home, there was a note on the door with a business card from a humane society police officer asking for us to give him a call."

I was tempted to follow up on that subject but decided to stick with the one for which I had come.

"No, it's..." I paused, pondering where best to begin without causing undue suspicion. Probably not *Do you happen to know if your uncle killed his lover, Paula Hart?*

"It's concerning the place for sale on the other side of the quilt shop. I read that it's been registered as the *Naylor Historic House*. I wondered if you and the owners were related."

"Oh, that." Jan fluttered a hand. "Why yes. Not the current owners but way back when. They were Uncle Christian's grandparents, or was it his great grandparents? I'm sorry, I can never remember my husband's ancestry. There are so many of them."

"Did they build this house too?"

"No, this and the one next door were built a few decades later by the Tithywide family if I recall correctly."

I took a sip of the lemonade which was too sweet and tasted vaguely of chemicals. "Who owns the old Naylor House now?"

"Not sure," Jan gurgled through her drink. With a dainty wipe of her mouth, she added, "I really don't bother about those things. My husband George might know. I can ask him."

"No, that's okay. I was just curious. It seems odd though," I put forth. "If that's your uncle's ancestral home, why wouldn't you be living there instead of here?"

"Oh, gosh, that's a long story. You can't possibly be interested."

"But I am." I smiled attentively. "I'm a bit of a local history buff."

"Okay, I'll give it a try. But don't quote me," she tittered. "The agency who is handling the sale probably has more information than I do."

She squeezed her eyes and cocked her head like a pigeon. "Uncle Christian moved in with us five years ago when we were living across town. He couldn't continue on his own anymore but refused to go to one of those senior homes. Though most of them are lovely nowadays," she said aside, "and he could have afforded the best. Anyway, he and George made a deal that he would pay our mortgage and come live with us. He's rolling in money, and let's just say that we're not, so it seemed like a good plan. It's not a bad arrangement. He doesn't require much care since he's basically healthy, and being an introvert, he spends most of his time by himself."

She paused for another sip of her beverage.

"Then out of the blue," she continued, "Uncle Christian got some wild idea about returning to his roots. He'd grown up in the old Naylor House before his parents sold it off and moved to Atlanta. He found this house and bought it, so here we are. The original homestead wasn't for sale at the time, or he would most certainly have got it instead."

"Has he thought about purchasing it now that it's come up on the market?" I asked.

"He was considering it. For a while he was going over there every chance he got, but then he seemed to lose interest. I'm kind of glad. This place is actually nicer, and besides, I don't think I could go through another move, even if it was just down the street. Moving is such a pain."

"Do you know if your uncle…"

"My husband's uncle," she corrected.

"Sorry, your husband's uncle—does he still know people in the neighborhood, friends from when he grew up?"

For the first time during the conversation, Jan Naylor looked uncomfortable. "No," she replied flatly. "No one. It was a long time ago. Folks move on."

"The Harts are still here." I was pushing it, but if she didn't know about the relationship between Christian and Paula Hart, she'd be none the wiser. And if she did…

She shrugged. "Uncle Christian never mentions them. That Pauleen woman invited us over when we first arrived, but Uncle Christian said he didn't want to have anything to do with them, and neither should we."

"That seems odd. Did he give a reason?"

"Pfft!" Jan waved a hand dismissively. "That old coot doesn't need a reason for what he says or does."

"So maybe he did know something about them after all," I suggested.

"Maybe, but George and I have lots of friends, and to be honest, those Harts are a bit too hippy-dippy for us. Did you know…" She leaned forward as if to confide a deep secret. "…all three generations of women are named Hart? The old lady was something else until she married Mr. Hart, but her daughter never married despite having a child of her own. That one's called Pet. Pet! What kind of name is that for a girl?"

I took a final sip of the syrupy drink, then placed it on the patio table. "The Harts seem very nice to me," I countered. "Their quilting projects help raise money for cat rescues and shelters."

Jan made a little face. "Oh, forgive me. I didn't mean to sound derogatory. That's a good thing they do, make things for charity. But you can't agree with everyone's lifestyles, can you?"

She was certainly right about that, and I'd just come to my own conclusion about the lifestyle of the Naylors. Jan was a prejudiced gossip, and the uncle, from what she disclosed, was a bossy recluse. I hadn't met husband George, but at that point I didn't think I wanted to.

What am I doing here? I suddenly wondered. Trying to get information that was none of my business and should be left up to the police? If there was something amiss with the Naylor family, it was hardly my job to chase it down. Meddling could compromise any real detective work that was going to happen. My time would be better spent getting hold of Detective Croft and apprising her of the letters in the Harts' attic. I should also talk to my mother about the corsage boxes. If by some quirk of fate she had known Paula Hastings when she was a girl, her insights could be useful.

It was time—past time—for me to bid Jan Naylor farewell and get on with things. Thanking Jan for the lemonade while silently vowing never to accept a beverage from her again, I headed out to the street. Frannie was just coming down the steps from the quilt house, so I paused on the sidewalk to wait.

"I thought you left," she said as she approached.

"I did, but then Jan Naylor caught me. She thought I'd dropped my scarf when I was there the other day, but it wasn't mine. I got talking to her about..." I realized I would need to fill my friend in on the attic caper, the unearthing of the suspicious letters, and the little box of dead flowers before anything would make sense. "Do you have time for a cup of tea at my house? There have been some new developments."

"Mmmm," Frannie hummed. "New developments, as in the murder of Mrs. Hart?"

"Pauleen and I came upon some things while we were in the attic. Well, really it was Mewella who led us to them, but that's another story. They may be significant. Anyway, I need to call Detective Croft, and I'd rather do it from home where I can get my thoughts in line. And I've got to get this tinny taste out of my mouth." I slapped my tongue across the roof of my mouth where the fake lemon flavor lingered. "So how about it? Tea with me and the clowder?"

"Sure, but only a quick one. I'm going to a movie matinée with some friends from my apartment building, and I'll need to dress."

I scanned her perfect teal tunic and wide leg linen pants, wondering how much more dressed up she could get without donning a ball gown, but that was Frannie—an outfit for every occasion.

"Then I'll meet you there?" I queried.

"Sounds good." She gave a capricious smile. "And Lynley…"

"Yes?" I shot back, suddenly apprehensive.

"I have something to tell you too."

Chapter 21

When a cat is first introduced into a new environment, she may be alert to every little sound. As she learns that those sounds don't represent danger, she comes to disregard them. The exception seems to be the sound of the vacuum cleaner.

If someone peeked through the window to witness the tranquil tableau of two old friends having cups of tea with cats sitting on their laps, they would never suspect those women were conferring about murder. But that's exactly what Frannie and I were doing—mulling over the clues to a murder most foul.

I'd told Frannie about the letters Pauleen had found in the quilt shop attic, giving due credit to Mewella for leading us to the extraordinary discovery. Frannie was properly impressed, as much by the cat's ingenuity as by the discovery itself.

"It makes sense," she said as she petted Little who had claimed her lap the moment she sat down on the couch. "And it goes right along with what I'd been thinking, that Mrs. Hart had a secret. But are you sure the relationship ties in with her death? Because I'm not. The idea of a murderous octogenarian seems farfetched. And I'm still having second thoughts about Gilda. I know the police let her go, but she is one weird lady."

"Gilda? Really?" My own lap cat Hermione mewed for attention, and I scritched her lush sideburns thoughtfully.

"Granted she's standoffish at the quilting sessions, and she was decidedly snippy with Mrs. Hart for no apparent reason, but…"

"That's what I wanted to tell you. After you left the quilt shop today, Gilda came back. She came back and went crazy."

"Crazy? How?"

"When she came to the door, she told Dora she needed to get something she'd forgotten in the workroom, so Dora left her to it. Then we started to hear noises, talking and quarreling. We couldn't figure out who she'd be conversing with—everyone was in the sunroom, even the cats. It was upsetting Pauleen, so Dora and I decided we'd better check up on her. We found her talking to herself—well, actually talking to Mrs. Hart's empty rocking chair. I only caught snippets of what she was saying, but it was as if she were engaged in an argument."

"She was arguing with herself? Out loud?" I understood talking to oneself—I did it often enough—but bickering with an imaginary foe was another matter. That behavior rang bells for various mental issues. "Did she explain what she was doing when you caught her at it?"

"That was weird too. When she realized she was being watched, she turned around, gathered up her things, and brushed right past us. She left without another word to anyone."

"That is odd, but again, it doesn't make her a killer."

"If only you could have heard the tone she was taking with Mrs. Hart's ghost."

"Ghost?" I exclaimed. "Now, Frannie, let's not get carried away."

"All right, spirit then, or essence. It may not have been visible to us, but whatever was in that chair certainly seemed real enough to Gilda."

"Maybe she was just running through things in her mind. She hadn't been very nice to Mrs. Hart lately, and now the old woman is gone and there's no recourse. Maybe she was trying to make amends."

"But amends for what?" Frannie scoffed. "For killing her?"

I gave Frannie an exasperated look. She was witty and wise, but when it came to crime, she was like Sherlock Holmes' companion Dr. Watson who regularly concocted some logical theory that Holmes would reveal as absolutely wrong.

"There was something else I wanted to tell you," Frannie continued. "Right before I left the Harts', Mark came by. He asked to see Pet, but she'd already gone to lie down. When I told him, he got all huffy and demanding."

I frowned. "That doesn't sound like Mark."

"I've never seen him that way, but he was really mad."

I caught a quick flash from my phone on the coffee table and picked it up just in time for it to ring. Hermione jettisoned from my lap at the tinkly sound. Little raised her head but laid it down again. She had grown accustomed to the instrument-that-sang. Hermione, a more recent addition to my cat family, had lived a quiet life with a complete recluse before joining my clowder and still wasn't sure what to think of objects that made strange noises all on their own.

"Hello, Carol," I said to my mother. "I was going to call you, but Frannie's here now. Can I get back to you in a little while?"

"Go ahead and talk," Frannie whispered. "I need to go to the powder room anyway."

She gently lifted Little and set the cat on my newly

vacated lap, then rose and left the room. After a brief look around, Little snuggled in as if she'd been there always.

"Never mind, Mum. Frannie's giving me a minute." I stroked Little's silky black sideburns. "What's up?"

"*It's Seleia,*" said Carol. "*She's in a terrible funk. She saw Fredric with another girl, and now she's sure he's about to jilt her.*"

I sat back against the couch. "Oh, dear. She told me he'd been avoiding her. Does she really think it's because of another woman?"

"*She does, but I'm not so sure. They were on the public street, and she says they were just chatting. Sounds innocent enough, but who knows? Either way, she's really depressed about it. You have to talk to her.*"

It was like my mother to make demands where she could have just asked nicely, but in this case, she was right—I should get hold of my granddaughter, and soon. If her beau was seeing someone else, Seleia would need support. That first love was the hardest to lose.

"Of course. I'll call her right when Frannie leaves. Thanks for letting me know. She's been on my mind, but I've been busy."

"*I heard you were off solving another murder,*" Carol harrumphed, ever skeptical of my propensity to sleuth.

"Where did you hear that?"

"*Halle told me. I ran into her at the cat café on Belmont Street yesterday. Oh, Lynley,*" she moaned, "*when are you going to learn to leave it to the police?*"

"Probably never, Mum. And it's not like I go down to the station and pick random killings out of their case files."

"*I know, I know, but be careful. What is it this time?*" she added as her curiosity surfaced. "*A body in a bedroom? A corpse on a golf course? A death in a department store?*"

"You've been reading too many cozy mysteries," I giggled.

"Then what?"

"It's a suspicious death of a friend's mother." I gathered my thoughts. "And there may be something you can help me with. The victim is someone you may have known, Paula Hart. Her maiden name was Hastings."

I heard an *emmmm* sound from Carol's end. "*Not that I recall. Where would I have known her from?*"

"High school. I found an old corsage box among her things that I swear is identical to the one you have stashed away in that little cloisonné chest."

The line went silent, though I could hear a faint tapping like fingernails on a hard surface. Then, even the tapping ceased.

"*I do know her!*" Carol exclaimed. "*At least I did back then. It's been so long. Oh, my goodness,*" she went on. "*Is she the murdered woman? Now that I think about it, I did read something on the newsfeed, but the picture they showed didn't ring a bell—just some old lady. Oh, I am sorry. I haven't seen her since we graduated, and I didn't know her well in school, but it's still a shock and a shame.*"

"Yes, it is very sad. Her daughter and granddaughter are taking it hard, which is why I'm helping them."

"*That's nice of you, dear. Please give them my condolences.*"

"There's one other thing, Mum. Did you know a boy named Christian Naylor from back then? He and Paula may have gone out together."

"*Christian? Now, him I remember! Handsome and older—of course by older I mean only by a few years. But he was out of high school and departing for college. It was all very heartbreaking.*"

"Heartbreaking? In what way?"

"Everybody loved him—he was so friendly and gregarious. And yes, he did date Paula for a time. He was quite stuck on her and she on him." There was a pause. "*But there were rumors.*"

"What sort of rumors?"

"Oh, I don't know, just hearsay that he could be jealous. I'm not sure why I'm even mentioning it—I never believed it myself. Such a gentleman." I heard Carol sigh, waxing nostalgic, no doubt.

"So what was the heartbreaking part?"

"*Well, she dumped him, didn't she?*" Carol blustered.

Regaining her composure, she said, "*Gotta run, dear. You'll call Seleia?*"

"I will. Thanks for the information. Talk to you soon."

Frannie came back into the room just as I rang off. "How's your mom?"

"She's fine. She's worried about Seleia though. Seleia's got the idea Fredric may be seeing someone else, and Carol wants me to talk to her. Not that there's much I can do about it if it's true."

"You can listen and be there for her. I remember the first time a boy dumped me for someone else. I thought I was going to die."

"You remember that far back?" I joked.

"Mind like a velvet trap!" she retorted with a laugh.

Returning to her seat, she finished off her tea in one long draught. "I need to get going, but there is one more thing I wanted to talk to you about before I go. I had an idea."

"Okay...?"

"The ShadowCat Auction is coming up. Obviously, Pet and Pauleen are in no condition to finish organizing the House of Quilts donations, so Dora and I volunteered to do it. We could use your help."

"The auction. Right! It would be a shame to have to back out now. What do you need?"

She leaned forward, a glint in her eye. "Everyone is really close to finishing their projects, but we need a place to do that. Would it be possible to have the remainder of our quilting sessions here?"

"Here?" I gazed around my big living room with its clutter of furniture, trying to imagine what it would look like as a workroom.

"If you moved things to the sides, there would be space for a worktable," Frannie went on quickly. "Not as large as the one at House of Quilts, but it should suffice. And there's the kitchen too, so really plenty of space. I'll help you pick up, and Mark can do the heavy lifting. I promise we'd make it as easy on you as possible." She gave me a sweet Frannie smile. "It's just that no one else has a place that would even remotely accommodate us, and renting is so expensive, even if we could manage to find a room on such short notice that isn't all the way out in Hillsboro or Aloha."

"I'll do it!" I said decisively. "But we'll have to decide on the date. I'm waiting to hear back from NWHS about rescheduling Elizabeth's therapy cat test, and this time, I've got to make it, or it will look bad."

"Will do. We'll need to transport things up from the Harts', but that shouldn't be too difficult. Everyone can collect their own projects and whatever materials they'll need. Thanks so much, Lynley. I'll tell the others."

Frannie picked up her purse and rose. "Don't get up!" she said as I made to join her. "Little looks so comfortable, it would be a shame to disturb her."

Frannie saw herself out, while I petted Little's beautiful

black fur and wondered what it would be like to have a houseful of quilters, one of whom might be a murderer.

Chapter 22

For people who strive to relieve the suffering of others, both human and non-human, there can be a cost. It's called compassion fatigue, a physical, emotional, and psychological exhaustion that develops from being overwhelmed by the seemingly never-ending misery of those they struggle to help. It has become an occupational hazard for professionals, such as psychologists, health care workers, and those in animal rescue.

Once Frannie had left for her matinée date, I sipped my tea, petted my cat, and considered what I would need to do to accommodate a quilt guild in my living room. I had card tables for those with lighter projects, and Mark could bring in a bigger table if he moved the cat tree and the rocking chair to the hallway. If I cleared off the antique table in the kitchen and added the extension leaves, some could work at that as well. There were advantages to owning a big house.

As I pondered the chore of shuffling furniture, my mind turned to Fredric, my stalwart helping hand. I'd enlisted the young man to assist me with various tasks such as hefting the monthly fifty-pound cartons of cat supplies in from my porch and shifting the new cat trees around the living room until I got them just right. Yes, Fredric would be happy to help me get ready for the quilters. Wouldn't he?

If he really is splitting up with my granddaughter, I

thought suddenly, *he might not be so enthusiastic as he once was.* If Seleia lost her boyfriend, would I also lose my handyman?

But Fredric was more to me than a heavy lifter—he was a friend. We'd enjoyed many a late-night discussion about life, the universe, and everything. He loved my granddaughter—or at least I thought he did. I may have felt concern at the start of their relationship because of Seleia's young age and his older one, but he quickly proved himself caring and reliable even to grandmotherly standards. It had been a long time since I'd questioned his intentions. Now I could think of nothing else.

Maybe Carol had got it wrong. Maybe Seleia was blowing things out of proportion. Still, a little twinge at the back of my mind whispered something was amiss. Fredric hadn't just been ignoring Seleia—he'd been quietly absent from my life as well.

Yesterday I'd convinced Seleia to confront Fredric, to find out what was going on in his mind instead of making up scenarios that might have been completely off the mark. She'd headed over to do just that, but I never followed up to see how it went. Kicking myself for not checking in about such an important matter, I reached across Little who was still sound asleep on my lap and picked up my phone.

Touching Seleia's contact icon, a white cat with one blue eye and one green, I listened for it to connect.

"*I can't come to the phone right now,*" came the familiar though disembodied voice. "*I'm off saving the world. Leave a message and I'll get back to you when I'm done.*"

"Hi, love. Call me when you have time. Nothing urgent. Just wanted to see how you are."

Clicking off, I sat for a minute, wondering if I should

follow up with a text, but I didn't want to alarm her. If she hadn't returned my call by dinnertime, I could try again then.

Little gave a purrumph and squirmed onto her back. She was not as little as her name implied, and my knees were beginning to tingle from the weight. I gently shifted her to the couch cushion. She opened one sleepy eye, then settled in among the pillows and returned to her slumber.

Taking up my phone and mug, I went to the kitchen and topped up my tea with a fresh bag and boiling water from the hot water machine. I would need all my wits about me for the next call, the one to Detective Croft.

Since the day was still spring-gorgeous, I decided to take my business out to the patio. It was early in the season, and I hadn't pulled my summer furniture out of the garage yet, but there was a folding lawn chair and a little tray table on the back porch, dry and ready for service. It didn't take me long to put on a sweater and get my makeshift phone desk set up under the latticework grape frame.

The grapevine that wound through the cedar slats was just beginning to sprout green. In the garden nearby, daffodils bobbed their cheerful heads, and the scent of the narcissi perfumed the air. The old plum tree in the corner was doing its best to bloom, and a few white petals floated on the surprisingly warm breeze. I set my phone down next to my teacup and breathed it all in.

Times like that it was hard to believe anything could go wrong. But things did go wrong. Chaos could happen anywhere, blasting lives into rubble and bringing lifetimes to an end.

There it was again, the morose feeling that was becoming more and more familiar to me. Was it age? Was it the state of the world? Was it compassion fatigue? Sometimes it seemed like no matter how many cats I rescued, how many family dramas I helped to work out, to say nothing of how many murders landed on or near my doorstep, there was always one more awful event waiting just around the corner.

Giving a determined sigh, I pulled myself together and picked up the phone. It had been a while since I'd called the P.P.D., but she was still right there in the list of contacts: Detective Marsha Croft.

I paused, thinking back to my first encounter with the savvy detective five years before. My initial impression had been of a stark, self-possessed woman who took her job way too seriously. But how else should a homicide detective approach such grisly work? Croft was a terrier and good at what she did. She had a sixth sense that she didn't mind using to help her capture her perps. And for some reason I never quite understood, her intuition had identified me as a helpful source. Detective Croft had listened to me in the past. I hoped she would listen now.

A little shiver ran down my spine as I punched the number, and it continued to prickle throughout the series of steps it took to reach a human who could connect me with my party. Finally a man came on the line.

"Detective Tim Schultz. How can I help you?"

"This is Lynley Cannon. I'm trying to reach Detective Croft."

"Detective Croft is out of the office. Can I take a message?"

"Do you know when she'll be back?"

"No, ma'am. I don't have that information."

I was disappointed, though I could have predicted the busy detective might not be sitting at her desk awaiting my call.

"I'm calling on behalf of Pauleen Hart concerning the case of her mother Paula Hart's recent murder."

"Yes, go on."

"I have—I mean, we have..." I was faltering, trying to pull my thoughts together into something that wouldn't sound like gibberish. "Pauleen and I discovered some information that might be pertinent to the case. Can you ask Detective Croft to call me when she gets back in?"

I gave my number and repeated my name, then rang off. I didn't like callbacks—they invariably came at an inconvenient time, like when one was standing a footstool or heading for the loo. I preferred texting and email, more forgiving methods of communication, but they weren't always appropriate. I'd just have to sit on my hands and hope Detective Croft would call when I wasn't in a compromised position.

After a few more minutes on the patio, I decided it was still a bit cool for a prolonged stay and went back inside to clean up the tea things and start the dishwasher. Though now I was expecting two calls, I jumped when the phone rang. Checking the screen, I was surprised to find an unidentified number.

As a rule, I refused calls from numbers that weren't in my contact list, but Detective Croft could be calling from outside her office, so I made an exception and clicked the answer bar.

"Hello?" I said cautiously, still poised to hang up if it turned out to be a robot.

"Lynley? Lynley Cannon?"

"This is she," I said, remembering never to say the word, *yes*, to an unknown caller in case they were scammers who record your voice, then use it to make it seem like I authorized something I didn't. "Who am I speaking to?"

"This is Dora. I'm at Pauleen's. Something terrible has happened! She wanted me to call and tell you."

I stopped cold, visions of horrors flashing through my mind.

"What?" I managed.

"The police are here," Dora hissed. "And that Detective Croft. They're asking all sorts of questions."

My tension eased, and now I felt annoyed. "That's bound to happen, Dora. It's nothing to worry about. They're just following through with their investigation into Mrs. Hart's death."

"No!" she shouted In my ear. Behind her I was beginning to hear shouts of another sort—people yelling in anger, or in fear?

"What do you mean, no? What's going on?"

"I told you. It's the cops. They've found another body!"

* * *

Dropping everything, I flew to my car and hastened down to House of Quilts. I didn't know how I could be of any help, but Dora said Pauleen wanted me, needed me. How could I refuse?

Besides, I was curious. As I dug deeper, Dora admitted she'd been premature about there being an actual body since no one but the police knew what was really going on, and they weren't telling. Something was up that required the presence of the medical examiner's van, however, and that couldn't be good.

I had to park two blocks away because of the glut of official vehicles taking up the street in front of House of Quilts. Then when I walked up from my car, a burly cop with an attitude refused to let me through. I'd just got my phone out to call Pauleen when I spied a familiar face, not at the quilt house but next door on the steps of the Naylor's.

Detective Marsha Croft paused to talk to a man in a brown suit. They exchanged a furtive dialogue, then he continued into the house and Croft came down to the street.

"Detective Croft," I called from beside the big officer.

Croft glanced my way, keen eyes locking onto mine. For a moment, she hesitated, and I wondered if she had forgotten who I was. Then the eyes narrowed, and she beckoned me to come. I pointed at my keeper, and her squint turned on him.

I saw no sign or gesture pass between them, but he tensed and grunted, "Go on. The detective wants you."

The indomitable homicide detective hadn't changed much since the last time I'd seen her. In fact, though I couldn't be certain, she may even have been wearing the same unremarkable gray suit. The drab clothing was a disguise, however. Tall, with lustrous black hair and a smoldering gaze, Croft could have been a fashion model, but she chose to underplay her beauty for the sake of her job. Her costume worked well, her only nod to feminine fashion the liberal use of bright red lipstick.

"Lynley Cannon," said Croft with that slight, unidentifiable accent of hers. "Here you are again."

"Detective," I returned. "Aren't you at the wrong house?"

"Wrong house?" she replied without understanding. "What would make you think that?"

"I'm sorry. I assumed you were investigating the death of Paula Hart." I pointed to the colorful facade where the trio of women hovered like three witches. "Or maybe there was a breakthrough in the case?"

Croft silently studied me, then taking my arm, she led me aside. "How are you involved with the Harts, Lynley Cannon?"

Straight to the point, as always. "I belong to their quilting group, that's all."

"That is all, yet you are asking me about the murder of their family member?"

"Well," I hemmed, "a friend mentioned I'd been close to a few murder cases before and suggested I could help them negotiate through this difficult..."

"Ah," she interrupted. "You are here to help. I should have known that, Lynley. You are very good at helping."

She was being sarcastic, but she did have a basis for it. I had been present at more than my share of crimes, always in the role of assisting someone acquainted with the victim.

"Christian Naylor, the man who lived there..." Croft pointed at the Naylors house, all mockery aside. "Did you know him too?"

Aha! I thought to myself. *So she does suspect Naylor!* She must have found out about his relationship with Mrs. Hart on her own. "No, I've never met the man, but I talked with his daughter-in-law a few times."

I stopped, my mind suddenly registered the detective's words. "Wait a minute. You said the man who *lived* there... *Lived*? Has something happened to Christian Naylor?"

Just then an ambulance pulled up and parked cattywampus in the street. Two medics hopped out and headed inside. They didn't seem to be in any hurry.

Croft blew a puff of air through her pursed red lips. "Christian Naylor is dead."

"Murdered?" I gasped in surprise.

Her eyes lingered on me. "Why would you think that?"

"I... I... It was just a wild guess."

"The autopsy will give the definitive answer, but it is possible you are correct." She shifted her stance. "Do you have any other wild guesses I should know about?"

My mind immediately flew to the letters from Mrs. Hart's hope chest, but I wasn't sure now was the time to bring them up. Though Christian Naylor could conceivably have had something to do with Paula Hart's death, Mrs. Hart was beyond bringing about the Naylor uncle's demise. Unless I wanted to believe there were two killers running around the Hawthorne neighborhood, I'd have to assume the pair were killed by someone else entirely.

"Wild guesses? I don't think so," I edged. "At least not right at the moment."

She eyed me suspiciously, as if she could tell I was holding back. Slipping her hand into her jacket pocket, she withdrew a business card, white medium stock with blue printing and a crest, and handed it to me.

"Give Officer Field your current information. I may wish to speak to you again."

Chapter 23

Lately we have seen an upsurge in people including cats in their family portraits. It's a challenge to the photographer, who must make the cat feel comfortable in the staged situation.

Croft turned on her boot heel and headed back into the house. As instructed, I handed Officer Field my card with my name and phone number listed beneath a photo of a distinctive black-and-white-faced cat. The man looked at the card, then back at me.

"Your cat?" he asked.

"Yes, that's Dirty Harry."

The burly cop smiled. "Boy, he's a beauty, isn't he?"

Instantly Officer Field rose several notches in my estimation. "I'll tell him you said that," I grinned.

Despite the exchange with the nice ailurophile cop, I was feeling let down that I hadn't managed to get more from Croft when I had the chance. Prying details out of the shrewd detective was as challenging as giving a cat a pill, but I could have tried harder. Too late now—perhaps a phone call when she was back in the office would yield better results.

I turned to survey the scene. A young policewoman was stringing yellow tape around the perimeter of the Naylors' front yard. There was no sign of the family themselves—they were likely sheltering somewhere to avoid the questions and stares. Aside from the police presence, locals had begun to gather. I noticed Colin leaning on his cane at the mouth of the alley, while in the other direction, Josie Brimm and her son were rubbernecking from the sidewalk in front of the sale house. Pet, Pauleen, and Dora had come out onto the steps of House of Quilts. Dora was waving frantically to get my attention.

"Yoohoo," she called out when she saw me look up. "Lynley, over here!"

With nothing better to do, I figured I'd answer her summons, after all she was the one who had called me to the scene. Besides, I had questions, and since Detective Croft was as closed-mouthed as ever, maybe the quilters could fill me in on what was happening next door.

Ducking back beneath the crime scene tape, I joined the ladies on the steps. "What's going on? Do you know?"

"We were hoping you could tell us," said Pauleen. "We saw you talking to the detective."

"Someone's dead," Pet blurted. "They are, aren't they?"

"Yes. It's Christian Naylor, but that's all Detective Croft would say. Except..." I hesitated—the words didn't come easily. "Except that maybe his death wasn't altogether natural."

A collective gasp rose from the three. Pet and Pauleen seemed genuinely distraught, this new calamity weighing on top of their own recent grief. Dora's gaze fixed on the street where the ambulance was pulling away with its grisly passenger.

"But you knew that already, didn't you, Dora?"

The small woman shot around, her eyes coming to rest on me. "Knew what?"

"That someone had been murdered. You told me on

the phone they'd found a body."

Dora blinked a few times in rapid succession. "What else could it have been? The detective, the coroner, police everywhere?"

"It's a déjà vu of when Gran died," Pet agreed.

"Except this time it wasn't our family," Pauleen cut in. "Thank the Lord for that! I couldn't take another loss."

Out on the street, the initial investigation was winding down. All but one of the cruisers were pulling away and driving off. With the excitement dissipating, the onlookers had begun to return to their homes, taking their speculations with them. Detective Croft was nowhere to be seen.

"It looks like that's about it. Why don't we go inside?" I proposed. "We can talk over a cup of tea."

Pauleen gave me a grateful look. "I'd like that. I didn't really know the deceased, but he was our neighbor. This is all too close—I'm beginning to feel a little woozy."

Dora was instantly at Pauleen's side, reaching for her elbow.

Pauleen gently pulled away. "I'm all right, but tea sounds like a good idea. Would you mind?"

"Of course not," replied Dora. "Any particular flavor?"

"Just the green in the Japanese tin. Thank you, dear. You're a lifesaver."

We headed into the house with Dora in the lead. Once in the shop, Dora broke off for the kitchen while Pauleen came to a halt in the middle of the room. Mewella, who had been watching her humans from her shelf by the screen door, hopped down to join us.

"Let's go up to the parlor," said Pauleen. "We'll be more comfortable there."

Without awaiting a response, she crossed to the stairs

and began to climb. Mewella ran in front of her, and Ridley, who had come in from the catio, followed his sister up the carpeted treads.

"We're going up to the parlor," Pet called to Dora. "Will you need any help with the tea things?"

"I'm fine," came the disembodied voice from the other room. "Be right up."

Pet and I mounted the steps to the little sitting room. Pauleen was already ensconced on the sofa, legs up on the ottoman, with Mewella on her lap and Ridley stretched long on the back of the couch looking regal. If I'd been a portrait photographer, I couldn't have asked for a more perfect layout, marred only by the frazzled look on Pauleen's face. The days of sorrow and worry had taken their toll.

"Another death!" she moaned. "When will it end?"

Pet dropped down next to her mother. "This is appalling." Turning to me, she asked, "Do you think the two murders are connected?"

I seated myself in an antique chintz-upholstered wing chair which I found to be unexpectedly comfortable. "That's a tough one. Since we don't yet know how Christian Naylor died, I hesitate to guess."

"But?" Pet prompted.

"But if there was foul play involved, as Detective Croft insinuated, it seems like too much of a coincidence not to be connected in some way…" I turned a questioning glance on Pauleen.

"I told Pet about the romantic letters from Mr. Naylor to her Gran," she replied to my wordless query. "And the not-so-romantic one."

Pet brushed a willful lock of hair from her face "I still can't believe it—my gran involved with a man. I don't mean back in high school—that's perfectly reasonable. She was young then. But now? She is... *was* in her eighties! Why, these last few years she barely ventured from her rocking chair. I mean, what was she doing? Leading a geriatric double life?"

I followed Pauleen's gaze to the window and the view beyond the filigree leaves of the maple tree. From that second-floor vantage, I could just see the tall buildings of downtown backlit by the setting sun. I hadn't realized how late it had become, but how could it not? The day had been long and arduous, and it wasn't over yet.

"How did we miss it?" Pet went on. "What kind of family are we?"

I remembered wondering the same thing myself—how could Pet and Pauleen have neglected to see what was going on right under their noses. But Colin had given me the answer, that the elderly became invisible to those younger folks busy with their lives. As long as Mrs. Hart appeared in the expected places at the expected times, no one would think anything was amiss.

"Speaking of the letters," I said, "I don't suppose you had a chance to show them to Detective Croft when she was here just now."

"But I did," said Pauleen. "I know I'd asked you to make the call for me, but then after you left, I decided it was really my job. That's what started the whole thing."

"What whole thing? I'm not understanding."

"Detective Croft wanted to see the letters for herself, so she came by. She spent some time looking at them and asked a bunch of questions that I couldn't answer. She must have thought there was something to them, but it was hard to tell. She's not very transparent, is she?"

"Not at all," I replied, recalling the many times I'd

been frustrated by the detective's unreadable expressions.

"Anyway, she took the letters and went over to interview Christian Naylor. Next thing I knew, we had police zooming into the street from all directions."

In the ensuing silence, I heard footfalls come down the hallway, and Dora appeared in the door holding a wooden tray.

"Tea's on." She set her burden on the coffee table and smiled up at Pauleen. "Just the green—no milk or sugar, but I did bring some lemon slices. I know it's not traditional, but a little citrus is good for us. May I pour you a cup?"

"Yes, please. And good idea about the lemon. I could use a pick-me-up."

Dora poured the dark chartreuse liquid into a porcelain cup, plopped in two lemon slices, and handed it to her friend. "Anyone else while I'm at it?"

With nods all around, we spent a few minutes organizing our drinks. Mewella decided there was too much activity for her liking and moved to a cat bed by the window. Ridley instantly usurped her place on Pauleen's lap, nosing at her teacup until she gave up and set it on the side table out of his insistent reach.

Dora pulled a cane chair from its place by the wall. "What did I miss?"

"Nothing much," said Pauleen. "I was filling Lynley in on Detective Croft's visit this afternoon."

"Oh, yes," Dora said with a crafty nod. "I'm glad I was here for that. It was such a strange thing, those love letters. I think they really opened the detective's eyes, don't you?"

Pet sipped her tea thoughtfully. "They did cast suspicion on Mr. Naylor. The lover spurned and all that."

"Exactly!" said Dora. "I'm sure she was about to make

an arrest." Leaning in as if divulging the deepest of secrets, she said, "What a surprise it must have been to find her prime suspect dead in his room."

I jerked my head around to study the small woman. Her face was aglow with delight.

"What did you say?" I stuttered.

"About what?"

"About finding the Naylor uncle passed away in his bedroom. How did you know?"

"Oh, I was just talking with Jan. That's why the tea took a little longer. She and George were going to their car—their house is a crime scene, you know. I went out to offer my condolences, and she told me. She gave me the whole story."

Now all eyes were on Dora, and she was lapping up the attention.

"Apparently," she began as if relating a tale, "Jan had been doing the laundry. George was out at one of his lodge meetings, and Veronica had gone to the mall with friends. When Detective Croft rang the bell and asked to speak to Uncle Christian, Jan was the only other person in the house. Poor dear," Dora sympathized. "She had no idea she was alone with a dead man."

"That's horrible," Pet exclaimed. "So gross!"

"Go on," I urged. "What happened next?"

"Well, Jan let the detective in and then went to call their uncle. His bedroom is upstairs, so she yelled from the bottom of the staircase. She was surprised when he didn't answer—I guess he usually taps his cane on the floor to show he's heard."

Dora paused to make sure we were listening, which we were.

"Jan started to go up, but Detective Croft stopped her,

and she went instead. She was up there a while, and Jan wanted to see what was taking them so long, but she'd been told to wait, so she did. She could hear muffled talking, which was probably the detective calling for backup or whatever they do when they find a body. Then Detective Croft came back and took Jan into the living room. George arrived home at that minute, so she asked him to sit down too. That's when she broke the news that Uncle Christian was dead."

"And murdered," Pet added.

"Jan said Detective Croft didn't mention a cause of death, but the fact they took his body to their morgue and not the funeral parlor made Jan wonder. And they told her and George to stay in touch—you know, the *don't leave town* bit."

Dora took a long draught of tea, thus concluding her narrative. "Well, there you have it. I guess we'll find out more in due time."

I was thinking Dora had found out quite a bit already, considering the events had only transpired within the last hour.

"Oh, there was one other thing," said Dora, bringing me back from my contemplations. "Their cat Clarice is sick. They were on their way to the vet's. It looks like she may have eaten something bad."

Chapter 24

Therapy cats need to tolerate situations that most cats would find frightening. They must be able to encounter hospital equipment, strange people, and new sounds and scents without panicking.

The morning had broken with the beauty that only can be found in those early days of spring. A crow hopped along the fence outside the window uttering guttural chirps at his brothers and sisters who had taken roost in the cherry tree across the street. The man in the house beyond stepped out to call his dog from the yard. A recycling truck rumbled past, huge as an armored elephant. I wondered how the driver avoided swiping the sideview mirrors of the parked cars, but he always seemed to manage.

"Lynley," said Frannie. "You look like you're a million miles away."

I turned back to the quilting table that now crouched in the middle of my living room, the crafting session successfully shifted from House of Quilts to House of Lynley. Initially I'd been skeptical of the arrangement, imagining all sorts of chaos and commotion, but it had worked out with amazing ease. Mark had come up with a six-foot table, and he and Dora, who despite her diminutive size, seemed strong as a horse, shifted my furniture so it fit nicely into my front room. The quilters had collected their projects and supplies from the quilt house, and now my place was bustling with creative activity. So far, the only issue had been Ruth forgetting her spool of pink thread. Luckily, I had a collection of sewing thread and came up with a color close enough to work.

I'd launched back into my white cat embroidery but soon found my mind drifting. It had been a little over a week since the deaths of Christian Naylor and Paula Hart, and my thoughts kept circling around to those two tragedies. That such a thing could happen at their advanced age was both depressing and scary. We were supposed to pass peacefully at the end of a life well lived, not be scythed down by someone on a killing spree.

On top of that sadness, or maybe exacerbated by it, I'd woken up with a sore back for no good reason. I took an aspirin, but even so, the pain lingered. Yesterday I'd suffered a headache, and the day before, I'd got a cramp in my foot that wouldn't go away. Such things weren't surprising at my age, but I couldn't help but wonder if that's the way it was going to be from now on—every day, a new ailment.

"Lynley," Frannie repeated. "Are you listening?"

I turned to find everyone staring at me—Mark, Ruth, Frannie, and even Gilda who had set up her sewing machine on my desk beside the cat tree. Emilio was perched on the top tier, watching her every move with great fascination. I hoped he wouldn't decide to make her square his quarry and jump down into the middle of her work.

"Mmmm?" I mumbled. "Sorry, I was woolgathering. What did I miss?"

"Ruth was asking when Elizabeth was going to take her therapy cat assessment test," Frannie filled in.

I turned to the woman on the couch, hand-sewing the

finishing stitches on her project. Today she was wearing a frilly pink sweater that made her look a little like a ruffled rose. The cat in question sat curled up on her lap.

"Her appointment is next week," I replied with some embarrassment for zoning out.

Ruth brushed a hand across Elizabeth's back. "She's such a sweet little thing. Anyone would be blessed to have her visit them."

"How does that work?" asked Mark. "Ouch!" he added after pricking his finger on a wayward pin.

"What, the test?" Mark nodded as he pressed a Kleenex over his tiny wound. "There are two parts to it. First, they go over her vet certification and give me a short interview to make sure I've read all the rules and know what I'm doing; then comes the evaluation itself, where I run Elizabeth through a set of mock situations that she might be faced with in real life. It takes about an hour in all."

"Poor kitty," said Ruth. "That seems like a long time."

"She's up to it. If she can't handle the assessment test, she wouldn't be happy as a therapy cat."

"I see what you mean." Ruth gave Elizabeth's cheek a rub, for which she received an audible purr. "You'll make it, won't you, sweetheart?"

"Speaking of cats," Mark put in, "does anyone know what happened with the sick one next door to the Harts' place? Clarice, I think it is."

Again the collective eyes were upon me. Why they thought I would know was beyond my understanding. Except I did know. In a fit of curiosity, I'd phoned Jan Naylor to see how they were getting along, which of course included the cat.

"You heard about that?" I wasn't really surprised since

word seemed to travel fast among the group, especially when it came to cats. Or murder. "She's fine. She'd ingested something poisonous, just as they suspected, but she'd taken very little, and the docs at Dove Lewis Emergency Hospital quickly flushed it out of her system."

Mark was fiddling nervously with his runner but not actually working on it. "Did she munch on a toxic plant or get into a cleaning cupboard?"

"Neither," I sighed. "It turned out to be the same thing that Christian Naylor consumed."

"The stuff that killed him?" Ruth gasped.

"I heard someone gave him a box of poisoned bonbons," said Gilda."

"That's the story," I confirmed. "Clarice licked one and got sick too."

"Lucky she didn't go the same way as Naylor," Gilda snorted.

"Gilda!" Ruth exclaimed. "The man died!"

Gilda paused her machine and shrugged. "Can't help if I like cats more than humans. Besides, I'm not trying to belittle the man's death. I'm just saying the poor cat was innocent. She didn't deserve to die."

"And Christian Naylor did?" Ruth returned.

Again the shrug. "Someone must have thought so or he'd be alive today."

There was an uncomfortable hush as Gilda's words hung in the charged air, then one by one, people shifted their attention to their projects. Gilda took up her machine sewing, and the stop-and-start hum served as a background to the strained silence. When the knock came on the front door, it was both a surprise and a relief.

I set down my embroidery, which was coming along nicely if I did say so myself, and went to answer. Peering outside, I saw Dora who had made a mysterious exit after setting up the table. Now she was back, the big smile on her face indicating her errand must have been a success.

"All good?" I asked as I let her inside.

"Better than good," she teased. "Come along and I'll show you."

She stepped through into the living room and raised her hand. In it, she held a fan of shiny paper tickets.

"ShadowCat Rescue has cordially invited us to the Black Cat's Ball! A thank-you perk for our donations to the charity auction."

She set the tickets in the center of the worktable. "Pauleen hopes everyone will come. We can bring a plus one."

I picked a ticket from the pile. Alongside the particulars of name, date, time, and the rescue's black cat logo, I was pleased to see a picture of a cat quilt.

I pointed to the image. "This is Pauleen's, isn't it?"

"Yes, it is," Dora cooed. "Isn't it wonderful?"

Even Gilda was impressed by the way the photographer had captured the repeating design of colorful cats on its intricate, patterned background. Under the picture the caption read, *Calicos on Calico, by Pauleen Hart.*

"That should go for a nice sum at auction," Mark commented. "Publicity always helps sell an item."

As people scored their complimentary tickets, Dora took her project from her bag and sat down at the table next to Frannie.

"How are Pet and Pauleen doing?" Frannie asked her. "I don't suppose they're up to coming today."

"No," Dora replied with an air of authority. "I asked them of course, but they send their regrets."

"I'm not surprised," said Mark. "Pet must be devastated. Pauleen too, of course," he added when he got a dirty look from Dora for excluding her friend.

"I'm not either," said Frannie, "but I'd hoped that since the session wasn't at their place, they might want to drop in for a bit."

"Pet's donation is finished, and so is Pauleen's, obviously." Dora tapped a finger at the quilt image on her ticket. "They had planned to do something more but decided under the circumstances to shift their efforts to a memorial quilt for Mrs. Hart."

"You've seen them often, have you?" Mark asked. "Pet and Pauleen, not memorial quilts," he clarified.

Dora sorted through a box of fabric squares for the ones she was piecing together. "Just helping out where I can. Pauleen is taking it hard, but of the two, she is the more accepting. Pet wavers between denial and absolute grief."

"I wish Pet would let me see her, comfort her," Mark lamented.

"She will, dear," said Frannie. "Just give her time."

"It's the not knowing," said Ruth. "Until they find out who killed that poor woman and why, they won't be able to move on."

"Has there been any news about Mrs. Hart's murder?" I asked. It wasn't subtle, but I hadn't been the one to bring it up.

"Lynley, really!" Gilda admonished.

"Oh, come on," I retaliated. "Don't tell me you aren't interested, Gilda. Like Ruth said, until the killer is found, we're all in an uncomfortable spot."

"What do you mean we're in a spot?" asked Mark.

"Don't you see?" I set my embroidery down on the

table. "Two people have been killed, one of whom was closely connected to this group. Until the police find who did it, we could be in trouble ourselves."

"By trouble," Frannie said, catching my implication, "you mean danger?"

"Well, yes, it's possible."

"Oh, please," Gilda muttered. "You can't think the murderer is going to strike again, pick us off one by one like in an old mystery movie."

"No," I admitted, my thoughts turning inward. "No, whoever killed Paula Hart and Christian Naylor had a motive, maybe to do with their December romance. What I'm more concerned about is that someone in our group..." I paused. Did I really want to say what was on my mind? Probably not, but I said it anyway.

"Could someone in our group—even someone in this room—turn out to be the killer?"

Chapter 25

Some cats are unaffected by disturbances when they're sleeping, while others will leap away in a huff at the merest whisper.

Ruth's quilt fell from her hands, sending Elizabeth tumbling off her lap in a sulk. Mark sat back in his chair with an *oof*. Frannie rolled her eyes, then looked away but not before I got the message: I was doing it again, placing myself smack dab in the middle of something that was none of my business.

"Well, it isn't me," Gilda shot out. "I already went through a police interrogation after Paula Hart died. And I never met the Naylor man, or any of the other Naylors for that matter."

"No, I didn't mean..." I began, but it was too late. I'd basically accused one of the quilters of being a killer, and nothing I could say would take it back.

"You think it's one of us?" Dora gasped. "Why, that's ridiculous."

"It is a bit fanciful, Lynley," Ruth seconded. "You talk about motive—well, none of us have one. We all cared about Mrs. Hart. And the neighbor—I don't think any of us knew him at all."

"You're right, you're right. I apologize." I stood and began to pace. "I'm just trying to figure this thing out."

"Is she always like this?" Ruth whispered to Frannie.

"Always," Frannie whispered back. "She's like a cat at

a mousehole when it comes to a mystery. Sounding things out is part of her process, and she usually gets it in the end. She's helped the police with their investigations more than once."

"No, Ruth has a point," I backpedaled. "None of us has a motive—that we know of. Nor do Pet or Pauleen."

Dora jumped at the sound of her friend's name. "Now you're accusing Pauleen of killing her own mother? Or Pet doing in her gran? It's bad enough to question one of us, but Pauleen? That's insulting, Lynley. It's absurd, and I'm not staying to hear any more of this slander." She rose and began sweeping her project supplies into her bag.

"Wait, Dora!" I caught her arm. "I'm sorry. I'm not accusing anyone. I can't even get a clear picture of what sort of person might have done it."

"Maybe the police are wrong and the deaths were accidents after all," Ruth put in. "Wouldn't it be wonderful if this were a big misunderstanding, and no one was murdered at all?"

That stopped the conversation, everyone staring at each other with blank expressions. Dirty Harry chose that moment to saunter into the room, look around, determine there were too many people for his liking, and go back out again.

"What do you think, Lynley?" Frannie asked. "Could that be true?"

"Why do you think I would know?" I retorted before I could stop myself. Yet, with the possible exception of Dora, Pauleen's best friend and confidant, I probably had more information on the cases than anyone else in the room.

It wasn't enough. What if Ruth was right and the initial investigators had been mistaken about Mrs. Hart's cause of death? According to Pauleen, she died when her head hit the corner of the fireplace hearth. Could she have fallen with such force on her own, or was she pushed? And if she had been pushed, was the pusher simply shoving her away, never intending for her to sustain a fatal blow?

As for Naylor, Detective Croft had all but said his death was suspicious. Poisoned candy from an anonymous gifter? Unless the poison was a natural form of toxin that had somehow managed to grow in the bonbons' fruit centers, murder seemed most likely. But again, had that been the plan? Could the perpetrator have been trying merely to make the old man ill?

I was second-guessing myself—third-guessing even. I needed more data if I were to work out whether the accidental death theory had merit or was just wishful thinking.

"Have any of you been interviewed by Detective Croft?" I asked abruptly. "Besides Gilda, I mean."

"I received a call from her office that she wanted to see me," said Ruth. "I'm going in early next week."

"I got one too," said Frannie. "They set up an appointment for Monday."

"Mark?"

"Not so far," Mark muttered.

"What about you, Dora?" The woman had made no more move to leave, but she hadn't returned to her workstation either. In fact, she seemed frozen in place.

It took her a minute to thaw, then she sighed and dropped back into her chair. "Yes, I received a call as well. I didn't answer it though."

"Why not?" asked Frannie. Dora just turned away.

"I set up my appointment right away," Frannie continued. "It didn't sound intrusive, just that the detective wanted to talk to everyone in the group in case we had something to add. Lynley, what about you? Did you get a summons?"

"No, but I should have." I paused to collect my thoughts. "I need to be interviewed as well, and I think now is as good a time as any."

"Excuse me a minute," I said, grabbing my phone off the sewing table and ducking into the kitchen before anyone could ask questions. I had an idea, if I could get Croft to go along with it.

Violet was lying on the linoleum beside her food bowl, ever hopeful. She blinked up at me with her liquid eyes, and I couldn't resist her plea. Crossing to the treat bar, I picked out a couple of her special diet treats and set them in front of her.

"Chew quietly," I told the big cat, "or we'll have the whole clowder in here clambering for goodies."

As if she understood, she soundlessly consumed the morsels. I gave her a pet, then turned back to my phone and my mission.

* * *

A few minutes later, I returned to the living room with my laptop computer. Moving my embroidery project aside, I set the laptop on the table. The cover was down but not all the way closed.

"I have Detective Croft on the call. She says she will talk to us now. Anyone who doesn't want to join in is welcome to wait in the kitchen. She's a busy woman so I doubt it will take long."

Though the entire group was eyeing me in shocked surprise, no one made to get away.

"Are we good then?" There were nods and an *I guess so*

from Mark, so I flipped open the laptop cover. On the screen we could see the detective against a virtual background of a mountain scene with the official Oregon State badge layered into the lower left hand corner.

"Who do you have, Lynley?" Croft asked as she squinted into the camera.

"These are all the quilters in our group aside from Pet and Pauleen—Ruth, Frannie, Mark, Dora, and you know Gilda."

Croft's hand filled the view as she fiddled with her controls, then she was once more front and center. "This meeting will be recorded. If anyone objects, please step away now."

Again, no one took the offer to give the session a miss.

"Each of you state your full name for the record."

The laptop was passed around as people dutifully gave their full legal names, most of which I'd never heard before.

"Thank you," Croft said when it came back to me. "Lynley, can you gather them together so I can see everyone at once? It will make this much easier on my end."

There was some shuffling as the folks at the table made room for Gilda and Ruth. Once everyone was situated, all attention turned to the small screen.

"I am Detective Marsha Croft, City of Portland Homicide Division, lead investigator into the deaths of Paula Hart and Christian Naylor." Her accent was more pronounced when she spoke officially, but as always, I couldn't place a country of origin. "I had planned to interview each of you separately and still intend to do so, but Lynley Cannon had the unconventional proposal of a group session, and I agreed. Lynley has a proven ability to come up with suggestions that work. Let us see if this impromptu round table will be one of them."

Croft's red lips managed the briefest of smiles. "All right, Lynley. This is your brainchild. Where would you like to begin?"

Though I'd come up with the idea of an online interview and succeeded in convincing Croft it was a good one, I'd never considered she might ask me to lead the show.

"Well, let's see... We were discussing the tragic deaths of Mrs. Hart and Mr. Naylor..."

"Yes, Lynley, I know that already."

"Okay, right." I took a deep breath and started again. "Among other things, we were talking about motives and how none of us had one. Then someone brought up an interesting question. Is there a chance those deaths were accidental?"

Croft looked down, then back at the camera. A slight scrunch of her dark eyebrows was the only indication that she had come to a decision.

"I will tell you what I can. We are currently treating both deaths as suspicious. The pathologist has determined Mrs. Hart could not have fallen with such force on her own. Bruising proves that some sort of thrust was involved. Whether the objective was to kill her, move her, or merely someone lashing out in high emotion, we will not know until the perpetrator tells us. One thing is certain, however. The act was one of malice."

"Just as I thought," Gilda muttered. "Death by murder either way."

"As for Mr. Naylor, his death was the result of ingesting poisoned candy," Croft went on, "candy delivered to him by an anonymous source that we have yet to trace. The deed was intentional, but was it meant to kill? One chocolate would have made him sick but not fatally so. He ate many, however, which according to his niece, was his usual habit. Did the poisoner know this? If so, then the objective was murder. Again we do not know." She paused to study her audience on the small screen. "But whether murder or manslaughter, both deaths are being considered homicides."

There was a short silence as people digested this information. For a time, they had allowed themselves to hope there wasn't someone in their community committing violence, but now faces fell and shoulders slumped as that hope fell away and reality set in.

"I have a question," said Ruth. Croft gave a nod. "Are you certain the two deaths are related?"

"What?" piped up Gilda. "You'd rather have two killers running around than one?"

Embarrassed, Ruth picked at a stray thread on her fabric.

"A good question," said Croft. "We are leaning toward that assumption, though we are keeping an open mind. But there are facts that support the one-killer theory and virtually none that lead us to believe they are separate crimes."

Mark rubbed his beard and straightened the neck of his Polo shirt. "Excuse me, Detective. Do you have a suspect?"

"Not as yet." Croft's mouth gave a little twitch. "We were about to look at Naylor for Hart's death, and still have questions in that area, but now he is dead as well."

"I don't suppose he killed himself," Gilda posed with a chuckle.

"Unlikely," the solemn detective replied without

missing a beat. "And it is time for me to ask the questions."

Gilda gave a harrumph but settled in her chair.

"Did any of you know that Hart and Naylor were involved in a relationship before it came to light through letters discovered in Hart's hope chest?"

Everyone began talking at once:

"No."

"Not a clue."

"I still can't believe it."

"Stop," Croft commanded. "One at a time."

The replies came more slowly, but the bottom line was that no one knew, suspected, or even imagined the old lady who sat quietly in her rocker by the window was having an affair.

"When did you last see Mrs. Hart?" Croft asked.

"It was at the quilting session," said Gilda, "the one before she died. But there was nothing odd about it. She was working on her knitting, like always. She did leave sometime after Lynley came back from chasing her cat."

Croft's eyebrows lifted at the mention of my cat, but she chose not to pursue it. "Did anyone see or hear from Mrs. Hart once the session was over?"

Gilda shrugged.

"I went home," said Ruth.

"I'd planned to go to the Crystal Springs Rhododendron Garden," Mark commenced, "but the weather was terrible. I went home too."

"I had a shift at Friends of Felines, the cat shelter," Frannie disclosed. "Mrs. Hart was gone by the time I left, but I didn't see her go."

"I did," said Ruth. Turning to me, she scrunched her eyebrows. "That was right after you came back with your little cat and told everyone about the heated argument you'd overheard going on next door."

"An argument?" asked Croft. "Please explain."

I thought back. "As Ruth mentioned, my cat Elizabeth had run off, and I went to find her. She'd started upstairs, and when I followed her, I could hear voices coming from the yard next door. A woman—likely Josie Brimm, the real estate agent in charge of selling the place—was berating a man for trespassing. Apparently, it wasn't the first time she'd caught him at it, and she was angry. I didn't pay much attention, but Ruth's right. It was when I came back to the workroom and told the others about the dispute that Mrs. Hart disappeared."

"You don't suppose it had anything to do with her leaving, do you?" asked Frannie.

Suddenly the exchange came into focus. I now knew the trespasser must have been Christian Naylor sneaking into the house to meet Paula Hart. Why he'd chosen his ancestral home for their rendezvous or how he'd managed to gain entry was still a mystery, but it seemed conceivable that hearing about the argument might have caused Mrs. Hart unease.

"Actually, I do," I mused, working to fit this new piece into an already complicated puzzle. "It may be that…"

"Hold a minute," Croft interrupted, looking to the side as her eyes fixed on something off-screen. She quickly muted the volume, but I could see her lips move in hurried conversation. When she turned back to us, her face was drawn.

"Something has come up. Thank you for your time."

The call abruptly ended, and the laptop screen reverted to the blue logo page. I stared for a moment before closing the cover.

"I guess that's that," I said uncertainly.

"At least we got some answers," Frannie said. "We know the deaths weren't accidental. That's something."

"Yeah," griped Gilda. "Something bad."

Just then, my phone rang. Checking the display, I was surprised to see the caller was Detective Croft.

Giving Frannie a wave, I took the phone through to the kitchen. "Detective?" I asked in lieu of an answer. "I'm glad you called back. I'd just thought of something else I wanted to tell you about the real estate agent Josie Brimm. I don't know if it means anything, but her scarf turned up at the Naylors' house. Jan Naylor thought it might be mine, but I recognized it as the one Josie was wearing when..." I cut off, not wanting to admit I'd crossed the yellow tape line and entered the murder house. Instead I said, "Jan said she'd never met the agent."

"What was that name again?"

"Josie Brimm of Holmes Homes. But..." I paused. "That isn't what you were calling about."

"No, Lynley, it is not. I have just received some information. I will leave it up to you how much you want to disclose to the others."

I froze in place. "Why? What's happened?"

"My sergeant has taken a call from Paulette Hart."

I tried to discourage the icy fingers that were creeping up my spine... and failed.

"Miss Hart wished to file a missing persons report."

"Missing persons?" I asked, dreading the answer. "Who's missing?"

"It is her mother, Pauleen Hart."

Chapter 26

Knitting, crocheting, and needlework are creative tasks that your cat may insist upon joining in on, not necessarily to the benefit of the endeavor.

Pauleen Hart had not been seen since eight o'clock last evening when Pet went out to listen to music with friends. Pet had come home late and didn't want to disturb her mother who she assumed was asleep. Surprised when Pauleen wasn't up the next morning at her usual seven-thirty, Pet went to look in on her and discovered she was gone.

"That's all I could get out of Detective Croft," I told the group. "She doesn't handle missing persons cases, so she may not know any more than that."

There was silence around the worktable, then Mark leapt to his feet. "I'm going to Pet," he asserted as he hurriedly gathered his things. "She might need me."

"No, I'll go," said Dora. If she needs anyone, it will be a close friend of the family."

"Detective Croft asked us to hold off visiting for another hour," I recounted, though I too had the instinctive urge to rush right down to House of Quilts.

"I wonder why?" posed Frannie, ever practical.

"She didn't say, and I didn't ask, but if she wants us to wait, she must have a good reason. They're probably sending someone out to interview Pet for details before beginning their search. A bunch of friends, no matter how well-meaning, would just get in the way."

Dora glanced at the clock on the wall. "All right, one hour. I wouldn't want to hold up the investigation. But I am going to call. Detective Croft didn't say not to call, did she?"

I wasn't sure if Dora was being sarcastic, but it was a moot point because she already had her phone out and was poking at an icon on the glowing face. Putting it to her ear, she stood stiffly, eyes still intent on the clock. After what seemed longer than necessary to assess Pet wasn't going to pick up, she reluctantly ended the call.

"No answer?" asked Mark.

Dora shook her head.

"You didn't leave a message?"

Dora turned on the man. "What am I supposed to say? *Hey, I heard through the grapevine your mom's missing. I want to come over, but the cops won't let me.*"

Mark lowered his eyes and began furiously sewing a light gray square onto the end of his runner. "I'm worried about Pet too, you know," he mumbled under his breath.

"Oh, this is terrible!" Ruth lamented. "Heartbreak upon heartbreak! What is the world coming to?"

The distraught woman looked on the verge of tears, and Frannie handed her a tissue. "Here, dear. Let's try to stay calm. I'm sure the police are doing whatever it is they do under these circumstances."

Ruth took the tissue and dabbed at her eyes, leaving a touch of mascara on the pristine white.

"I'm sorry. I don't know why I get so emotional. There just seems to be so much sadness lately. And I'm not talking about out there in the world..." She flung an arm up in an expansive gesture. "It's all right here in our own back yard. This group used to be so pleasant, my go-to place for serenity. Now every time we gather, it's something else... Something else..."

"Oh, Ruth, quit," Dora admonished. "It's not about you."

Ruth's mouth fell open in shock. "No, I know that. I didn't mean..."

"Can Pet even file a missing persons report if the person hasn't been gone for twenty-four hours?" Gilda posed. "Or is it forty-eight?"

"That's a fallacy," Frannie said. "Something made up for television. In fact, there's no waiting period at all. Those first twenty-four hours are the most significant in finding someone who's gone missing."

"Oh, my word!" Ruth gave a whimper. "What if the person who killed her mother and the old man has struck again? What if he's hurt Pauleen too?"

"Hold on, Ruth. Let's not get ahead of ourselves." I pulled off my glasses and rubbed the bridge of my nose, suddenly grasping why Detective Croft had left it up to me whether to announce Pauleen's disappearance to the group. It might have been better if I'd waited the hour until people could actually do something besides sit and worry, but it was too late now—the cat was out of the bag.

"We don't know if she's actually missing," I reasoned. "Pet must be on edge after everything else that's happened, so maybe she's jumping the gun. Pauleen might have gone out for an early morning walk—it's a beautiful day after all. And as you said, there has been so much stress lately. Maybe she just needed to clear her head."

"That's right," Frannie furthered. "She's probably fine and we're fretting for nothing."

"It's nearly noon now," said Gilda. "If she left before

7:30, that would be some walk."

Mark put down his work and fidgeted in his chair, the subject clearly making him uncomfortable. "She could have gone to visit a friend."

"Or across town to explore the stores and the art museum," Frannie took up.

"Maybe," Ruth conceded. "I did hear her talking about the new exhibit of impressionist painters."

"She may even be back by now," said Gilda. "It's not like the police are going to phone and give us an update."

I sat down at the worktable and took up my embroidery. Hermione hopped into my lap and began vigorously batting at my thread, so I tucked it away again. "I know everyone's concerned, but we've got an hour before we can do anything if we follow Detective Croft's instructions. Let's assume everything will be okay and concentrate on our projects until then. The auction is coming up, and we've all worked so hard. It would be a shame not to finish our pieces in time."

"That's the first practical thing I've heard all day," said Gilda, moving back to her sewing machine and picking up where she left off for the online call with Croft.

"How can you be so cold?" Dora shot out. "I thought you liked Pauleen."

"I do like her, but I'm not going to get my knickers in a knot until I'm certain something is wrong."

"And you don't think Pet declaring her missing is wrong enough?" Dora seethed.

Gilda gave a huff, adjusted her material under the presser foot of her machine, and bore down hard on the foot pedal. The mechanism sprang into action, pulling the fabric askew. "For goodness sake!" she blurted. "Now look what you made me do."

"I?" the little woman shouted. "I made you do? Why..."

"Here now," Mark said, half-rising from his chair. "Let's just do what Lynley suggested and concentrate on our projects. I'm sure we'll get a call any minute telling us Pauleen is fine. In the meantime, the last thing she would want is for us to fight about her. Am I right?"

Dora looked complacent, while Gilda took a deep breath and began picking out the wonky stitching with a seam ripper.

"And she'd want for us to finish our donations," Mark continued. "It would be awful if she came back to find we'd missed the deadline, and all her hard work making the arrangements with ShadowCat was for nothing."

With sighs and murmurs, the room settled. People took up their needles and thread, their scissors and chalk and rulers, and got to work. I picked up Hermione and carried her into the kitchen where I proceeded to make a good old pot of tea.

Chapter 27

Sitting quietly with a cat can be soothing to a troubled mind.

It had been a difficult hour but a productive one. I was able to finish my white cat embroidery without any more help from Hermione, and Mark appliquéd it onto his table runner, declaring his project complete. Gilda finalized the machine stitching of her mini-quilt, leaving only the handwork around the edges, a tiny masterpiece of craftsmanship that was sure to bring a tidy sum in the auction. Frannie and Ruth were nearly done as well, with another hour's work at the most. Dora was the only one who was having problems.

Between watching the time and swearing to herself, the small woman had managed to run out of thread, attach the wrong pieces together, and have her cutting wheel slip, ruining the cat shape she'd been fashioning. Finally my old mantle clock chimed one. Glumly she stuffed her things into her bag, stabbing herself with her thread snips as she did so, and left without another word.

"Well, she's off," Gilda needlessly commented.

I sighed. "She really does love Pauleen. This must be very hard for her."

"We all love Pauleen," Gilda retorted, "and you don't see any of us being rude about it."

I didn't mention that Gilda, herself, tended to be rude in general—she was right this time. Dora could have at least said goodbye.

"There's still no answer on Pet's phone," said Ruth. "I tried Pauleen as well, but it goes straight to voicemail. Do you think we should drop by and offer our help?"

"What kind of help would that be, Ruth?" Gilda snapped.

"I don't know. Moral support?"

"Humph. I, for one, am going home and leaving the police to do their job." She rose and began packing her sewing machine into its wheeled carrier. Then she straightened. Coming up beside Ruth, she put a hand on her shoulder in an unusual show of compassion. "I'm sorry. I'm worried too. Will you let me know what happens?"

Ruth looked up gratefully. "Of course, Gilda."

"I'm going to take off, too," said Mark. "I have a one-thirty appointment I can't miss. Will someone get my donation to ShadowCat?"

"I will," said Frannie. "I plan to finish mine up and then make an appointment to drop it off. I can take yours too."

"Thanks." He hesitated. "Keep in touch."

I was pacing. I knew I was pacing, but I couldn't stop. I really wanted to hop down to the quilt house and find out the news on Pauleen, but I didn't wish to seem like an ambulance chaser. Besides, I had guests. I couldn't very well tell them to scram just because I felt the need to assuage my curiosity.

Frannie came to my rescue. "You should probably go see if Pet is all right, Lynley. I'm not sure how much help Dora will be in her current state."

Yes! my mind cried. "But what about you and Ruth?"

"I can stay while we finish our quilts, then lock up

when we leave."

"You don't mind?"

"Not at all. I'll even give the cats their afternoon snack if you like."

"Frannie, you're a lifesaver! And I'll call and tell you the minute I know something."

I gave her a peck on the cheek, slipped her the key, then grabbed my bag and coat and was out the door and down the stairs to my car.

* * *

I pulled up in front of House of Quilts ten minutes later. It really was the most beautiful spring day, and I paused to linger in the shadows of the red maple that draped its branches like living lace above the walkway. Now that I was there, I didn't feel all that comfortable about visiting Pet. I worked better when there was action, and consoling someone whose loved one had gone missing required a passive approach. *Buck up*, I told myself as I climbed the steps and rang the bell. *Not everything is about me.*

I was a little surprised when Pet answered the door. I'd assumed that by now Dora would be deep into her caregiver role which should include door duty.

"Oh, it's you, Lynley," Pet mumbled as she unlatched the screen to let me in. She looked like a lost cat, her lovely hair down in tangles and a coffee stain on her rose-colored caftan. Bags around her eyes spoke of an anguish that began long before today, and I realized how Pauleen's disappearance was just another blow to someone already hurting.

The black cats were waiting as Pet led me into the sunroom. She scooped Ridley into her arms while Mewella padded along at our feet.

"They're such a comfort," Pet said without turning. "I don't know what I would do without them."

"Yes, I'm sure they are," I agreed without a second thought.

Once in the bright sunny room, Pet sank heavily onto the bench and picked up a mug of something dark from the side table. Ridley hopped up next to her and curled against her thigh.

"There's coffee, if you want some. In the kitchen. But do you mind getting it for yourself?"

"I'm fine," I said, looking around, "but where is everyone?"

"Everyone? Oh, you mean the detective? She left a little while ago."

"And Dora?"

Pet glanced up in surprise. "Dora isn't here. Was she planning on coming? I could really use the help."

That was unexpected. An hour before, Dora had been more than keen to get to Pet. What could have happened in that sixty minutes to make her change her mind?

"Well, yes, I thought she was. The group was at my place for a quilting session when we heard the news about your mother. Dora wanted to come right over, but Detective Croft asked us to wait an hour to let the investigators do their job, and Dora complied. Once the time was up though, she rushed right out. She didn't say where she was going, but I had assumed she was coming here."

"Nope," Pet said flatly. "I haven't heard a word from her. I had my phone switched off for a while, but there were no messages. I know she's mainly my mom's friend and all, but I thought maybe…"

"I'm sorry. Is there something I can do?" I offered.

"Not really. Just be here, I guess. I'm so worried about Momma. And then to have that awful detective asking those ridiculous questions..."

"They have to ask questions, Pet. They need to gather as much information as possible so they can figure out what happened to Pauleen. That's how it works with missing persons."

Pet turned to me, eyes even darker and face even paler than a moment ago. "I filed the report and told them everything I could think of—that her bed hadn't been slept in, and that she never goes anywhere without telling me... The last time I saw her, and what time I realized she was missing... All that stuff. The officer wrote it down on his tablet and was very positive and comforting. Everything seemed okay until your Detective Croft showed up."

"Detective Croft? But she's a homicide detective."

"Yeah, right," Pet said with a coldness that caused me to shiver, "but she must be a very poor one. She's decided that my wonderful, beautiful, kind and loving mother may have killed my gran!"

I was taken aback. "What? Why would she think that?"

Pet stroked Ridley and stared out into the garden. "Detective Croft says my mother's disappearance might not be accidental. She thinks she may have run off on purpose, because she is guilty of murder!"

With that, Pet broke down and buried her face in Ridley's silken fur. As if the cat knew how much she was hurting, he snuggled his head against hers.

I sat in stunned silence. Never had it crossed my mind that Pauleen was the killer. There were so many reasons that could not be the case. But in spite of myself, my mind began running through memories to see if there was something I'd missed. Were there times Pauleen had lacked emotion over her mother's death? Times she expressed disgust and resentment about the liaison with the next door uncle? Could those subtle antipathies have masked a larger rage, one that could have led to murder? If Marsha Croft was considering that angle, there must be evidence to support it.

"What exactly did Detective Croft tell you?" I asked carefully.

Pet sat up, plucked a tissue from the box on the bench beside her and dried her eyes. "I don't know. I can't remember. It's all a blur."

"Pet, it can't be as bad as you think. Croft has to explore all potential suspects, and statistically murders are often committed by friends or family. Your mother's sudden disappearance could seem suspicious—to someone who doesn't know her, that is," I added quickly, noting the anger brewing in Pet's narrowed eyes. "But meanwhile, it's also a missing persons case. Once they find your mom, everything will be clear. You'll see."

Pet's burst of fury deflated into a bone-racking sigh. "They told me to stay home in case she comes back."

"That's good advice."

"But I can't just sit here, Lynley! I'll go crazy. I already feel like I'm crawling out of my skin."

"I have an idea. Do you have a pen and paper?"

Pet gave me a questioning look but pulled a little box from the bottom shelf of the wicker coffee table. Opening it, she produced a pencil and a yellow notepad and handed them to me.

"Perfect! Now, try to think of any places Pauleen might have gone, and I'll write them down."

"I already went through this with the cops," Pet grumbled.

"I'm sure you listed the obvious ones, but let's dig deeper, the stranger the better. Friends, favorite walking routes, favorite shops. Does she volunteer anywhere? Belong to any clubs? Anything that pops into your head, no matter how far-fetched it may sound. Indulge me," I concluded. "It will be better than sitting around, and we just might come up with something good."

"I guess it's worth a try. Like you said, I have nothing else to do."

The list started off slowly with Pet's faltering thoughts, but it soon began to take off as she remembered more and more. Since Portland had an efficient mass transit system, we decided not to limit ourselves to places within walking distance. Pet seemed to take heart in the process, sometimes becoming sidetracked by memories of spots she and her mother had gone in the past.

We were both smiling over a story about the time Pet and Pauleen rode the little train at the Oregon Zoo. Pet didn't say how old she'd been, but I gathered she was a child at the time. It was doubtful Pauleen would retrace those particular steps today, but suggesting locations was only part of the exercise. The real point was to draw on the past to distract Pet from the scary present, and it seemed to be working.

We were actually enjoying ourselves with Pet doing the talking and me jotting down notes so when the doorbell rang, we both jumped.

Pet's eyes grew wide, and she tensed as if turned to stone.

"Would you like me to get that?"

By the time she managed to nod yes, I was already headed for the door.

Thankfully it was someone I knew. "Dora, you made

it."

"Lynley," Dora said curtly. "The door was locked."

"Pet's in the sunroom. I came down after the session. I thought you'd already be here."

"There was something I had to do first. I'm here now." She pushed by me. "Pet," she called out. "It's me, dear."

I followed Dora into the sunroom where she had shed her yellow coat and was already fussing. "Oh, your coffee is cold. Let me get you a fresh cup. I heard about your mother. Have the police been here yet? What are they doing to find her? You must be worried sick. Has there been any word?"

Pet, who was used to Dora's well-meaning blather, took it in stride. "No more coffee, but a cup of hot tea would be nice. I think there's some chamomile in the tea basket. Would you mind?"

"Coming right up in a jiffy," Dora said as she scampered for the kitchen.

I made a quick decision. "I'm going to take off now, Pet. You seem to be in good hands, and I should get back home."

"Oh? Oh, sure. I'll be okay. I feel better for making that list. Do you think I should give it to the police? Some of it is a bit bizarre."

"I don't see why not. Sometimes the smallest clues lead to a big discovery. Tell Dora goodbye for me?"

I beelined for the door and let myself out. I wanted to make sure Frannie had locked my house up properly, but there was another reason for my swift departure, a purely selfish one. I preferred not to be present when Pet told Dora that the homicide detective suspected her best buddy Pauleen of being a murderer. I predicted she wouldn't take it well, and though I felt bad about leaving Pet to cope with a ballistic Dora, I figured that fuming at Detective Croft might be cathartic for both the women.

I was just to my car when Josie Brimm appeared on the porch of the Naylor House.

"Hey!" she shouted. "Hey, you!"

I turned to look for the recipient of Josie's annoyance, but there was only me. A moment later she was down the steps and in my face.

"You did it, didn't you? Sicced the cops on me?"

I took a step back. "What?"

"It had to be you. Telling them about my argument with the old Naylor fellow? That I dropped my scarf at his place? Now they think I killed him."

"Detective Croft questioned you?" Josie nodded so violently I thought her bun would come undone. "Did she take you in to the station?"

"Naw, but she said not to leave town, and you know what that means!" She mouthed the word, *suspect*. "She didn't say who had blabbed on me, but I know it was you."

"I'm sorry. I never meant to incriminate you. I just told her what I knew."

"Well, you know nothing. That old man kept creeping onto the property and hanging around scaring the clients. I told him to leave, that's all. But then when my sale fell through, I had another idea. If he was so interested in the place, maybe he'd want to buy it himself. I went by to talk to him, but he got irritated. I wasn't going to stick around for that and must have dropped my scarf as I left."

Her eyes squinted into slits. "So now, Miss Busybody, unless you want to buy or sell a property, stay out of my business. Ya hear?"

Chapter 28

Some cats find comfort in a cave or nest bed. The enclosed design with its soft fabric walls gives them a sense of security.

The next few days were busy ones. I'd called Fredric to ask if he could lend a hand with some gardening jobs, but I couldn't get hold of him, so I ended up doing the work myself. I really hadn't needed the help, but it was an excuse to see the young man because, let's face it, I was curious. It had been two weeks since Seleia went to confront him at his duplex, but all I'd been able to get out of her about the meeting was a rant on the pitfalls of love, relationships, and men in general.

Garden work was interspersed with shifts at the shelter where I was working with a very shy kitty named Fluffy. Fluffy and I were at a critical point in her socialization. I'd finally been successful at luring her out from her cave bed to let me pet her. Once she was accustomed to doing that on a regular basis, I could move her on to the next step — sitting in my lap.

I'd also volunteered to help Frannie take the quilting donations to ShadowCat Rescue in preparation for the auction that was to be the highlight of the upcoming Black Cat's Ball. I'd visited the secretive shelter once before and knew she might have trouble finding the hidden acreage secreted behind the modest single-family home.

It was nice to see ShadowCat's proprietors again.

Skelter, an aging hippie who now devoted his time to the underappreciated black cat population, and his partner Reese, the burly cat lover with the fascinating tattoo of a recumbent cat on her chest, had built the little shelter into one of the most respected—and most mysterious—rescues in the country.

Skelter had given me a bear hug, then graciously accepted our offerings and logged them in with the rest of the donations. Reese offered to show Frannie and me around the grounds, a rare treat we couldn't refuse. We'd spent the next hour touring the wooded gardens and cushy kennels. Seeing so many black-colored cats in one place seemed somehow magical.

On the way back home, Frannie and I talked more about the auction and how much fun it had been to craft something with our own hands that was going to help cats. We marveled at each donation: Pet's framed applique; Ruth's study in pink; Gilda's mini-quilt which was nothing short of a work of art. Mark's table runner that had initially struck me as plain came to life once it was all together. With my white cat embroidery at the center, it was a masterpiece of simplicity, fit for any home, no matter the décor.

"Your *Cali the Calico* needlework really made my piece stand out," Frannie commented as we motored down the quiet side street with her at the wheel. "It seemed sort of blah without it."

"Oh, I didn't think so," I differed. "I loved the way you fit those cat shapes together. I never knew you sewed."

"I haven't for a long time, but I used to do it a lot when I was younger. I made my own clothes, and for a while, I even sold a few of my creations."

"Pauleen must have delivered her quilt some time ago,

since it was photographed for the posters and tickets."

"Yes, Thankfully she got it in before..."

Frannie's voice trailed off as she fixed her eyes on the road.

"...before everything went to howdy in a handbasket?" I finished for her.

She nodded. "Before some of it, at least."

Then, as I knew it inevitably would, our conversation came around to Pauleen's disappearance.

"It's been nearly a week and still no word," said Frannie. "What does it mean?"

In movies, it would mean one of two things, I thought to myself. *Either Pauleen is the killer on the run or she's dead.* But this wasn't the movies, and I still held out hope. "You know the police aren't going to apprise us of every little lead. They may be closer to finding her than we think."

"I've been talking to Pet regularly since it happened, just to make sure she's okay and she knows we care. As of yesterday, there hadn't been any ransom demands, and no Jane Does have turned up in the hospitals."

What about the morgue? I nearly added but caught myself in time. No one wanted to contemplate that prospect.

I stared out the side window at the houses and gardens we passed by. With Frannie driving, I could enjoy a leisurely view, but my mind wasn't on the colorful azaleas or the blossoming cherry trees.

"That would indicate she went willingly," I mused.

"But where could she have gone? And why? Do you think..." Frannie faltered. "Do you suppose Detective Croft is right? She killed her mother and her lover and ran for the hills?"

"I can see why that scenario might make sense to the

detectives—Pauleen Hart disappears after two murders were committed—but no, I don't believe that's what happened."

Frannie pulled onto a main street, only to get stopped by a red light. "But then who did it? And why? And where is Pauleen? There are too many unanswered questions," she huffed, resting her arms on the steering wheel. "It's baffling."

"There's a pattern though, and I'm beginning to see it."

I paused to gather my thoughts, which were as scattered as a handful of cat treats tossed across a floor. I needed to process them, one by one, until they resolved into a satisfactory snack.

"The footprint on the carpet of the sale house where Mrs. Hart was killed? It was small. It could have been Mrs. Hart's, but it also could have belonged to the killer."

"So the killer could be a woman," Frannie filled in.

"Exactly!"

"Or the footprint might have been Mrs. Hart's."

"Exactly," I repeated with less enthusiasm. "But then there was the ring, gold with a diamond, like an engagement ring. We know Christian Naylor had a thing for Paula Hart, and we also know from the realtor that he often hung around the sale house, his ancestral property. What if he and Mrs. Hart had a rendezvous, and he gave her the ring?"

"Okay, except hanging around isn't the same as breaking and entering. There's no way to know if he was actually inside the house."

"Yes, I think there is," I countered. "There was a candy box on the coffee table at the crime scene, Mr. Naylor's favorite kind. I thought it was a staging prop until I learned of his penchant for those fruit filled bonbons. That pretty well proves he was in the room the night Mrs. Hart was killed."

Frannie slowed for a pedestrian walking a dog. "But how did he get in? I'm sure the real estate people kept it locked up tight."

"He could have been watching Josie or one of her coworkers punch in the combination to the lock box."

The dog walker gave us a wave as she stepped onto the curb. Frannie waved back and we were on our way again.

"Even so," Frannie began, "according to the letters you and Pauleen found, Mrs. Hart had broken up with him."

"So that could be why the ring was tossed into the potpourri bowl and not on her finger."

Frannie nodded thoughtfully. "Might her rejection have made him mad, and he killed her? You mentioned your mother telling you he was the jealous type back when they were kids. Maybe he was violent as well."

"It's possible, but that was decades ago. Seems like he should have mellowed with age. People do, don't they? And there's the fact that someone killed him too. I refuse to believe there are two people running around doing murder. It's just not the way most folks reconcile their differences."

"So one person murdered both of them... but why?"

"The most logical reason would be to put a stop to the liaison between the lovers... and stop it for good."

"But who would care enough to kill?"

That was where my calculations fell short. *Could it be the daughter? The granddaughter? One of the quilters? One of the Naylors?* Suspecting Josie Brimm made no sense. She was all about selling her property, and committing a murder in the living room would be counterproductive, no matter how badly she wanted to end the trespassing.

Besides, killing Christian Naylor when he might have purchased a property from her was unimaginable. That left...

"There is something you should probably know," Frannie sighed. "Mark has a police record. It's not common knowledge. He told me in confidence and asked me to keep it to myself. So far I've honored his request, but..."

I sat forward in surprise. "What did he do?"

"It was years ago." Frannie hesitated.

"What did he do, Frannie?"

"He was charged with fighting in public. He was given a fine and community service since it was a first offense. I don't think he has anything to do with the killings," she added quickly.

This was an unexpected turn. Mark had always seemed so innocuous, but every once in a while, I'd got the feeling his bland façade was just that—a façade.

"He has small feet."

"Pardon?"

"Mark has small feet," I repeated. "What if it was his muddy footprint in Mrs. Hart's murder room?"

"Enough murder talk," Frannie proclaimed, pulling to the side of the street and coming to a stop. "It's depressing me because I don't have any answers and I'm worried about Pauleen and I hate that there is a killer loose in our city and..." She heaved a great sigh. "And we're going to get an ice cream and forget all our troubles, at least for a little while."

I gazed up at the shiny pink and white sign and wished it were that easy for me to get my mind off a troublesome matter. Still, it wasn't fair of me to burden Frannie with my obsessive thought process.

"Good idea. And we can talk about that new dress you bought for the Black Cat gala, and maybe you can give me a hint as to what I might have in my mothball closet that I could wear without looking too much like last decade's news."

We entered the little shop and were soon ensconced at a table by the window with our desserts. Frannie had ordered a two-scoop of pistachio almond fudge, and I'd indulged in my favorite, coconut lemon ice in a dish instead of a cone. Even though the spring day was still on the cool side, the cold treat was refreshing and welcome.

"Have you decided who your plus one for the ball will be?" I asked Frannie through a mouthful of zesty lemon.

She took a lick of her pistachio ice cream. "I'm probably going alone. I purchased my ticket ages ago, before I knew we'd be given free ones. I'd thought to bring you, but now you have your own. What about you?"

"I'm taking my mother. She wanted to come, and how could I say no?"

"Carol is good company. You could do worse," Frannie teased.

"You know it!"

I scooped a spoonful of my tangy concoction up in the tiny plastic spoon and savored the creamy texture. "Are the rest of the quilters planning to be there?"

Frannie gave her cone another lick, then wiped her mouth demurely with a pink napkin the size of a business card. "Ruth is coming with her husband. Mark plans to come solo—I think he hopes that in the social setting, he can finally have a chance with Pet."

"So Pet's coming?"

"I don't know. She was undecided last time we spoke. I think she wants to. I can understand why she's hesitant, but it would be nice for her to get out. Everyone will be so appreciative of her work. It could only do her good."

"What about Dora?"

"I doubt Dora would miss it though I haven't heard definitively one way or another. She's still very upset about Pauleen."

There it was again—no getting away from the tragedies, no matter how much ice cream we consumed.

"It won't be the same without Pauleen," Frannie went on. "You know she was supposed to accept an award of merit for all the donations House of Quilts has supplied ShadowCat throughout the years. Now the duty will fall to Pet."

"Is Dora still helping Pet out?"

Frannie frowned. "I'm not sure. I know she's been working the shop, but as to how much help she is otherwise, that's another matter entirely."

I paused, spoon halfway to my mouth. "Why do you say that?"

"Well, she's so upset about Pauleen, I'm not certain she's much of a comfort to Pet. You know how Dora is—not always thinking before she speaks. Pet told me she was grateful for the assistance running the store, but Dora's constant chatter was getting on her nerves."

Just then, a young man came through the door, jostled by a six-pack of small children all yelling at the top of their lungs.

I looked at Frannie and she at me. "It might be time to finish up and get on our way," I said softly, though there was no danger of being overheard against the gleeful ruckus.

"I think you're right," Frannie agreed, taking a last bite of her waffle cone. "I'm finished."

I scooped a final smidgen of melted lemon ice from the bottom of the paper bowl, then rose and dumped it in the trash receptacle. Frannie and I exited onto the sidewalk and the relative quiet of the city.

"Oh, there is one good thing to report," Frannie said as we strolled unhurriedly to the car.

"I can always use some good news."

"Veronica has given up her claims on Ridley. She came by the quilt house the other day with a bouquet of daffodils and an apology. She said she understood now that Ridley belongs with the Harts. It was an eloquent little speech—something along the lines of, she will love him always, but she knows Pet and Pauleen are giving him the best home ever."

"Nice!" I commented. One problem solved, though still several more to go.

Chapter 29

Besides the common nickname of House Panther for black-colored cats, they are also called Voids because their fur seems to absorb light like a black hole.

The week had gone by uneventfully. No new deaths or disasters, but also no word on Pauleen or the couple killer. Now that the projects were signed, sealed, and delivered to ShadowCat, I saw little of the quilters. Even Frannie had been absent, off for a short vacation to the coast with a friend. But tonight all that changed. Tonight we came back together at the Black Cat's Ball.

I stood before the massive, glass-walled kennel watching the black cats. There must have been a dozen of them, prowling amongst the potted plants and lounging in assorted beds. A big male was shimmying up an authentic-looking tree to join his cohorts in the branches. On the floor sat a young volunteer inconspicuously reading a book, but I noted she kept a vigilant eye on the clowder. Whoever had outfitted this temporary environment was a bit of a genius, because they all looked happy and content in their novel environment, including the human girl.

The spacious kennel was an unexpected treat in the Riverfront Suites' otherwise-plain convention hall. The gala's event committee had tried their best to festoon the huge room with cheerful adornments, but there was no getting around the dullness of the place. I suppose the hotel felt the need to maintain a certain amount of genericism, but one would think a five-star conference center could have come up with a more exciting base color than Portland gray.

The architectural feature that saved the otherwise bland room from complete banality was a wall of windows facing onto the Columbia River which flowed just below the hotel itself. Outside, a balcony ran the length of the building with viewing chairs and chaise longues. It would have been a perfect place to relax were the day nicer, but the weather had taken another turn, and the cement-colored panorama now rivaled the gray interior of the ballroom.

"Hey, Linnie, you having a good time?" someone asked over my shoulder.

I turned to find Reese decked out in a sequined ballgown, her elaborate tattoo showing prominently above the low scoop neckline. Her dark locks were done up in a high pony, and the most exotic black cat earrings I'd ever seen hung from her ears.

"This is amazing!" I exclaimed. "I didn't know you would be bringing cats to the event."

"It was Skelter's brain baby. What would a Black Cat's Ball be without black cats?" She did a Vanna White toward the glass. "These are a few of our more outgoing residents. They're all adoptable if you feel the need to add a house panther to your family."

"Thanks, but I already have three. It's a good idea though. They show beautifully in that gorgeous setting."

She gave a lopsided smile. "I'll be sure to tell the boss."

I cast my gaze across the crowd and back to the cat display. "How do you handle adoptions in such chaotic surroundings?"

"Oh, we'll talk the cats up here at the event, but potential adopters have to go through the normal channels at the shelter tomorrow," Reese said, reading my mind. "Nobody can scoop a cat tonight on a tipsy impulse."

With that, she swept off in a dazzle of sparkles. Though I'd only ever seen her wearing manly clothing, this new look gave a whole new dimension to the woman.

Speaking of manly clothing, I spied my friend Halle coming through the door. A proud member of Clan Mackay, she'd taken the opportunity to wear her great kilt, five and a half meters of tartan wool folded into pleats, then wrapped around her waist with the excess tossed over her chest and shoulder. Her wife Barb was equally spectacular in a simple silk dress of a dark blue that exactly matched the tartan's indigo stripes. Though Frannie had helped me choose a long-skirted cat print frock I'd bought for some forgotten party, I suddenly felt underdressed compared to Reese and the Mackay-Pratts.

"Lynley!" Halle called across the room.

I waved and went to meet the couple. "I didn't know you were coming," I said after hugs and greetings.

"Wouldn't miss it. A good cause, and when you told me about your quilting efforts, I had to come see for myself."

"The auction items are all up there." I gestured to a long table at the front of the hall. "Our quilts are on display at the end nearest the stage, but there are plenty of other things as well. Yoga baskets, spa packages, autographed books, designer jewelry, gift certificates, an antique Royal Doulton tea set... Someone's even donated a trip to Best Friends Animal Sanctuary in Utah, all expenses paid."

Halle's bushy eyebrows rose. "Impressive, but I want

to see the quilts. You'll have to show me which one is yours."

"I didn't make one, but the embroidered patches on Mark's runner and Frannie's mini-quilt are mine. Cats, of course."

"Everything here is cats," Barb commented, taking in the décor which was also heavily cat-themed.

"Where are you sitting, hon?" asked Halle.

"We have a spot up near the front. Please join us. It's my mother Carol, some of the quilters, and an older couple, Colin and Mary, neighbors of House of Quilts. Don't worry, nobody bites."

"Sounds good if you have the room."

"They're jumbo-sized tables," I commented as I led Halle and Barb through the throng.

"So they are," Halle replied, pulling out a chair for Barb, then sweeping the bulk of her kilt to one side so she could sit down as well.

I made introductions, and soon everyone was talking together like old friends.

"Hey, I heard about something we might look into for our next projects," said Ruth. She had brought her husband Don, a nice-looking man in a gray suit with a pink carnation in his lapel. Ruth herself was decked out in a pink designer outfit with gray accent, and the prim pair reminded me of a matching salt and pepper set I'd seen once at a novelty store.

Frannie adjusted the gardenia pinned on the shoulder of her teal satin gown. "What's that, Ruth? I'm excited to get started on something new."

Ruth leaned into the table as if disclosing a secret. "Have you ever heard of cat fur felting?"

This brought a round of shaking heads and murmurs

to the negative.

"It's the latest thing," she went on. "I bought a book on it. Basically it's like any other felting except you use cat fur. The results come out soft and subtle, and the tones depend on what color fur your cats have."

"How do you get the fur?" asked Halle. "You don't have to shave the cat, do you?"

Ruth cringed in horror. "Goodness me, no! It's the fuzz you comb out of your cat's pelt during their regular grooming sessions."

"You could probably do a whole sampler with our Sedgewick's leftovers," said Barb. "Especially in the spring when he sheds his winter undercoat."

"I had a cat who shed a lot," Dora put in, not to be outdone. "She was a white cat, and the hair got everywhere. You wouldn't think white fur would stand out as much as it does."

Dora had shown up at the last minute, grabbing a chair and plunking herself down as if she had run a marathon. Her rumpled yellow dress did nothing to discourage the image.

"Dora, you made it," Frannie greeted.

"There was a hold up at House of Quilts. You know I've been taking care of the shop for the past week," she put in smugly.

"Now we're only waiting on Mark." Frannie gazed around the big room. "He told me he was coming. I wonder what happened."

Dora sniffed. "Probably changed his mind when he learned Pet wouldn't be here."

"I'm sad she decided not to come," said Ruth, "since this is her big night."

Dora turned and looked down her nose at the woman.

"Surely she has every reason not to want to expose herself to the public."

"I know." Ruth cast her eyes floorward. "I was just hoping she'd feel up to it. We would all be so glad to see her."

There was an awkward silence as everyone's thoughts were hurled back to the goings-on of the last few weeks. The gala was supposed to have been the guild's ultimate hurrah, the culmination of months of hard work. But now the mentors of that work were absent. Mrs. Hart was dead. Pauleen was missing. It wasn't surprising Pet didn't feel like joining in the triumph after such a mountain of tragedy.

Frannie gave Ruth a soft nudge. "She may come after all. Last time I spoke to her, she was undecided."

Dora gave a harrumph while the rest of the table fell silent.

"Oh, I was meaning to tell you, dear," my mother said, cutting through the gloom. "I finally had a chance to compare that little corsage box you found in Mrs. Hart's hope chest with my own. It is an exact match. I was reasonably certain it would be when you described the embossing on the top, but I wanted to make sure."

"Seems Carol went to high school with Mrs. Hart," I explained to the others. "She actually knew her back in the day."

"Knew *of* her would be more accurate," Carol corrected. "We had some classes together, but it was a big school, and she belonged to different clubs than me. I did look her up in my old yearbook though. I found a photo of her at the prom. You'll never guess who she was with."

"Christian Naylor?" I asked and she nodded yes. "But he didn't go to school with her, did he?"

"No, he'd already graduated. They made a darling couple though."

"His family must have been in the original Naylor House at that time." I turned to Colin. "Were you living in the neighborhood then?"

Colin laughed and straightened his orange striped tie. "No, I grew up in North Portland. Mary and I came to Southeast after we got married."

"A sad thing, his passing like that," said Mary. "Even if we didn't know him well, no one should have to have their lives ended on someone else's whim."

"Sad," Carol agreed. "You never think those things will happen, and then, *blam*—they do."

"I can't believe you're talking about this again," Gilda scolded, returning from the bar with a tall fizzy drink. "This should be a happy night. Can't we just have a few hours without bringing up the past?"

"Have you folks ever considered," Dora commented out of the blue, "that everything's happened for a reason?"

"A reason?" Gilda blurted, her mood turning even more sour. "What reason could there possibly be for two murders and a kidnapping?"

"I'm just offering the possibility that there may be a greater meaning to it all."

"What, Dora? Are you trying to tell us it's all part of some cosmic plan?"

"You don't believe there's a plan?"

Gilda sniffed. "Not if it involves hurting people, I don't."

"That's not what I meant," Dora stated before turning away in a sulk.

"We don't actually know that Pauleen's been kidnapped, do we?" Frannie offered.

"What else can it be?" Ruth lamented. "The idea of Pauleen as a killer on the run is unthinkable."

"Don't get upset, Ruth," her husband soothed. "Like Gilda said, this is a night for celebration. No one knows what's really going on, so trying to second guess the police is only going to lead to frustration."

"You're right, Don. I'm sorry."

"We're all on edge," Frannie consoled. "It's understandable that we're worried."

Gilda tapped the table distractedly. "If only we knew more about the whys and wherefores. Then it might be easier to accept the facts and move on."

Halle skewered me with a twinkle in her eyes. "Ask Lynley about whys and wherefores. She's probably got the whole thing figured out."

"Me?" I was caught off guard with that one. "Wait, no."

Halle ignored my objection, confiding in a slightly dramatic tone, "Lynley always knows. She's got a sixth sense when it comes to crime."

"I do not," I shot back unconvincingly.

"You can't deny it," said Frannie. "You always get there in the end. Why, just the other day, you told me you'd detected a pattern to the Hart affair. Do you think you know who did it?"

I found ten pairs of eyes on me. Most were expectant, though one—if I didn't know better—seemed almost angry.

"Yes, if you know who the killer is," Dora taunted, "then tell us—please."

I was about to disavow all knowledge of who may or may not have killed and/or kidnapped three victims when the screech of a microphone split the air.

"Sorry, sorry," came Skelter's booming, amplified voice from center stage. The old flowerchild had gone all out for the gala with a leather jacket, a tie-dyed silk shirt, and numerous strings of beads and bells hanging around his scraggy neck. His sparse gray hair was gathered into a ponytail, and the earring he wore in his left ear rivaled Reese's spectacular cat dangles.

"I hope everyone's having a great time here at the Black Cat's Ball," he called out to an enthusiastic round of applause. "We sure are. And I know you want to get on with the festivities, so I'll make this short. The auction will be coming right up in a few minutes. You've still got time to look over all these magnificent offerings. Make sure you got your wallets out for generous bids because one hundred percent of the proceeds go to the care of the cats at ShadowCat Sanctuary."

I breathed a sigh of relief, off the hook for the moment as the focus shifted from me to the auction items, the black cats, and the ShadowCat shelter. This time when I gave a quick glance around the table, I found all attention had moved to the man at the microphone.

All but one.

Dora was staring at the cat enclosure. Slowly her head swiveled until her gaze was aimed directly at me.

Chapter 30

A domestic cat in good condition can sprint up to thirty miles per hour. No wonder we can't catch them when they run!

Everyone but Carol had left the table to give the auction items one last perusal before the bidding began.

"What about you?" I asked my mother. "Aren't you going to check it out?"

Carol took a sip of her mock-tail, something orange and icy. "I really don't need anything, dear. I already have more belongings that I can comfortably squeeze into my little condo."

"But need isn't the point of an auction. It's fun to see if you can outbid other people without getting ahead of yourself. And besides, it's for charity."

Carol cocked her head and gave me a mischievous look. "There is that rare book of Scottish Clan tartans by R. W. Forsyth. I was thinking it would make a nice addition to my Highland collection, even if it isn't solely about the Mackays."

"You may have to bid against Halle for that one."

"I assumed as much. I plan on bidding it up as high as I can go without breaking the bank, then letting her have it. That way the rescue will get top dollar. And if I do manage to win it, all the better."

"That's the spirit!" I exclaimed.

"And I did rather like the Royal Doulton set," she went

on. "I've always had a weakness for violets."

"It is really nice. Did you notice the maker's mark is missing the traditional crown? That means it's from the 1920s. It's rare to find a set that old in such good condition with the teapot and both creamer and sugar bowl intact."

"All right, you sold me," Carol said. "I'll go take one more look." Pushing to her feet, she smoothed the back of her dress, a dark blue jersey crepe that she had owned ever since I could remember. Despite its age, it was of a style that gave her an air of timeless elegance. "What about you, dear? Aren't you going to bid on anything?"

"I'm going for Pauleen's cat quilt. If I get it, that will be my entire budget right there, but it will be worth it. It's such a beautiful piece."

Carol bent down and slipped her hand over mine, "And all the more meaningful after everything that's happened."

"Is still happening," I remarked. "Pauleen is still out there somewhere."

"You believe she's okay?"

"I do," I nodded. "I have to."

I watched Carol vanish into the crowd, imagining what I would feel like if she disappeared without a trace. The fear would be unbearable. That was what Pet had been going through since Pauleen went missing. The anxiety of not knowing... Was she hurt? Was she dead? Was she running away from something? Would Pet ever see her mother again?

My morbid contemplation was broken by the sound of a woman screaming. The scream was followed by a shriek. People started yelling. Someone was barking orders with others shouting back. In an instant, the room was buzzing with commotion.

A fire? was my first panic-charged thought. But fire would have triggered the alarms. Besides, I didn't smell smoke.

A man with a gun? In a city the size of Portland, violence could crop up anywhere, even in the most unlikely places. But that, too, seemed farfetched. People's reactions were less of fright and more of concern.

I sprang to my feet but couldn't see anything beyond the milling crowd as they surged this way and that. I was about to go after my mother when I picked out a flurry of yellow shooting toward me.

"What's going on, Dora? Do you know?"

"It's the cats!" she panted, grasping the chair back to steady herself. "Someone's let the cats out of their kennel! Poor things are scared to death and running away in a panic."

My heart fell. The big convention hall had several entrance doors, many of which were wide open—a frightened cat might dash off to just about anywhere. They could hide. They could get lost. They could even be hurt.

"Skelter and his crew are doing their best to corral them, but the place is too big, and there's not enough manpower."

"I can help," I replied without thinking.

"That's what he was hoping you'd say. Come on. Follow me."

Instead of heading into the thick of the chaos, however, Dora began for the north wall. She paused when she got to the door to the balcony. Checking to make sure I was following, she opened it and slipped through.

"Come on," she commanded. "One of the cats got out here, and we have to find him before he leaves the property and becomes irretrievably lost."

I took in the long promenade with its cement parapet. The view of the river was spectacular. At any other time, it would have been entrancing, but right now it seemed fearsome. If the cat became frightened and jumped off the edge, it could be the end.

"How did a cat get out here anyway?" I asked as I followed.

Dora was already about halfway down the walk and had stopped to peer over the edge.

"Look there!" she cried in lieu of an answer.

I rushed to join her. The coping was cold on my bare arms as I leaned in to see where she was pointing. Though the parapet was high enough to prevent an accidental fall, the vista was disturbing to someone like me with an uncomfortable fear of heights.

The hotel had been built on the slope of the riverbank with another full floor beneath the conference room. Looking down, I could see the edge of a patio jutting out. Beneath that was the river. At six hundred feet wide, it looked more like a massive lake than a moving body of water, but every so often, a branch or log would scud by, proving the treachery of the current. If a cat fell in, there would be no saving them.

"Down there!" Dora pointed to the row of lounge chairs just visible beyond the balcony's overhang. "Do you see him?"

I scanned the row but found no sign of a cat. "Where? Is he still there?"

"He just scooted back under." She bent precariously across the parapet, then straightened up. "You're taller than me. See if you can catch sight of him."

Swallowing my acrophobia for the sake of the poor lost cat, I splayed myself over the wide coping to view the spot where Dora was pointing. The exercise was useless, to say nothing of scary.

"I don't see any cats."

"Lean a little farther. It would be a shame to lose him now."

I straightened up and faced the small woman. "Wouldn't it be better if we just went on down to the lower level? There's a staircase right behind you."

"Good idea. I'll go while you keep an eye out to make sure he doesn't run off somewhere else."

She smiled but made no move to leave.

"Uh, okay, I guess that makes sense."

"Then get on with it. I'm not running all the way down if he's gone already."

Since there seemed to be no way around it, I returned to my balancing act, bracing my body as I leaned over the edge once more.

"I'm sorry, Dora, I still don't see…"

"Here, let me help you." Was it me, or did her tone sound unexpectedly malevolent?

I felt her hand on my ankle, then suddenly I was being pulled upward, lifted off my footing. My glasses began to slip, and before I could grab them, they tumbled to shatter on the hard tiles below.

In an instinctive panic, I squirmed to wrench free, but the grip only tightened. Fingers closed around my other ankle, pulling both my feet off the ground and tipping me forward. Since much of my weight was already hanging over the edge, it took only leverage to send me the rest of the way.

Suddenly I was flying through the air, arcing out toward the clay-gray swirls of the river. A shockwave shot through my system, and I struggled as I fell, an utterly futile fight against gravity. In my wildest dreams, I never imagined that being pushed into the Columbia by a two-time murderer was how I would meet my end.

Chapter 31

Make sure to arrange for your cats' care in case you become incapable of caring for them yourself. Put it in writing and update it every few years or when anything changes.

I was going down—there were no two ways about it. Then a thought shot through me with the intensity of a lightning strike—my cats! My cats would miss me if I died. I'd made arrangements for their care in case something happened to me, but it wouldn't be the same. I was the only one who knew old Dirty Harry's little foibles. I was the single human that shy Big Red felt he could trust. Tinkerbelle would miss her therapy visits with the patients she'd grown to love. And Little, my sweet Little. I imagined her sitting by the window in the front hallway waiting for me to come home—a wait that would be in vain. I couldn't put them through that. I refused!

In that split second revelation, I found I had some control over my flailing body after all. Twisting, I drove my weight inward, away from the river and toward the lower patio. It worked! Instead of a watery landing, I hit down on top one of the cushioned lounge chairs. There was a crash, and I dropped a foot farther as the chair collapsed. *I'm alive,* I thought to myself right before I passed out.

* * *

I came to in a blaze of pain. I couldn't recall what had caused such agony, nor could I pinpoint the source of the hurt. It was as if someone were jumping up and down on every part of my body all at once—with boots on!

Then someone *was* on top of me, and I remembered everything.

"Dora!" I blurted, my voice a mere squeak. "What are you doing?"

"Darn it, Lynley," she huffed as she worked to shove me toward the river. "You were supposed to go all the way over. How the heck do I get rid of you now?"

"What?" I croaked. "Get rid of me? Why...?"

Her reply came just as I figured it out for myself.

"Because you know what I did," she hissed. "You know I killed Paula Hart and Christian Naylor. And if I don't kill you too, you'll tell."

The irony was, I hadn't known. I'd never guessed. I never even had an inkling there was anything amiss with Dora the quilter until a mere hour ago. Even then, it had been only little glimpses: her angry glare when Halle joked that I'd figured out the killer's identity; her unexpected allegation that the deaths might have happened for a reason.

"You're wrong," I began, but I knew it was too late. Now that she'd confessed, it ceased to matter when I'd put it together. Her role in the two deaths was certain.

The smaller woman had given up wrestling me around by brute force and was now tugging at the broken lounge chair. The two front wheels were still intact, and if she could heft up the back part enough to get it moving, she'd be able to roll me to the edge of the patio, tip the chair the rest of the way, and down I'd go. I had little doubt she could do it. She was stronger than she looked and hopped up on blood lust. I, on the other hand, felt weak as a kitten and fragile as broken glass. My attempt to rise and run resulted in more pain than I could endure. If I were to save myself, it wasn't going to be in a fair fight.

The hurting receded slightly beneath my utter panic, and I managed to sit up. "Wait! Dora! Hold on, don't do this. You don't want to be a murderer."

Dora stopped pushing and heaved a few ragged gasps. "I am a murderer, Lynley. I've already taken two lives. One more isn't going to make any difference."

It'll make a big difference to me and my cats, I thought blackly, but that point was moot.

One thing I'd learned from mystery shows as well as a number of real-life crimes—keep the bad guy talking for as long as possible because occasionally miracles happen.

"Why, Dora?" I persevered. "Why did you do it? I thought Pauleen was your friend."

"Friend?" Dora guffawed, taking the bait. "What do you know about friends? Pauleen and I are more than friends. Pauleen is my life. She means everything to me."

"Oh, really? If she means so much, then why did you kill her mother? You saw how grief-stricken she was over it."

"It would have hurt her more if her mother's ridiculous love affair with Christian Naylor had been allowed to continue. Don't you see? That old man was trying to take Paula away from Pauleen. I couldn't let that happen."

"So you decided the solution was to kill poor Mrs. Hart? Why didn't you go after Mr. Naylor instead? Surely that would have been easier on Pauleen."

Dora sank down onto the lounge chair opposite me. "Paula was an accident. I only wanted to scare her. That old lothario had asked her to marry him. He'd given her a big fat ring. She was thinking about doing it even though she'd broken up with him. I needed to convince her that marrying Christian would devastate Pauleen. I guess I got carried away. I pushed her—just the slightest of nudges, you see—but she fell backwards. Her head hit the edge of the fireplace hearth. I was sorry that happened."

So many questions were coming to mind. *Why was Dora at the sale house in the middle of the night? Where was Naylor when Dora was terrorizing his true love?* But Dora was already rising to her feet. It was only a matter of seconds until she turned her attention back to the task of doing away with me. I had to keep her engaged. If I maintained the dialogue long enough, someone might come...

"What about Christian Naylor, Dora?" I pushed on. "You can't claim his death was accidental."

"Christian had left for home by the time I confronted Paula, but he might have seen me. I couldn't take the chance. He had to be dispatched before he said anything to make trouble between me and Pauleen. I knew Pauleen would forgive me for what happened to Paula," Dora went on, "but the truth that I was the instrument of her mother's death, no matter how unintended, would have been stressful for her. I didn't want her to have to go through that. Better she didn't find out it was me who pushed Paula in the first place."

Dora smiled, a creepy, canny grin. "That's when I came up with the idea of the fruit bonbons. There was a box on the coffee table, and Paula offered me one before... you know, *the death*," Dora whispered, glancing from side to side as if afraid someone might hear. "She mentioned Christian was addicted to them. I admit, they were good. What is it the young people say nowadays? They were *to die for...*" She giggled to herself. "I didn't think about it at the time, but seems like it was meant to be."

I was fast realizing just how unbalanced this little woman was. Paranoid in some ways, and oblivious in others. There was probably a name for that particular mental illness, but I didn't need a psychologist's diagnosis to convince me she was dangerous.

The adrenaline was wearing off and my pain returning, centering in my neck and torso. I could still move the neck a little, so I guessed it wasn't broken, but I wasn't as sure about the ribs. I'd begun to shake uncontrollably and not just from being underdressed in the overcast chill.

I glanced hopefully up and down the long patio, but we were still quite alone. If I was to win this battle of brain and brawn before I went completely catatonic, I'd better come up with something more effective than banter.

"What have you done with Pauleen, Dora? Did you kill her too? Is that why the cops can't find her? Because she's already dead?"

Though my voice came out little more than a squeak, the words made their impact. Dora reeled back as if she'd been slapped.

"Dead? Killed? How can you think that, Lynley? I would never..." she gasped. "Never in a million years harm a hair on that woman's head. Don't you get it? That's what this whole thing has been about. All for Pauleen, my lovely Pauleen."

"But you did something with her, didn't you? Because I can't see you just allowing her to run off on her own. You weren't about to let anything happen to her that you didn't orchestrate yourself."

"If you must know," Dora harrumphed, "she's resting

comfortably at my place."

"At your place?" I sniffed. "What, tied up and drugged in a locked room?"

"Of course not. She is there totally by her own will."

"Oh, so she just up and left her family for a week with no word? Come on, Dora. I find that hard to believe."

"It's true! I merely had to convince her she needed to lay low for a little while."

"And how exactly did you do that?" I challenged.

Dora gazed out over the broad river. "I told her," she said guardedly, "that maybe the murderer was after her, and that her family might get caught in the crossfire if she were still around. I convinced her she was best off remaining incommunicado until things got straightened out."

The shaking was getting worse, and I could feel my concentration slipping away. Whatever impact I was hoping to make on Dora's conscience, I needed to make it soon.

"But they will never be straightened out, Dora," I said through chattering teeth. "Don't you see? You'll have to let her go eventually. The police will figure out you're the perp. If they haven't done so already. Detective Croft is smarter than you think."

"No!" Dora spat. "No, that won't happen." She took up pushing at my chair again. "It... won't... happen..." she grunted with each violent thrust.

I let myself fall back on the lounge chair, my energy spent. There was nothing more I could do, nothing I could say. Unless someone came to rescue me right that minute, I'd be with the logs and branches in that cold, dark river floating my way to the open sea.

I could no longer move my neck without agony, so I

settled for shifting my eyes left and right. Where was everybody? Where were the runaway cats?

Then I realized, as I should have long before, that there were no cats. It had been a lie from the beginning, a ruse to get me outside where Dora could do away with me. She was the one who opened the kennel doors as a distraction. She had let the cats out, uncaring of their fates. She had organized the entire chase scenario, with my demise as the finale.

Just as the wheels of my chair hit against the guardrail, a single ray of sunshine broke through the cloudbank, setting the river asparkle. I managed to shift myself just enough to gaze upriver toward the distant snow-covered peak of Mt. Hood. I'd known that mountain all my life, grown up in its shadow. The tableau was comforting, and I found I was no longer afraid. My consciousness was failing, but it didn't matter anymore. What happened now was beyond my control.

I felt my body rise as Dora leveraged the chair against the rail. Maybe she wouldn't be able to get me over the top. Maybe she would. I tried to care. I *did* care—I just couldn't do anything about it.

Suddenly Dora gave a shrill scream and reared away from me. The chair tumbled back to the ground sending a jolt of pain through my body, but I wasn't the only one with a problem. Dora cried out again, whirling madly in her own personal anguish. At first, I couldn't tell what was causing it. Then something alighted beside me on the lounge chair—a black cat. The one was followed by another. For a moment they lingered, skewering me with their wild green eyes; then the pair leapt away and raced down the patio, disappearing from my limited view.

Dora was crying and writhing in a weird, arrhythmic

dance. As she spun, I saw bright red stripes forming across her shoulders and down the back of her yellow dress.

Through the pounding in my ears, I began to hear voices from the balcony above.

"Where did they go?"

"I think they went this way."

"Oh my gosh, did you see them jump?"

I raised my eyes upward to find Reese and Skelter hanging over the railing.

"Yo, Lynley, did you see two black cats run by?" Skelter called to me in all innocence.

I began to laugh. *You mean those two beautiful angels who just saved my life?* I wanted to reply. What came out was a garbled and gasping, "Help!"

"Hey, that doesn't look right," Reese said to Skelter. "I think she's hurt."

Skelter's eyes narrowed onto Dora whose jerky movements seemed nothing short of crazy. "What's that other woman doing? That don't look right either."

* * *

I must have passed out again, because the next thing I knew, the police were taking Dora away in handcuffs, and a young paramedic was kneeling beside me, asking where it hurt. Though I was tempted to say *everywhere*, I knew that would be unhelpful, and help was what I needed the most.

"We're going to stabilize your neck and move you onto the gurney," the EMT said in a quiet voice that was instantly reassuring. "Is that okay?"

"Yes," I whispered. "Thank you."

Skelter's craggy face appeared in place of the medic's, but instead of my eyes, his gaze was directed at my midriff.

"Hold on and let me collect these cats," he directed the EMT. Then he broke into a grin. "Awww, they look so comfortable, I hate to move 'em."

I couldn't see any cats from my reclining position, but I could feel them. Soft fur tickled my bare arms, and patches of warmth pressed up against my sides."

"The black cats?" I whispered.

Skelter nodded. "We'd been chasing these two all over the darned hotel. I thought they were in trouble when they threw themselves off the balcony. Now come to find them sleeping next to you like nothing's happened. You are a special cat lady, Lynley Cannon."

Then Reese, too, moved into my field of vision. "And not a crazy one either," she added with a lopsided smile.

Chapter 32

Cats can sense when their humans aren't feeling well and will often come to sit with them while they convalesce. Either that or ignore them completely.

There are reasons we can't go back to the past, and we shouldn't want to. People get hurt. Sometimes people die. Christian Naylor had tried to go back, and see where it got him. He wanted to recapture his youth, and it seemed as if Paula Hart may have wanted that too. How bad would it have been to let the old couple reunite? Dora claimed it would have devastated Pauleen—that's how she justified her crimes—but was it true? I doubted it. Sadly we would never know.

No, you may not be able to go back again, but you can go on. That's what I was doing, had been doing since the incident two weeks before. I'd been calling it *the fall*. How was I to tell people I was nearly murdered at a charity auction? There were way too many details that would need to be explained, questions to be answered. Maybe someday the story would come out, but not today. For now, it would just be *the fall*.

The sound of the doorbell broke through my musings.

"I'll get it," said Carol, who had designated herself my personal nurse.

Though limited by a sprained neck and three cracked ribs, I really didn't need a fulltime caregiver, but Carol was intent on helping, and when my mother was intent on something, there was no dissuading her. Besides, I appreciated her attention. It hurt to move, so other than the physical therapist's exercises and necessities such as going to the bathroom, I spent most of my time on the loveseat by the front window surrounded by cats. I had accomplished one thing though. With Frannie's help, I'd made it to Elizabeth's assessment test and was now the proud partner of a second registered therapy animal.

Oddly enough, despite the pain, that awful sense of impending age had disappeared. I'd heard it said the mystery of life isn't a problem to solve but a reality to experience. Yes, life was a sequence of stages. I needed to embrace time's passing and enjoy the moments as they came.

I sat forward and peered out the window to see who was on my front porch. My movement disturbed Elizabeth, and with a kitty huff, she shimmied down onto the carpet where she settled with her back to me.

"Sorry, sweet one," I told the cat.

I hefted myself up a little farther. Through the glass, I saw Frannie holding a large, flat box. The door opened, and Frannie pushed inside. *Curious*, I thought to myself.

My gaze drifted across the street to Fredric's duplex. Fredric and Seleia were standing out front, deep in conversation. The young man had been evasive for some time, but it looked like she'd finally got him talking.

"Here you go," Frannie said as she breezed into the room, bringing my attention back to the box. "Where do you want it?"

"What is it?"

"It's a surprise." She set her burden on the ottoman. "From all of us in the guild."

I watched as she took off the lid. There, nestled into yards of white tissue paper, was Pauleen's gorgeous cat quilt.

"We knew you planned to bid on it at the auction, but then you didn't get the chance. So we did it for you!" Frannie puffed out the chest of her Burberry jacket and shook her platinum curls. "And Pauleen added a little something." Frannie flipped back a corner of fabric to reveal a row of embroidered script. Peering closer, I picked out Pauleen's bold signature, the date of completion, and the words, *For Lynley*.

"Wow," I exclaimed, tears springing to my eyes. "That's amazing—I'm overcome!"

And I was. The experience with the Harts had left me raw, but Pauleen's beautiful quilt and the thoughtfulness of those who had procured it would go a long way toward healing those wounds.

"Please thank everyone for me, Frannie."

"I'll tell them you'll be doing that yourself very soon." Frannie replied as if it were fact.

"How is Pauleen doing? I've wanted to go by but…" I made a sweeping gesture down my broken body.

"She understands, Lynley. She feels terrible that someone she thought was her friend caused you such harm."

Harm, yes, Dora had done that, both mentally and physically, but it was the last thing I wanted to dwell on at the moment.

"And Mewella and Ridley?" I asked, diverting the conversation.

"They're fine. There haven't been any more incidents with Veronica. In fact, Pauleen and Pet have begun to let the girl visit, under their supervision of course. Pet says she's well-behaved with the cats, and they like her too, so…" She shrugged. "I guess it's all good."

"And the quilting guild? How is everyone?"

"They're good too, each in their own way. I haven't heard much from Gilda, but Ruth and her husband are on vacation in Paris. And you'll never guess—Mark asked Pet out on a date! He's been mooning over her for ages, but this is the first time he's got up the gumption to do anything about it besides following her around like a lost puppy."

"Did she go?"

Frannie nodded enthusiastically. "I gather they enjoyed themselves and are going to try it again."

The thought of those two lonely souls spending time together made me happy. Whether it grew into something more or not didn't matter as long as they gave themselves the chance to find out.

"And to think," I ruminated, "I was beginning to suspect Mark was the murderer."

Frannie started. "You did? Because of what I told you about his trouble with the law?"

"Not really. It was little things. He always seemed either blasé or frustrated, an odd combination that kept me guessing. I'm glad I was wrong."

"It's good to know you can make a mistake every once in a while, dear," Carol declared. "Proves you're human like the rest of us."

We all had a laugh at that one, except mine was only a giggle since laughter made my ribs hurt.

"Has the group begun working on new projects yet?" I asked.

"Not yet." Frannie took a seat on the edge of the couch by my feet since Carol had installed herself in the easy chair where she could watch over me like a cat with a bug.

"Pauleen and Pet are still working on getting their business in order now that Mrs. Hart is gone," Frannie continued. "They closed the shop for the month of May and plan to do some updating and remodeling, give the place a fresh look. I'll let you know when we start up again. Maybe you can try sewing a quilt next time."

"Baby steps, please," I said, "but yes, I think I'd like to learn. I was impressed by everyone's results. Your donations must have brought in a tidy sum at the auction."

"*Our* donations," Frannie corrected. "You worked on them too. Your embroideries were a real hit. The event was a huge success."

"Harrumph," my mother grumbled. "I can't say I'm pleased by the outcome. My daughter off to the hospital, and all those poor cats running everywhere! I never even got to bid on my tea set."

Frannie turned to Carol. "It was terrible, but you can't blame ShadowCat. It was Dora's fault, and no one else's. And hopefully our Lynley will resist any more sleuthing in the near future. Eh, Lynley?"

I wasn't paying attention. My full concentration was trained on the couple across the street. Fredric and Seleia were still conversing, but now Fredric seemed to be doing most of the talking. After so long ghosting my poor granddaughter, that was a good thing, right?

"Lynley?" Frannie urged.

"Sorry, what did you say?"

"She said she hoped you weren't planning on getting involved in any more crimes," Carol said flatly. "And I second that."

"N-no," I stuttered. "Of course not. But I never plan it—it just happens."

"The Jessica Fletcher of Southeast Portland," Frannie joked.

I smiled, but Carol just snorted and looked away.

I pulled my legs up onto the couch trying to find a position that didn't send twinges through my ribs and failing. Looking at the clock, I saw it was time for another painkiller. I didn't like to rely on them, but without something to take the edge off, I felt like a cracked walnut. Thankfully the non-addictive ibuprofen worked as well as the stronger stuff.

"Carol, would you mind bringing me my pain meds and a glass of water?"

"Sure, dear, or would you like iced tea instead? I made some earlier when you were having your nap."

"Sounds good. Frannie, care for an iced tea? It's such a beautiful day. We could go out on the patio…"

I moved to rise but didn't get far.

"One thing at a time," Frannie soothed. "The patio can wait until after your pill kicks in."

Chapter 33

The cats who saved Lynley may be fictitious, but cats do save people's lives. Cats have been known to fend off attacking dogs, chase a bear up a tree, and alert people of fire, gas leaks, and diabetic seizures. One cat, when his person fell from a wheelchair, is credited with dialing 911.

Carol bustled into the kitchen where I could hear the rattle of the cupboard and refrigerator doors. A few minutes later, she returned with three tall glasses of icy amber beverage. Also on the tray were a sugar bowl, a plate of lemon slices, three long-handled spoons, and my bottle of meds in a Japanese bowl. How she managed all that in such a short time I'd never know.

She shifted the quilt box off the ottoman and set down the tray. Deftly, she opened the pill bottle, shook one of the pills into the bowl, and handed it to me along with a drink.

"Help yourself, Frannie," she said as she heaped a generous spoonful of sugar into her own and stirred it diligently. The white granules swirled in the dark liquid like an underwater tornado.

"One good thing came out of the chaos at the ball," said Frannie, taking a glass. "All the shadow cats got adopted. Your hero cats were the first to be snatched up, both of them together. They are now living in a cushy condo in the West Hills with a catio overlooking a protected bird garden."

"That's wonderful," I exclaimed. "I couldn't believe waking up with those sweet kitties beside me. They saved my life, I'm sure of it."

"It sounds like the perfect happy ending." Frannie put a hand on mine. "Do you feel like telling us about it?"

"Yes," said Carol. "You've been so quiet. It's not healthy."

My mother was right. It was time to get everything out in the open.

"I don't know," I began slowly, "it all happened so fast. One minute I was sitting at the table with you, Carol, and then someone let the cats out, and it was instant turmoil."

Carol nodded vigorously. "It certainly was. When I returned from checking the auction items, you'd already left."

"Dora came running up asking me to help catch some cats that had gone out onto the balcony. Of course I said yes. I had no inkling of her true motive for getting me outside," I confided. "She told me the cats were on the lower level and made me look over the rail. Next thing I knew she'd got me by the ankles and was trying to push me off. It was sheer good fortune that... that it didn't turn out worse."

I recalled the fall and the miracle landing on the chaise longue and gave an inadvertent shudder. "But when Dora realized her plan had failed, she wasted no time coming after me again. She almost had me, too. I was sure I was headed for the murky deep. It was terrifying, but the next part of the story makes me smile."

I paused for a breath. I hadn't done so much talking since the accident, but I needed to go on.

"That's when my little angels arrived. The cats must have been running down the balcony in a panic and leapt off the edge. They landed on Dora, claws first. It would have hurt like crazy. Skelter and Reese were there, but I don't remember much else. My memory is blurry."

"If it weren't for those cats..." Frannie mused.

I wouldn't be here today, I finished to myself.

I don't know whether it was telepathy or coincidence, but that was when my three black kitties strode into the room. Little leapt up beside me, carefully avoiding my hurt ribs, while Tinkerbelle and Emilio placed themselves at either end of the loveseat like onyx sphinxes.

"Look at that!" said Frannie. "You have guard cats right here at home."

Carol remained sullen. "That Dora woman was insane," she grumbled though she did take a moment to pet Tinkerbelle who was sitting nearest. "How had no one seen it before?"

"Hard to say," I commented. "It's likely her instability increased slowly over time."

Frannie touched a perfect eyebrow. "Pauleen noticed Dora had gotten awfully clingy of late. She remarked on it before Mrs. Hart's death. She didn't remember exactly when it started but mentioned that Dora's well-meaning attention was beginning to smother her. She wasn't sure what to do since, for years, Dora had been such a steadfast friend."

I sighed. "Obsession is bizarre. It can progress from an innocent fascination into something disturbing and even dangerous."

"I have a question," said Carol. "We know why Paula and Christian were at the Naylor Historic House in the middle of the night, but what was Dora doing there?"

"I have no idea," I replied. "I've wondered about it myself."

"I know that one." Frannie took a dainty sip of her drink. "I heard the full story from Ruth who got it from Gilda who got it from Pet who'd been allowed to read Dora's original confession to the police."

Both Carol and I looked at her in astonishment. "Do tell," we said simultaneously as only a mother and daughter could.

"Apparently, Dora was coming home from a late concert at the Keller Auditorium," Frannie began. "She was driving up Hawthorne, and naturally as she drove past House of Quilts, she glanced over. She saw Christian Naylor coming out of the house next door which of course was supposed to be unoccupied. Dora pulled over to assess the situation and spied Mrs. Hart through the window."

"I can guess what happened next," I proposed. "Dora, figuring anything to do with the Harts was her business, parked her car and went right on in."

"Pretty much," Frannie agreed. "It had just begun to rain. The door was unlocked so she rushed inside to find Mrs. Hart by the fireplace admiring her new engagement ring. Mrs. Hart told Dora about Mr. Naylor's proposal and how, despite her earlier misgivings, she had accepted. Well, Dora went ballistic and must have blacked out. The next thing she remembers was Mrs. Hart on the floor, blood pooling from her head onto the granite hearth. Dora pulled the ring off Mrs. Hart's finger and flung it away, then hightailed it out of there. Because she was still wearing her driving gloves, the police never found her fingerprints at the scene."

"She just left without attending to Mrs. Hart?" Carol

gasped. "Without seeing if she was still alive?"

"Dora swears she could tell by looking that Mrs. Hart was dead." Frannie shrugged. "But who knows? Pet and Pauleen are livid that she didn't call for help."

"When Dora was trying to kill me," I said, ignoring a sharp glare from my mother, "she said she'd been worried that Christian Naylor might have witnessed the murder. She killed him so he wouldn't expose her."

Frannie looked doubtful. "But she didn't send him the poisoned chocolates until days later."

"I doubt Christian saw anything" Carol muttered, "because wouldn't he have alerted the police? And he never did."

I ran an idle hand across Little's back. "It must have been her guilt driving her. She wasn't thinking logically by then. She saw conspiracy everywhere. Why, she was certain I'd figured out she was the murderer, when in fact I didn't have a clue. On the other hand, she firmly believed that Pauleen would forgive her for killing her mother, which is equally as absurd."

"Paranoia verses pronoia," said Frannie.

"Call it what you like," Carol seethed. "It's just plain madness to me."

"No doubt about that," I agreed. "And then there's Pauleen's abduction-that-wasn't-an-abduction. Dora had Pauleen totally under her spell. How many days was Pauleen missing while everyone, including the police, feared the worst?"

"And it turned out Pauleen could have left Dora's any time she wanted to," Frannie furthered. "The woman had her convinced terrible things would happen to herself and her family the moment she contacted anyone. Pauleen still hasn't recovered from it. The doctor thinks drugs may have been involved."

"Poor dear," said Carol. "Such trauma upon trauma. It will take time to mend."

"She's strong," said Frannie. "She's already improving, but you're right. It could be a long road."

"I'll write her a card," Carol pronounced, believing that all occasions, especially sad ones, could be made better by a pretty note card sent through the good old-fashioned U.S. Mail.

I turned my gaze to the window. Outside, the wind ruffled the leaves of the almond tree, and the sun glanced off the peach-colored stucco front of the duplex across the street. Seleia and Fredric were still standing by the steps, but now Fredric's back was toward me with Seleia obscured in his shadow. Then he stepped aside, and I felt my heart speed up...

Seleia was crying!

"Rats!" I exclaimed as I pulled myself to my feet, my pain overcome by anger. *That man is making my baby cry*, was my only thought. No way was I going to stand by and let that happen.

Among questions and protests from Carol and Frannie, I hobbled to the front door, flung it wide, and levered myself down the steps to the sidewalk. As I shambled across the street with the determination of a geriatric attack cat, Fredric and Seleia turned to me in surprise.

"I don't know what you're up to, young man..." I began, then stopped in my tracks. Both Fredric and Seleia had smiles on their faces.

But they weren't just smiling—they were *beaming*. Despite the tears on her rosy cheeks, I don't think I'd ever seen my granddaughter so radiant.

Seleia took my arm to steady me. "Grandmother,

should you be walking, and so fast?"

"What's up, Lynley?" Fredric put in. "Do you need something? Can I help?"

"I... I thought..." I studied the two before me, searching for signs of distress and finding none. "What's going on here, Seleia? Your face is wet."

Abruptly she flung herself into my arms, and indeed she was sobbing her heart out, but not for the reasons I'd imagined.

"Oh, Lynley, isn't it wonderful?" She pulled away, this time embracing the man beside her. "Fredric has asked me to marry him!"

I was struck wordless, then I smiled too. "And what was your answer?"

"He's not letting me give my answer for seven days. He says I have to think it through before I make a final decision. Isn't that smart of him, grandmother?" She gazed lovingly into her beau's—possibly soon to be her fiancé's—eyes.

"That is very smart." I gave Fredric a wink. "He is a very smart man—sometimes."

But I wasn't about to let him off the hook just yet. He'd caused Seleia a good amount of worry by not confiding his intentions sooner. "Is that why you've been so rudely avoiding my granddaughter?"

Fredric looked down at his feet. "Yeah, I didn't handle that part very well, did I? But I needed some space to think. Marriage is a big step, you know." He said it so seriously that I had a hard time to keep from laughing. "And I was afraid she'd say no."

"And now you're not?"

He ran a hand through his red locks. "Talk about smart, Seleia is the smartest woman I know. Whatever she decides will be right, and I'll stand by it."

"We're not going to tell anyone just yet though," said Seleia, "in case... Well, we're just not."

I glanced back at my house where Carol stood in the doorway with Frannie peering over her shoulder watching our every move. "That may be difficult..."

Seleia's eye followed my gaze. "I see what you mean. I guess you'd better tell Granna."

"Would you like to tell her yourself?"

"Not right now. Fredric has to get back to work, and I have class in half an hour."

"Then I'll leave you to it." I gave her a kiss on the cheek and patted Fredric's arm. "I do expect a full account sometime in the near future."

The couple said their goodbyes, and Seleia escorted me back across the street to my door. As she left for her car, I found myself thinking not about the past but about the future. I had little doubt that when the week was up, Seleia would say yes. I was happy for her, ecstatic even, yet a part of me felt sad. The little kitten girl was all grown up now. Soon she would be making a home of her own.

"What happened?" Frannie burst out the minute I came in the door. "Is everything alright?"

"Well, yes, as a matter of fact, it is. Seleia has some big news..."

"Fredric's popped the question," said Carol.

I looked at her in surprise. "But... how did you know?"

She stared back, then blinked. "How come you didn't?"

With that, my mother picked up Emilio and hugged him to her. The big black cat snuggled into her arms as she carted him off to the kitchen.

"Cookies," she called back to Frannie and me as we stood dumbfounded. "This calls for a celebration."

THE END

A Note from the Author

Thanks so much for reading my eleventh Crazy Cat Lady Mystery, *Crafty Cat*. I hope you enjoyed it. If you did, please consider leaving a review on your favorite book and social media sites. Reviews help indie authors such as myself to gain recognition in the literary jungle. Thank you in advance for your consideration.

Want more cozy cat mysteries? Look for more books in my **Crazy Cat Lady** series. Don't worry—the books need not be read in order. Just pick a plot that interests you and start reading.

"...Each book drew me right into the story and kept me intrigued and guessing all the way." —Catwoods Porch Party

Or check out my **Tenth Life Paranormal Cozy Mysteries** involving a septuagenarian and a ghost cat in a small coastal town.

"This is the sort of cozy mystery that you like to curl up with on a rainy day with a cup of tea." —Verified Reader

For sci-fantasy fans, there is my **Cat Seasons Tetralogy**—Cats saving the world!

"Mollie weaves a story that blurs the lines of mythology, spiritualism, mysticism, science and reality that took me into another world." — Ramona D. Marek MS Ed, CWA Author

About the Author

Cat Writer Mollie Hunt is the award-winning author of two cozy series: the **Crazy Cat Lady Mysteries** featuring a sixty-something cat shelter volunteer who finds more trouble than a cat in catnip, and the **Tenth Life Paranormal Mysteries** involving a ghost cat. Her **Cat Seasons Sci-Fantasy Tetralogy** presents extraordinary cats saving the world. She recently released a COVID memoir which she calls, "an ode to the very real and healing presence of cats."

Her cat writing has earned various honors, including CWA Muse Medallions and World's Best Litter-ary Awards. She is the recipient of the prestigious Michael Brim Distinguished Service Award (CWA) and the Catalyst Council Connect to Care Award, celebrating a true story of the profound connection between a shelter cat and its adoptive pet parent. Her book, **Cat's Paw**, was a CIBA Mystery & Mayhem Semi-finalist.

Mollie is a member of Sisters in Crime and Willamette Writers, as well as being on the board of the Oregon Writers Colony and Northwest Independent Writers Association (NIWA). She is also the librarian for the Cat Writers' Association. Mollie lives in Portland, Oregon with her husband and a varying number of cats. Like her cat lady character, she is a grateful shelter volunteer.

About the Cover Art

"Greetings!" by Leslie Cobb

This cover, like the other books in the series, features artwork by cat artist Leslie Cobb. The piece is titled, "Greetings!" and is one of her Best Friends Animal Sanctuary series. The black cat's name is Scooter, and he was the official greeter in the Best Friends Cat World lobby.

© *Leslie Cobb* www.lesliecobb.com

Made in the USA
Middletown, DE
29 October 2024

63536044R00149